A TEXAS-SIZED FAKE OUT

MICHELE DUNAWAY

SPECIAL EDITION

Recycling programs for this product may not exist in your area.

ISBN-13: 978-1-335-18027-8

A Texas-Sized Fake Out

For questions and comments about the quality of this book, please contact us at CustomerService@Harlequin.com.

Harlequin Enterprises ULC
22 Adelaide St. West, 41st Floor
Toronto, Ontario M5H 4E3, Canada
www.Harlequin.com

HarperCollins Publishers
Macken House, 39/40 Mayor Street Upper,
Dublin 1, D01 C9W8, Ireland
www.HarperCollins.com

Printed in Lithuania

“We’re going to need to kiss.”

Madi’s bluebonnet-blue eyes widened. “What?”

“If we’re dating, we’re going to have to kiss.” Wyatt tried to backpedal. “This isn’t me trying to kiss you. But the committee won’t believe we’re in a relationship otherwise. People who date, kiss.”

“True.” Her teeth tugged her bottom lip under. Her light nibble destroyed his concentration. “They do.” She loosened her arms, straightened and drew herself up to her full height. “Well, let’s do it. Get it out of the way.”

Now it was Wyatt’s turn to be surprised. “What?”

She shrugged. “Let’s kiss. We’ll get the awkwardness over with now, while we’re in private. Because as you said, as soon as we pretend to date, they’ll be scrutinizing us through a microscope. We’ll be feeding the grapevine and all eyes will be on us.”

“I’m glad you realize that. They’ll be hard to fool.” He resisted the urge to cover his mouth and check his breath. She might as well get him at his worst.

“We’ll approach this clinically,” Madi decided. “I’m a doctor. I can see the human body as a person while also controlling my own body’s reaction. Suffice to say, I quickly learned to hide my shock, surprise or disgust when facing people.”

“I hope kissing me doesn’t fall into the latter category.” Wyatt tried to keep his tone light, but she was starting to give him a complex. No woman had complained since he’d first kissed Nicole during middle school. Then again, why was Wyatt worried about his male pride? They were fake dating. It would be a fake kiss.

Madi’s face had heated but she boldly stepped forward like a defiant man headed to the gallows. “Okay, I’m ready. You can kiss me.”

Dear Reader,

A few summers ago, I spent a week in the Panhandle of Texas. I had the chance to do two things on my bucket list: hang out with fabulous authors who became good friends and visit Palo Duro Canyon, which is the second-largest canyon system in the United States. Because I wanted to return to a favorite spot and because the places I travel often become settings for my stories, *A Texas-Sized Fake Out* takes us to the Panhandle and to the town of Legacy Canyon.

Legacy Canyon is a place that's great for second chances. It's a chance for Wyatt to be a better dad to his newly adopted twin boys than his father was to him. For Madi, it's a chance to escape the perfectionism by which she's lived her life. She's tried to meet not only her parents' high expectations, but also her own. However, there's a small catch. Legacy Canyon has a group of meddling matchmakers known as The Committee, who not only organize the annual Lasso for Legacy rodeo every September, but also every other event in town. And this group knows that Wyatt and Madi are perfect for each other. So when Madi and Wyatt decide to fake date to sideswipe The Committee's efforts, the two quickly realize there's a fine line between truth and fiction, and that the line easily blurs.

I hope you enjoy joining Wyatt and Madi as they go on a journey of big-city girl meets country boy at heart. Let me know by visiting my website, micheledunaway.com, where you can also subscribe to my newsletter.

Michele

In first grade, **Michele Dunaway** wanted to be a teacher. In second grade, she wanted to be a writer. By third grade, she decided to be both. Now a bestselling author, Michele strives to create strong heroes and heroines for savvy readers who want contemporary, small-town adventures with characters who discover things about themselves as they travel the road to true love and self-fulfillment. Michele loves to travel, with the places she visits often inspiring her novels. An avid baker, Michele describes herself as a woman who does way too much but never wants to stop, especially when it comes to creating fiction, or baking brownies and chocolate chip cookies. She loves to hear from readers at micheledunaway.com.

Books by Michele Dunaway

Harlequin Special Edition

Legacy Canyon

A Texas-Sized Fake Out

Love in the Valley

What Happens in the Air
All's Fair in Love and Wine
Love's Secret Ingredient
One Suite Deal
Room for Two More
The Playboy Project

Visit the Author Profile page at Harlequin.com for more titles.

To Jodi Thomas, Jolene Navarro,
Candace Havens and Teri Wilson. We'll always have
the West Texas Writers' Academy at WTAMU. And
Candace, thank you for being there when I needed it
most (besides driving through the canyon).
Cheers to more success for all of you!

Chapter One

One thing was certain, Wyatt Larrabee thought as he drove into town—Legacy Canyon never seemed to change. Even in the dead of winter, the stuck-in-time tourist trap where Wyatt had spent his impressionable formative years looked as frozen as the ground covered with a one-inch dusting of mid-January snow.

He loosened fingers stiff from driving as he passed Samson Hardware, Cooke Dry Goods, Molly's Bakery and the headquarters of Lone Star Savings and Loan. The famed town square dating back to the 1890s showcased historic storefronts with timber frames, weathered wooden exteriors and broad front porches complete with railings covered in blue-and-white snowflake bunting. In February, the theme would swap out for Valentine's Day, then the next would be St. Patrick's Day followed by Easter, etc., etc. September was always the Lasso for Legacy rodeo, the amateur and professional charity event that had truly put the town on the map. Wyatt had participated once, much to his father's eternal shame. Worse, he'd competed in barrel racing and been knocked out in the first round.

Just another failure in the long string of disappointments Wyatt's father had had to endure from his firstborn. But Wyatt was a grown man, and a father now himself, with the proof being the eight-month-old twins riding along in the back seat of his SUV. Wyatt certainly hadn't predicted this life-changing event six years ago when he'd moved from Legacy Canyon to Denver, but he didn't regret his boys.

Had it really been that long since he and his father had exchanged harsh words that neither regretted? If Wyatt was truly honest, the verbal blows still felt a bit like yesterday, especially after his dad had called adopting the twins foolish, said that Wyatt was throwing his life away. Said Wyatt should find some nice woman, settle down and have his own flesh-and-blood kids. That latter part had stung and turned Wyatt into a defensive Papa Bear. His own father's attitude had provided the strongest reason Wyatt had skipped visiting the Larrabee Ranch this past Christmas, much to his mother's eternal disappointment. Just another sin added to a long list.

But he'd wanted to spend his first holiday alone with his twin sons as just the three of them. Even if the boys were too young to remember his first attempt at Christmas decorations and their presents, Wyatt would remember. When his memories faded as the boys grew, he'd be able to look back at the photos of them in their Santa suits, and smile.

Besides, the day after Christmas the stress had started. Not only had the decorations been tucked away into plastic tubs, but Wyatt had also begun the process of packing his life into cardboard boxes. Moving back to Legacy Canyon had been a hard decision, but he'd had to admit he needed help. He couldn't do it alone, and he was man enough to make the hard decisions that were in the best interests of his family. So he'd finished out the work year before saying goodbye to his viewers, his coworkers and the meteorology job he'd truly enjoyed, and pointed his car toward Legacy Canyon. His mother was thrilled and ready to babysit. Wyatt's dad hadn't said a word, probably warned to stay silent by his wife.

As for his father's idea of Wyatt dating? His work hours had made that near impossible. Worse, when he'd been approved to adopt the twins, the woman he'd been seeing had balked. Told him he was a fool and dumped him flat. Good riddance. Wyatt didn't have time, anyway. Dating was a nice thought, but not a priority. His first priorities slept quietly, unaware of their new home, or that someone had once called the town's architecture "saloon-style on steroids" and run the risk of being chased out of town. Wyatt snickered because the description fit.

Besides, when he did eventually find "the one," she'd understand and accept that he and the twins were a package deal. She also wouldn't want him for being a TV news personality. She'd be fun, yet serious when it mattered. She'd embrace his eccentricities and his passion for the weather. He wanted his marriage to be affectionate and caring. He wasn't on board with all that soul-mate stuff, not with his parents as role models. But if he and his bride were both friends and physically compatible, and if they got along well, then he believed they could develop a deep bond, one rooted in trust and respect. While love wasn't something he had truly understood until he'd met the boys, it mattered. He would not bring just anyone into their lives.

A ringing sound interrupted the music, and Wyatt answered the phone call. "Hi, Mom."

"Wyatt. Just checking in on you."

"Driving through town now."

"Can you stop at Brayden's? Your grandfather's prescription's ready. Says they'll meet you at the door."

His grandfather had cancer, but the treatments were working. His grandfather's poor health had been another strong factor in Wyatt's decision to move home. "I can pop by. It's just ahead. Call them and tell them I'm here."

"Okay, see you soon."

Wyatt pulled the SUV to the curb. Today was Wednesday, which meant fewer tourists and therefore, more available parking. Brayden's Drugs had been in the same location for generations with a loyal clientele that would go nowhere else. The car idling, Wyatt gazed out the passenger window. He couldn't see anyone inside the glass door. He checked the dashboard clock. A few minutes later, he checked that the boys were still sleeping, turned off the car and climbed out. Probably faster to run in and out. Be two minutes tops. Key fob in his pocket, he locked the car and stepped onto the curb, and ran smack-dab into someone. He instinctively righted himself and reached to help her.

"Watch where you're going!" She shrugged him off and secured the lid on her coffee.

Embarrassment mixed with annoyance at her sharp tone, but Wyatt prided himself on being a gentleman. "I'm so sorry. Are you okay?"

As she lifted a head covered with caramel-colored hair, Wyatt found himself staring into the most captivating blue eyes he'd ever seen, despite the fact that they were glaring at him. They reminded him of the bluebonnets that bloomed every spring. Wyatt blinked in response as the full lower lip of a bow-shaped mouth dropped. "I'm fine."

Then a pretty gaze a man could drown in narrowed. "You're not going to leave your car there, are you?"

"What?" Wyatt had no idea what she meant.

Despite his having five inches on her, she held her own. She pulled her winter peacoat tight, then she pointed to the rear passenger window. "Your children are alone in the car."

"It's locked. They're sleeping, and I'll only be a—"

She cut him off. "It doesn't matter. You never leave children unattended. What if it's a hot car? Do you know how fast those heat up? How many kids or pets die each year?"

Her scathing words had him off-kilter, as if his mother had scolded him. And, yes, he knew the number. He often gave his viewers the same warnings and statistics when the temperatures climbed. "It's winter," he pointed out.

As if proving the point, a twenty-mile-per-hour wind buffeted them and his car. Since the winds covered the high plains year-round, the locals in this part of the Texas Panhandle called the nonstop gusts "God's blow dryer." If he'd been in front of the camera, he'd describe today's weather as cloudy with a high of thirty-two with winds from the southwest. By tomorrow, the temperature would be in the upper forties and the snow would be gone.

"It's still freezing. You don't leave children. Ever."

"Of course not!" Wyatt snapped. "I'm picking up medicine for my grandfather. In and out. What type of father do you think I am?"

Her arms folded and the peacoat bunched at her shoulders as she silently judged him.

"Wyatt?" Matt Brayden, who'd attended high school with him, stepped out holding a white paper bag. Wyatt exhaled his relief. "Here's your grandfather's medicine. Tell him I said hi, and I hope he's doing better. Let's catch up now that you're back." Matt shivered in his white pharmacy coat, then took note of the woman. "Ma'am." He disappeared back inside.

"Ma'am," Wyatt echoed, holding the package like a shield. He left her on the curb, went to the driver's side and climbed in. The electric engine made no noise as it started. He could still see her standing there, then she began to walk as he drove away.

Who did she think she was? He didn't know her. This was Legacy Canyon. As for his being a father, he was already a better dad than his own standoffish father. Fuming at being found lacking, he ignored the rest of the town square, which was lined with art galleries, antique stores and other such tourist temptations. He planned to give his kids the best upbringing, and in order to be more present, he'd chosen to come home. It was a small sacrifice to make, leaving a large-market weather-forecasting job for one a short distance away in Amarillo, whose airport had a mere eight gates.

How dare she judge him! He always put his kids first. Instead of discussing mile-high conditions to his 5:00 and 6:00 a.m. early morning newscast viewers, soon he'd be telling the area locals about the weather affecting the region's flat terrain and lack of natural windbreaks. In the TV industry, the backward move could be seen as a demotion.

But his sons—how strange yet powerfully fulfilling that word sounded—came first. And they were too young to notice or care that the strongest winds would peak by early spring. The twins would be a year in April, beginning to pull up and soon to be walking according to the parenting book he'd read. Already they were saying "da," "ah" and "ooh," although they were noises, not words. Their first smiles had been a like a punch to the gut, in a good way. The love he'd experienced at that moment? Words couldn't come close to describing how enraptured he'd been, how determined he was to be there for his sons, to experience every milestone.

He glanced in the rearview, as he'd been doing the entire drive—the normal seven hours had taken nine with the stops he'd needed to make for diaper changes. The mirrors attached to the back headrests allowed him to see into the rear-facing car seats. Noah and Ethan slept with chins tilted onto their chests. Tiny fists that his could swallow had curled. Soon, their puffy baby cheeks would be covered in kisses by a grandmother and great-grandmother eager to meet them. The jury remained out on Wyatt's dad. Joe Larrabee marked the fourth generation of Larrabee cattle ranchers in the Texas Panhandle. Wyatt had been the first to break the streak, leaving for Denver to follow his dream.

But then, fate had sent him these angels, meaning he now had a new dream. The boys might be the children of a distant cousin who'd passed far too young, one Wyatt hadn't even known that well, if at all, but the boys had Larrabee blood. And they'd been in foster care. And his cousin had named Wyatt their guardian in her will, for reasons he still fully didn't understand minus the fact he'd always been the face of the Denver TV station's foster-and-adoption programming. But from the moment he'd held the twins, he'd loved and wanted them. After a lengthy process, they were legally his, with his name secure on their birth certificates in the line that read *father*.

Wyatt's hands worked the leather-wrapped steering wheel, and he drove away from a town square decorated in snowmen and snowflakes. The Larrabee Ranch was five country miles outside of town, so he'd take the next left onto the county highway for the final stretch. A soft sigh of sweet, dreamy slumber came from the back as Wyatt waited for a green left arrow. He tamped down his anxiety. His father had been correct about one thing: babies were a lot of work.

He tried to erase the woman's pretty image. He hadn't needed a judgy woman around his age to make comments today. He tried to let it go, but found it difficult. Why was her rebuke under his skin? He'd been fending off well-intentioned, and some not so well-intentioned, women for months. Once the Denver news station had aired a story on the double adoption as part of its commitment to helping children find a home, female admirers had poured out of the woodwork, a situation made even worse after the national news rebroadcast the story. The subsequent attention was annoying rather than flattering. Overwhelming instead of helpful. Trying to work full-time and be a full-time single parent was stressful enough, but he'd been unable to go to the supermarket without attracting notice and people wanting to touch his sons. Thankfully, the Larrabee Ranch had gates and better protections.

As the town gave way to the wide-open fields that belonged to the cattle ranchers, Wyatt leaned forward over the steering wheel. Despite the snow, the area had been in drought the last two years, and dry, brown grass poked through the layer of white snow. He studied the remains of a gray sky blocking the sunset as he drove through the gates onto Larrabee Lane. The former dirt-and-rock, one-mile drive was now plowed clean. Above his head the light, snow-covered branches of the half-century-old, fifty-foot-tall honey locusts created a magical winter canopy. He reached the *Y* and took the right fork, toward his childhood home. If one pictured a rectangle of nearly one hundred thousand acres of land, his mother and father lived in the lower right corner on five dedicated acres. His Uncle Silas was somewhere to the left, and his brother, Caleb, more to the center right. His grandparents lived more toward the center, and his grandparents had an additional twenty thousand acres of their own.

Alerted to his presence by the security cameras, his family stepped onto the wide front porch that ran around three sides of a rambling two-story house decorated in colors similar to the town storefronts. His father's frown accompanied a green plaid shirt and tan corduroy jacket. Joe Larrabee had shoved his hands into the front pockets of a pair of worn blue jeans spread in a bow-legged stance. The ever-present Stetson topped a full head of graying hair. Everyone said thirty-two-year-old Wyatt looked like a carbon copy of his father at that age. Wyatt had the same jet-black hair, same Roman nose, and same brown eyes with gold flecks. He didn't have the same dedication to the ranch, which remained a bone of contention. Thankfully, Caleb had stepped into that gap. But Wyatt didn't see his younger brother among the welcome party, but then again, they had nothing in common minus the fact they were both parents. They'd catch up at some point. They always did.

Wyatt waved to the onlookers waiting on the porch, a gesture two of them returned. His mother wore slacks and a long-sleeved sweater. She rubbed her arms against the cold. Born and raised in LA, his mom was proof that while you could take the girl out of the city, you couldn't take the city out of the girl. Wyatt wasn't surprised to see that his eighty-year-old grandmother was already moving spryly down the front steps. In clear contrast to Wyatt's mother, she wore snow boots and blue-jean overalls with a red polka-dot T-shirt underneath. An unbuttoned black parka covered everything. Clarissa Larrabee was a force of nature in her own right, and without hesitation she tugged open the back door of the car the moment Wyatt had put the vehicle in Park and turned off the engine. Cold air swirled inside. She peered at Ethan.

"Ooh, look at how cute they are! Much more adorable in person. Aren't you so cute! So sweet," his grandmother cooed at the sleeping Ethan. She made to reach for him but stopped. "You will let me hold both of them, yes?"

Wyatt climbed out of the vehicle. "Once they're awake, of course. We've had a bit of a rough go lately, as both are getting their top incisors. I'll let you carry him inside if you'd like, and I've got Grandpa's medicine."

"Good, good. Let's get these precious bundles inside."

"Yes, hurry. It's too chilly out here," his mom called, stepping off porch. His dad disappeared back inside.

Standing five-six to Wyatt's six-one, his grandma straightened as Wyatt rounded the car. She took the medicine he handed her and shoved it in a coat pocket. "You did good, my boy. Very, very good." She lowered her voice for his ears alone. "Don't let your dad get to you. He'll come around, you'll see." Then, smiling, she opened her arms. "Now, come here. Don't think I'm letting you get by without giving me a quick hug. Then let's get them inside out of the cold."

"Yes, ma'am." Arms that felt less strong than they had over a year ago enveloped him, giving him a tight squeeze before she leaned back to size him up. "You're thinner but nothing some home-cooked food won't cure. The organizing committee sent casseroles."

"They sent multiple casseroles," Wyatt's mother murmured as she edged closer. "Because, well…" She paused. Considered her words carefully. "Because they're your grandmother's friends," his mother said diplomatically from her spot on the sidewalk.

Officially, the organizing committee was an ad hoc committee—as if fifty years of being a committee could still be considered ad hoc—consisting of civic-minded women and store owners who worked for the betterment of Legacy Canyon. The group not only organized the Lasso for Legacy charity rodeo, but also put together other community events. Unofficially the committee also served as the town's welcome wagon, grapevine and gossip central. If anything happened in Legacy Canyon, everyone knew about it within seconds. That was critical during times of crisis. Not so helpful when Wyatt had tried his first and only cigarette during eighth grade. So much for looking cool in front of his friends.

He smiled at his grandmother. "Tell the committee I said thank you. I'm going to love not having to cook. I consider it a victory that I can make the scrambled eggs my boys like."

"Oh, don't let them hear that, they'll keep dropping things off," his mother said.

Wyatt covered Ethan's face with a blanket and lifted the car seat from the base. Months ago, he'd fumbled with the contraption. Now, he unhooked the seat with ease. His grandmother reached for the handle.

"They wanted to make sure you were fed well and not eating fast food or carryout," his grandmother said cheerily as she started for the house. "You know how they are."

He did. For better or worse, so did everyone in Legacy Canyon. He went to retrieve Noah. "And I'm grateful. Truly."

"I'll pass on your thanks," his grandmother called as she climbed the porch steps. "There's enough to feed you for a month, so we put the dishes in the cabin fridge. You can choose which to freeze. I'd eat Betty's beef Stroganoff tonight. She makes a mean one, but for some reason it won't keep. Not sure why." With that, the force that defined his grandmother hustled through the heavy wood front door. Wyatt's father had long disappeared.

"You can toss it if you want." Wyatt's mother's pink-tinged lips thinned and she gave another shiver. "It might not be to your liking."

"It'll be delicious. You're getting cold. Let's get inside." Wyatt tucked the receiving blanket around Noah. He and his sons would be living in "the cabin," which was the name for the two-bedroom guesthouse located about one hundred feet from the main house. He lifted the car seat, closed the door with his foot and carried his son quickly inside. His mother followed, rubbing her arms until she closed the front door behind him.

Wyatt glanced around. Like the town, not much in his

boyhood home had changed. A formal dining room to the left awaited dinner guests. A Western-themed living room on the right contained family photos of various generations on the fireplace mantel and a bookcase filled with nostalgia from his dad and Caleb's rodeo days. The kitchen was straight ahead, past a wide flight of stairs. Beyond that was the family room addition. He set the car seat on the hardwood floor next to Ethan's. As his mom bent to peer at Noah, Wyatt shed his coat. "He's adorable," she said. "I've already missed so much."

Guilt twinged at not having visited in the past seven months. But once the social worker had contacted him last May, saying she had infant twins whose mother had named him their guardian, he'd been busying with the foster and adoption process.

"How is Grandpa?" Wyatt asked as he hung his coat in the closet. His grandmother passed him hers.

"He has more good days than bad," his grandmother answered, her pragmatic nature not allowing her to sugarcoat anything. "So far the cancer's stayed gone. The medicine's helping, so thanks for getting the refill. He'll be glad to see these guys. The thought of seeing your boys, of seeing you marry, gives him something to fight for."

"Uh-huh." There it was. That pressure to marry.

Clarissa continued cheerily. "He's napping now or he'd be here. And I told your father to unload your luggage, so he probably went out back to unlock the cabin first before heading to your car," she said, answering Wyatt's unasked question as to where his father had gone. "I told him to make himself useful. Besides, I wanted some uninterrupted time with my littles before the two of you start butting heads. Aren't you the sweetest thing," she cooed to Ethan as Wyatt juggled both car seats.

They moved into the kitchen and Wyatt set the seats on the kitchen counter.

"That is Ethan," he told his mother and grandmother as they crowded around. "This is Noah. These are my sons. You can tell them apart because Ethan has this little dimple in his cheek and his eyes are darker."

"Oh, I see it," his grandmother said.

"They are beautiful." His mom fingered the strand of pearls skimming her collarbones. "I love them already. Let's get some food in you, and then we'll help you get settled."

"Yes, ma'am." Wyatt had no problem agreeing. He was hungry and the boys were starting to stir. "Once they wake up, would you like to hold them?"

Clarissa never stopped looking at the babies. "Of course, we would. What kind of question is that? Been waiting forever for great-grandchildren and now I got two more teeny ones. Emma's two and, well, we never see Kate since your sister stays in Chicago for the holidays. We send presents, though. But it's not the same."

Emma was Caleb's daughter. Wyatt's niece, Kate, was five, and her mom, Kristen, was a veterinarian. Whereas Wyatt and his father butted heads, Kristen and their mom were like bighorn sheep. She'd followed Wyatt's footsteps in leaving Legacy Gap to blaze new trails in a big city.

"I like the new high chairs." He nodded toward the breakfast nook.

His grandmother grinned. "Your mom and I figured we'd need them with the babysitting and all. And wait until you see what your mother and I did with the cabin. Fixed it right up."

"We shopped at Bundle and Bloom, the baby boutique on the square." While Clarissa might be more forthright, Wyatt's mother was not one to be left out, and had learned to hold her own. She'd decided to assert herself.

Wyatt had never heard of Bundle and Bloom. "Is that new?"

"Been there about two years," his mother said. "Excellent quality. And if they don't have it, they can order it."

"Huh. Good to know we have a local place." Then again, he hadn't been looking for baby items the last time he'd visited and he hadn't driven all the way around the entire square today.

"It's an excellent store. Marya Brennan, she's a friend of mine, started the place after she permanently retired from teaching," his grandmother said. "You remember her, don't you?"

How could he forget the infamous Mrs. Brennan? She'd caught him and his friends smoking behind the middle school, and when she'd surprised them, he'd inhaled wrong. She'd pounded his back and told him she was calling his mother. While Wyatt was bent over wheezing, his friends, who hadn't lit up, had scattered, even though Mrs. Brennan knew them all and called their mothers, too. As punishment, the entire group had had to give up a Saturday to clean the entire campus. Wyatt had never smoked again.

"Anyway, gave her something to do and the shop does really well," his grandmother continued. "Did you have Mrs. Brennan as a teacher? She taught journalism at the high school."

"She'd moved to the middle school by then."

"Oh, that's right. She was a principal."

"Yeah. I had Mr. Bradley for journalism. He's the one who inspired me to go into broadcasting."

Ethan began kicking his legs, making the quilt fall off. "They need a diaper change, and they'll be hungry." He reached into the diaper bag and retrieved two baby spoons, two jars of sweet-potato baby food and a fresh banana. He put them on the table and the strap back on his shoulder. "Where can I change them?"

"I moved the old nursery changing table in the spare room," his mother said, her eyebrows knitting together when Ethan started fussing. Noah had opened his eyes and was looking around, and Wyatt knew Noah's lower lip would start quivering soon. Juggling the diaper bag and both car seats, Wyatt went into the spare room, where he discovered his mother had created a nursery complete with two cribs. "This is nice," he said.

"Thanks. I wanted something so that when you work they could stay here, if that's okay." His mother seemed hesitant.

"That's one reason I came home," Wyatt reassured her. "And we'll cross that bridge when we come to it. For now, do you want to fill these sippy cups with water and cut up this banana?"

He swore his mom lit up like a firecracker. "I would love to."

"Perfect. That way I can feed them when I get done."

His grandmother passed his mom and stepped into the room. "Isn't this nice? She's very excited about the prospect of babysitting."

"I noticed. I'm glad one of my parents is." Noting the

changing table already held the correct size of diapers and a container of wipes, he lifted Ethan and placed him on the table. “My father has made it clear he isn’t pleased with my choices. All he wants is for me to settle down and man the ranch. Oh, and find a wife and have *real* kids.”

“He’s my son, so I can say he’s hardheaded. But he’ll come around.” His grandmother’s prediction contained a confidence that Wyatt couldn’t echo.

“You mean the way he did when I said in ninth grade that I planned on studying meteorology and being a weather forecaster?” He’d gotten an earful about how the ranch needed him, how it was his destiny, his legacy, like the canyon off to the east.

Clarissa made funny faces at Noah, who watched her with wide-eyed interest. “You’re as headstrong as he was. Neither of you knows how to back down. You’re both as stubborn as the land. Perhaps this will mark a new start for you two.”

“I hope so.” They needed a reset. Their arguments had increased once Wyatt had begun to exercise his own agency, be his own person, finally out from underneath his father’s thumb. When he’d chosen to leave the TV station in Amarillo for the far larger Denver market, he and his father had stopped speaking for almost two weeks. “I’ll try if he does.”

“You aren’t opposed to dating, are you?” his grandmother asked instead of acknowledging his conditions. “You’re young. Handsome. A Larrabee.”

An awkward laundry list if ever there was one. He made a goofy face at Ethan, who grinned. “With what time? I’m not opposed to dating, but I’m not finding some woman to raise my boys because they need 'a woman's touch.'"

Still irked by that particular commentary from his father, Wyatt began to unsnap Ethan's pants. He'd grown adept at swapping the diapers, quickly covering that part of baby boys that could let loose an arcing stream if one wasn't careful. He'd learned that lesson the hard way. A new mom who anchored the newscast had laughed at his story and explained what to do.

"Your dad only want what's best for you. Always has. If the two of you could get your heads out of your…well, you know, you would both realize you have a lot more in common than you think."

Ah, the second woman to criticize him today, but he'd allow this one since he loved his grandmother. "Well, I'm here, back in Legacy Canyon, so maybe it'll happen. I'll make an effort. Best he's going to get. Remind me to tell my mom to expose then cover before the fast swap."

Clarissa tickled Noah's sleeper-covered foot and he grinned. "She'll remember. She did raise you, Kristen and Caleb."

"With the help of the bunkhouse cook as our part-time nanny."

"Your mother wasn't perfect and you won't be, either. No parent is, and everyone needs help."

"Touché," Wyatt acknowledged. He'd used a nanny in Denver.

"Now, these babies…that's another story. They are perfect. Perfectly adorable. Gimme. I've waited long enough."

Wyatt passed a changed Ethan to Clarissa. Holding him close to her chest, she blew bubbles at him. The outgoing one of the twins, Ethan immediate reached for Clarissa's thick black glasses. "No, you don't," Wyatt's grandmother said as she pushed them back onto her nose. She held out a rattle instead.

"Da da da," Ethan babbled as the rattle shook in his fist.

His grandmother grinned. "I can see this one loves music. Will he play the saxophone like you did?"

"No idea. Another bridge we'll cross when we get to it. We do like listening to the classics. They particularly like the London Symphony Orchestra."

"Classics, huh?" Clarissa cooed at Ethan as he continued to shake the rattle. "We need to get you into some country classics, like Reba and Dolly. Maybe some Merle."

"They've heard them. I'm no heathen. Did I tell you I got to meet Luke Bryan when he came by the station before a concert?"

"Ooh, your daddy thinks he's a big shot meeting a celebrity," Clarissa teased, rubbing her nose into Ethan's belly.

Wyatt set Noah on the table and unsnapped his pants. The second born by six minutes, Noah's deep brown eyes blinked as Wyatt changed him. Wyatt ran his hand over the top of a head covered in soft blond hair. "Shall we find out if your grandma has your food ready? No worries, little buddy. Baby food, she can do. That's why she had a cook and still does."

"Da," Noah said with a wide grin that showed his bottom two teeth.

"That's right. I'm your Dad," he confirmed. At some point, it would click.

Soon Wyatt had both boys strapped into their high chairs eating pieces of banana. Wyatt alternated between spooning pureed sweet potato into one mouth and then the other.

"It's good to have babies in the house again," his grandmother said as Ethan drank water from his sippy cup. "Tomorrow morning you should go into Bundle and Bloom. Since you sold most of your stuff and babies grow so fast, I know you'll need things. Are they crawling?"

Knowing the cabin was already furnished, he'd moved only the essentials. "Yes, but not far."

"That'll change quickly." His mother hovered on the periphery, participating but not intruding. Wyatt never doubted her affection, but she'd never been touchy-feely in the way his grandmother was.

"I believe you. They've already grown so much." When it was clear the twins were done eating, Wyatt began the process of cleaning messy fingers and removing the high-chair trays. He suppressed a yawn. "I know we said we might do dinner, but can we rain check? Say until tomorrow? I'd like to get them settled in. And I should probably eat Betty's Stroganoff so it doesn't go bad." His mother appeared slightly crestfallen by his choice. "Do you want to hold one? Carry him over to the cabin for me?"

He'd never seen his mother appear truly excited, until now. Sadness morphed to joy and she stepped toward him. "I would love that."

Since Ethan was kicking, she unbuckled Noah and lifted him from the high chair. "Come here, sweetheart." Noah immediately began crying and reached for Wyatt.

“Maybe take Ethan,” he suggested. In contrast to his brother, Ethan immediately began to smile.

“Aren’t you the cutest thing,” his mother cooed as she settled him onto her hip. “I’m your grandmother and I love your red shirt.” Ethan made a razzing sound.

They bundled the kids into coats and hats for the short walk, and soon after, the group entered the cabin. Five minutes later, after a round of hugs and kisses for him and his sons, his mother and grandmother said their goodbyes. His dad had unloaded the car, and set the suitcases and boxes to the left of the front door. Wyatt decided to unpack everything but the essentials tomorrow. And his grandmother was right in that he could use a few things from the baby store, starting with a stroller. They’d borrowed one from a friend in Denver and had returned it when they’d left.

“Let’s see what we’ve got to work with.” He unpacked the play yard and set Ethan and Noah inside. Once they were secure, he took inventory. His mom and grandmother had babyproofed. The outlets had safety covers. The former open-to-the-room fireplace had new glass doors secured with a child lock. Corners had bumpers. Electrical cords had been secured. The cabinets had safety latches. Heavy furniture had either been removed, or secured to the walls. A wood coffee table with rounded edges had replaced the glass one.

The smaller, second bedroom had two cribs and a changing table similar to what was in the main house. However, he’d need a gate or two. A small bookcase for the growing collection of children’s books. A rocker was a must, as was a small dresser that would fit inside the closet. He assumed Bundle and Bloom would have furniture he could order. The boys would enjoy an outing into town, especially as the weather would be warmer. Maybe he'd ask his mother if she'd like to go with them. See if being with her grandsons might loosen her up. Wasn't that what his coworkers had said? That their own parents had done one-eighties when they'd become grandparents? *Like, who knew my mom could be fun?* one had said.

With his sons happily gnawing on the soft teething toys he'd put in the play yard, Wyatt microwaved some beef Stroganoff, which turned out to be so delicious he had two helpings. As he ate and watched the twins, he continued to make a list. Any stroller needed to be something that would handle the long ranch driveway and town sidewalks, along with some of the gravel paths of the nearby parks. He didn't remember the brand he'd used, but it had had all the bells and whistles.

Since the twins still ate formula about every four-to-six hours when awake, he prepped seven ounces for each. After their feeding, he cuddled each boy in his lap as he read aloud from a board-book version of *Goodnight Moon.* Then, after another changing into fresh diapers and bunny-themed sleepers, he set the boys in their cribs, checked that the baby monitor worked, started some soft classical music and flipped on the night-light. If he was lucky, which he normally wasn't, they'd sleep a good eight to nine hours, especially as it was past their usual bedtime.

Hopefully, this move to Legacy Canyon meant that their family's routine would shift for the better, especially as he no longer had to wake up around 1:30 a.m. to get to the news station by three. Leaving the rest of the luggage and boxes for tomorrow morning, Wyatt unpacked his carry-on suitcase, stored his toiletries in the medicine cabinet and wandered into the bedroom to check on the twins. He found them fast asleep, their chests rising and falling smoothly, their tiny fists above their heads. His heart overflowed. They were marvels. The closest thing to seeing an angel was a sleeping baby. And he had two. His sons.

They were his family. His future. He'd lay down his life for them. As for dating? He meant what he'd said. As much as the idea of holding a woman held appeal—and in his single days Wyatt admittedly had enjoyed sex—life was different now. The boys came first. He'd willingly chosen this path and was all in.

Whether his father liked it or not.

Chapter Two

"You really should take it easy." Dr. Madison Brennan heaved what had to be her thousandth sigh in less than an hour—and Bundle and Bloom wouldn't even open its doors for another fifteen minutes. At least her grandmother was not standing on a stepladder, like where she'd found her yesterday. "Please." Maybe pleading would work since the well-intentioned chiding had not.

"The doctor says that my arm is just fine." As if to demonstrate, her seventy-eight-year-old grandmother moved past carrying two boxes perched precariously. "And we have to restock since we did so well at Christmas and New Year's. Hardly any returns. A miracle."

"Still, let me take those." Madi moved swiftly and retrieved the oversized square boxes before they toppled to the floor. "The doctor also said no heavy lifting."

"They weren't heavy."

That assertion was debatable and suspect. Madi planted her palm on the lid and worked to keep everything steady as she set the boxes next to a display of infant snowsuits. "You're only two weeks past having the cast removed and still in physical therapy. You need to take it easy."

"I'm fine." Her grandmother's vinegar came through

loud and clear. "You don't need to worry. You can stop questioning your elders."

"Never." Because Madi did worry. Owing to the nature of the facture, her grandmother's arm hadn't healed as quickly or as well as her medical team would have liked. While a broken arm took an average of six weeks to mend, it could take up to twelve for older adults, and her grandmother's injury fit that bill. "Don't make me pull the doctor card on you," Madi warned. While she made her tone teasing, she meant every word. Then again, what type of a doctor was she really, if she'd failed one of her easiest cases?

"I can hear you thinking," her grandmother said. A feisty gray-haired dynamo standing five-five to Madi's five-seven, she began slicing the seam of a box. "What happened was not your fault."

"No, but it triggered an audit of my work just the same." And while that had revealed no performance lapses, Madi still felt the residual guilt on a personal level. She'd failed a child who'd needed her. If she couldn't make a simple diagnosis—of appendicitis, of all things, something so textbook—what good would she be with more complicated pediatric illnesses? Or as a doctor in one of Boston's top practices? She still hadn't accepted the job offer because of the lapse.

"I should have ordered an ultrasound the first time. I knew better." Madi pried the lid on the second box and withdrew a stack of Valentine's Day–themed onesies that had My Heart Belongs to Daddy on them.

"So could your supervising physician," her grandmother pointed out. "Ultimately, he's the one that made the diagnosis it was constipation and sent the child home."

"She was my patient. She was in pain." The mistake haunted her. Madi had wanted to be a pediatrician as long as she could remember and here she was, burned out at the age of thirty-one. "The surgeon said he could see the appendicitis when he opened her up. We're lucky it didn't burst. Thank goodness that mom was persistent."

The mother had brought the child back to the ER three days later with the same symptoms and seen another attending pediatric resident, one whose attending physician had listened and ordered an ultrasound. When her cohort had determined it hadn't looked correct, he'd contacted the surgeon, who'd agreed. The child had suffered three more days of pain because Madi had missed the obvious.

"I should have tried harder. Maybe pressed more." Instead, she'd sent the girl home, gone off her shift and then straight into a very boring date her parents had arranged with the son of a one of their friends. They'd eaten rubbery chicken at some charity gala while both sets of their parents had hoped it would work. It hadn't.

"Stop it," her grandmother ordered. "All the blood work was in the normal range. It was not your fault. You were a resident under a supervisor."

But this was the type of mistake Madi obsessed over. Always had. She was a perfectionist raised by two overachieving parents who, while they'd doted on their only child, had at the same time demanded she meet the highest of expectations. Her father, a renowned cardiac surgeon, had been delighted his daughter had followed in his footsteps and entered the medical profession. Driven to excel, she'd not only attended one of the country's best medical schools, but she'd also worked hard to secure a residency at Boston's top children's hospital. Certainly, the sixty-to-eighty-hour weeks had been brutal, and she'd survived on little to no sleep and half as much food. But she was in her zone. Learning from the best.

She hadn't realized she'd been on a path to burnout and depression. When her residency ended, Madi had been at a crossroads. She'd found herself unable to commit to the prestigious job offer she'd received from a friend of her father. She'd had the worst time on yet another date her parents had arranged. She didn't want to become part of some country-club social set. At loose ends and questioning how to solve the problem, when she'd learned her grandmother had fallen and needed help with the store, Madi had volunteered. She still worked with infants and toddlers, but instead by selling their parents high-end merchandise instead of treating them medically.

It had been a break she needed, and the practice had given her until the end of February to accept their offer because everyone, including her, knew she'd say yes. Her father didn't understand why she hadn't already, and told her she would have still had the same start date of mid-March either way.

Madi knew it didn't make sense, but escaping to Legacy Canyon without making a commitment had been a great way to get out of Boston for the holidays. Running the shop was fun and different, and while she eventually would like to find a nice guy and have both love and a career, Legacy Canyon had been the break she needed. Well, minus all the matchmaking attempts by her grandmother's well-meaning but persistent friends. Those had been annoying, and so nonstop that she was running out of decent excuses. Unfortunately, her grandmother's friends didn't understand the word *no*, even when uttered endlessly.

The man from yesterday popped into her head. When she'd told her grandmother about what had happened, she'd shrugged and said, "This is Legacy Canyon. Matt brought out the stuff. The kids weren't in danger."

She would have called the police and child services if they had been.

"How are those coming along?" her grandmother called.

"Good. Almost done." Madi studied her handiwork. Adjusted a onesie to make it line up perfectly. Then moved another. Her grandmother had built a thriving enterprise, and helping her keep it running until she was completely healed was Madi's focus. Not dating. Not her future. After the frenetic pace of residency, she was taking one day at a time.

"Oh, I love those! They're perfect for my niece and nephew." Madi moved aside as one of her grandmother's employees plucked two of them from the display, creating a messy pile. The store would open soon, and even though it was a Thursday, because of its location directly on the square, Bundle and Bloom did a brisk walk-in business. Madi began to straighten the remaining onesies.

In a tourist destination like historic Legacy Canyon, it was never too early to sell upcoming holiday-themed merchandise, which is why her grandmother was putting out the green-and-white shamrock bibs. Her grandmother glanced over. "Perfect. The rest of those will be gone by this weekend. It's the Snowball Festival, you know."

Which was why there was a table up front with baby items decorated in snowflakes and snowmen. "Is that another committee project?" Madi was losing track of them all.

"The committee likes to stay active. There's at least one event a month. You'll go with me, of course."

Madi sighed. "As long as you stop trying to fix me up."

"Who, me?" Her grandmother blinked innocently. She made to grab an empty box from the floor, but Madi beat her to it.

"Yes, you. I'm rather tired of it." Madi held the box out of reach.

Her grandmother pouted. "We just want you to find someone."

"And I will, on my timeline. Besides, you know I'm not staying. But I will attend. The events you and the committee put on are lovely. The rest, not so much." Madi had liked the community tree lighting, which had come complete with Santa, a holiday toy drive and Christmas caroling. "No more of 'this is one of my good friend's grandsons who happens to be single that you must meet.' Promise me."

"I promise," her grandmother said.

Suspecting her grandmother had crossed her fingers behind her back, Madi lifted the empty boxes and carried them to storeroom. By the time she returned, the store was open and filled with customers. She was so busy, she lost track of time. After a huge group of tourists purchased almost the entire stock of Baby's First Valentine's Day bibs, Madi headed toward the storeroom to retrieve more. She did a double take as she went by a mirror and shoved some loose strands of her shoulder-length, dark brown hair behind her ear. Thankfully, she didn't appear as washed out as when she'd arrived. Most of the stress lines around her blue eyes had faded, as had the dark circles once bigger than nearby Palo Duro Canyon.

She grabbed another box of bibs and passed her grandmother as she carried them out to the sales floor.

"I'm going to use the restroom," her grandmother said. "Since it's lunchtime, it's gotten pretty quiet."

"Already?" She glanced at her watch.

"Yes. Just one customer over by the strollers. Set those bibs down and go see if they need help."

Besides baby and toddler furniture, strollers were also high-ticket items, with some costing in the low four figures. Amazingly, people bought them. However, many also came in, browsed and then ordered online in an attempt to get the item cheaper. Madi would wait to see if the shopper—she found it odd that it was a man—wanted any help. He was probably purchasing something for a gift. Maybe for his wife or sister. She'd remind him that Bundle and Bloom shipped nationwide, too. She quickly restocked the bibs on the display table.

Her grandmother reappeared and nodded toward the shoppers who'd just entered. "I'll get them. You go sell a stroller. We don't keep customers waiting."

Keeping him in her periphery, she made her way over. "Hi, may I…?"

"Ah, ah!" Two sets of legs clad in different colors of winter puffer pants kicked out from the seat of a flimsy umbrella stroller.

"Da!" Another distinctive voice. Twins.

Madi took a better look. It was a double stroller holding two blond-headed twin boys. Was this their…? Oh, my.

"You!" The word burst out. She'd recognize him anywhere, and she closed her mouth so that her jaw didn't wobble like that of a beached fish. Yesterday, she'd been focused on the kids inside the car. Today, she got a good look at the man who'd thought it okay to leave them there. As her body's reaction roared to life, and this time it wasn't in anger, she worked to keep her wits. She'd had multiple hot dads come through the pediatric ER with infants, toddlers and even teens in tow. But he was something else entirely, in a class of his own.

Chiseled nose and cheekbones. Full lips. Dark brown eyes the color of warm chocolate she wanted to drown in—in his case, not a silly cliché. He stood about half a foot taller, and the jet-black hair curling at his nape made her fingers itch to touch it. And when he smiled, his teeth were so white and perfect he could be on television. The innate confidence he wore like a second skin was tempered only by the way he was looking around the store like a lost puppy.

"And look, it's you." Even his voice was deep, with a husky, sensual quality that gave her shivers despite the seventy-degree indoor temperature. His cadence was perfect as his words washed over her. "You work here?"

"I do. I see you actually have your children with you today." She winced as the words came out harsher than intended.

"I had them with me yesterday, too. And wasn't leaving them locked in a car. Despite what you might have thought."

Well, that told her, didn't it? She gathered her bearings. Handsome men were a dime a dozen in her parents' crowd. She'd grown up around them. She could handle him, even if it was to run him out of the store. Then again, he was a potential customer, and selling something would help the bottom line. She'd upset her grandmother if she lost this sale.

"Are you looking for a stroller?" That sounded so lame, as if being in his orbit had crossed the wires in her brain. Best she ignore her racing heart.

"I am definitely looking for a stroller. I'm standing by them." Was he deliberately goading her? He pointed to the umbrella stroller. "This one isn't really built for Legacy Canyon."

Madi held her temper. Whoever he was, he lived here. The pharmacist had come out, greeted him and handed him medicine. That meant her grandmother would lose a long-term customer if Madi botched this, or told him to take a hike. "I assume you'd like one stroller that's built for two. Or would you like two strollers?"

"As it's just me pushing them both, definitely need one built for two."

"A double stroller then."

"Yes. Seeing as I have two sons." He waited patiently, and Madi's perfectionist nature inwardly screamed at her flubs.

"Yes, I can see them. They are cuties."

"I'd like to think so." He stood there watching her.

Madi rubbed her hands on her thighs, the chino fabric smooth underneath her fingers. She was clearly failing this sales encounter. Couldn't get her bearings, especially after yesterday. "So did you have any preference as to a model?"

He pointed. "I was looking at this one."

It was one with a four-figure price tag. "Shall I show you some of the features?" *Please say no.* Onesies, she could handle. Not strollers with more features than a high-end sports car. She had no clue how the contraption worked. That was something they didn't teach in medical school.

"Do you recommend it?" he asked instead. "Seeing as you're a kid expert."

Madi gritted her teeth. "Listen, it seems like we got off on the wrong foot and—"

"Da da da!" One of the twins began kicking, while the other blew raspberries. Distracted, Mr. Hot Dad leaned down to wipe his son's mouth with a burp cloth. The movement made his shirtsleeve inch up his left arm, showing a well-defined forearm lightly dusted with dark hair. She didn't see a ring, not that that meant anything. Many men didn't wear wedding rings so that they didn't get caught in machinery. Or whatever. She'd made that mistake before. She also needed to stop staring at him like a cat finding the cream. She wasn't some spellbound teenager—she was a doctor. Smarter than this. And he had left his kids inside a car. How would she know he wasn't leaving the curb? She'd seen too many instances of parents forgetting to check the back seat.

"So, yes or no to recommending this," he prompted, his deep brown gaze fixating on hers. "I don't have all day."

"Uh, y-yes? S-sorry." Caught staring, she stammered out the words and began to fiddle with the stroller's handle.

"You'd use it with your own children?"

"I don't have children, but my grandmother owns the shop and she only stocks the best merchandise. We're not about the quick sale. We're about making lifelong friends."

"A good slogan. Sounds like something she or her husband would have said."

There was a slight twinkle in his eyes, and she couldn't tell if he was serious about her grandfather, or if he'd known him, or if he was making fun of her. She played it safe. "Thank you. It's the truth. And are you sure you don't want to look at any of the others? We could order them in and…"

A shake of his head ended that suggestion. "I need a stroller today. Like now. Cut the tags off and walk out the store with it now. Can't lose any more bad dad points, like being mistaken for leaving my children alone."

"I didn't know if you needed to consult with your wife or anything before you made your purchase."

As he arched an eyebrow, she bit the inside of her lip. She sounded like she was fishing for information. "Do you know who I am?"

"Should I?" She was from Boston, and while Legacy Canyon was small, she hadn't met everyone. "And should it matter?"

Where was her grandmother? She knew the strollers she stocked far better than Madi did. Even if this man planned on swiping his credit card for the easiest sale ever, she was floundering and shouldn't be. She was a pediatrician. She erred on the side of caution. Minus ordering that ultrasound, that was. She tried to concentrate but the second twin began wiggling. The man replaced the pacifier that had fallen out of his mouth. He straightened, turned to her and withdrew a folded piece of paper. "No wife, much to my father's eternal disappointment. It's me and the boys. I'll take the stroller. I also need everything on this list. Today. Can you handle that?"

"Okay. I mean, yes." Ignoring the way her heart gave a jump, she took the looseleaf sheet from his hand. The surprise sizzle that was created when their fingers grazed meant the paper slid out of her grip. She caught it and her eyes widened as she looked at the sheet. "You need all of this. Today."

"Is that a problem? This is a baby store, right? It's why my grandmother sent me."

She sensed his impatience. Bristled slightly. "Of course, this is a baby store. I'm sure it's not going to be a problem."

"No, but you're judging me again for not having all this. I just moved home. We figured we'd buy it when we arrived."

"That's fine. I..." Where was the control she exhibited in the ER? Where was the compassionate yet impenetrable doctor who had confidence in her skills? She was flailing like a person trying to escape quicksand. "My grandmother would be thrilled to..."

Mr. Hot Dad who just moved here cut her off. "Perfect. And since these guys are getting antsy, I'll have you do the shopping and arrange for a delivery later this afternoon. I'll either open an account or leave my credit card. Your grandmother is friends with mine. She'll vouch for me."

He wiped another mouth and replaced the Binky. "If there's nothing else?"

Across the store, her grandmother was ringing up a sale on the iPad that served as the register. She claimed it was easier than making a daily trip to the bank, so her grandmother had gone cashless. "I need to find out if we can deliver today."

A twin began to whimper. "Hold on, Ethan," the man

said. He rummaged into his backpack and handed his son a clear sippy cup full of a white liquid. Formula, Madi assumed. As if knowing his brother had gotten something, the other twin began to fuss until he had a sippy cup in hand, too, the pacifier once again falling, this time to the floor.

Madi bent to grab it at the same time the twin's dad did, and they clocked heads. "Ow." She saw stars. Her hand reached for her forehead and she staggered back slightly. This man was dangerous. Literally.

"Are you okay?" His hands went to her shoulders, his touch sending a jolt down her spine, one that momentarily took her mind off the fact her head hurt. As he steadied her, that deep brown gaze roamed over her. "How many fingers am I holding up?"

"Two, and stop that." She was the doctor here.

He dropped his hand, but only to push some hair off her face. "The red is already fading."

This must be what people meant when they swooned, which meant she was in danger of becoming a bad romance cliché. "I'm fine." As he released her, she rubbed the spot on her forehead. "No worries." *Nothing that some acetaminophen wouldn't fix.* "I'll be okay." Not really. She'd made a fool out of herself, which triggered her every insecurity. Despite her mortification, she remembered her manners. "How's your head?"

"I'm hardheaded, so I think you took the worst of it. I'm sorry that happened. Clearly, we had the same idea. We probably need to stop meeting like this."

If he hadn't come in, they wouldn't have met at all. At least his words didn't sound as harsh as before, as if he'd softened his attitude after his accidental attempt to knock her out. Her heart raced, but Madi couldn't decide if the adrenaline was from being bonked on the head or the fact that he'd almost touched her again.

"Well, I'll be! Wyatt Larrabee! Your grandmother told me you were coming." Madi's grandma had finally made her way across the store. Her face lit up like a firecracker when she spotted the good-looking man in front of her.

Madi wished the floor would swallow her. This was Wyatt Larrabee? She'd heard about the Larrabees. They were one of the town's founding families. Ignoring the fact he stood over a half foot taller, her grandmother sized him up. "Let me get a good look at you. My. My. No wonder the camera loves you. When did you get back?"

"Arrived yesterday evening, ma'am." He had a voice that resonated. Tremors that were as unwelcome as an earthquake passed through her.

Her grandmother's smile widened. "I tell you, son, you are much better-looking in person. Your grandma brags on you all the time. And here you are in my store."

"About that…" Wyatt began.

"We'll fix you up." As her grandmother turned to her, Madi straightened. "Wyatt here used to do the morning weather in Denver. Now, he'll be working in Amarillo. What…five and six?"

"Yes. But evenings instead of mornings. Wanted to be home more for these two. Which is why I need stuff."

Madi had been right about him being on TV. Why not? He had the *it* factor. A presence that commanded. She thrust the sheet of paper toward her grandmother, who made no move to take it. Madi rustled it slightly. "This is what he needs. He's buying a stroller and needs everything on this list. He needs us to shop for him and deliver."

Ignoring Madi's outstretched arm, her grandmother clasped her hands. "You're in the right place. Not to worry. Madi will shop and will deliver everything we have in stock to you this afternoon. Make sure you don't have any questions about anything."

"I will?" Madi asked. When had she become a delivery driver? And she wanted to be as far as possible from Wyatt and the fact he made her stomach topsy-turvy.

"Of course, you will. I've known Wyatt since he was a baby. His grandmother and I are on the committee together."

Madi's eyes narrowed in suspicion. Surely, her grandmother wasn't going to play matchmaker again, especially after Madi had told her no more before the store opened. Madi planned to be in Boston by the middle of March, at the latest. She wasn't staying. Even if Wyatt might be the type of guy for whom a woman would want to change her plans. But not her. Some other woman.

Her grandmother's smile never wavered. "You have to help, Madi. You were just telling me about how I needed to do less and you know the doctor won't let me drive yet."

Madi managed to hold her temper as her own words came back to haunt her. Her grandmother smiled at Wyatt. "I broke my arm a while back and it's still healing even though the cast is off."

"I hope you're doing better."

"Oh, I am. But Madi will need to take the van and drive things out." As if knowing she'd pulled a fast one, her grandmother's eyes reflected a hint of mirth. "Wyatt's staying at the cabin on the Larrabee Ranch. It'll be easy to find." She gestured to the stroller Wyatt had chosen. "We'll put Wyatt's sons in this one because it's the best. Even though it's a display, I unboxed it yesterday and no one's even used it. It's fate. Like it's been waiting for you to arrive."

Or because Wyatt's grandmother had made a phone call to her coconspirator. Madi folded her arms. This smacked of committee meddling.

"Perfect." Wyatt seemed far more amiable now that her grandmother had decided things. "I'm meeting my grandmother for lunch at Bantry's. I think that's down the boardwalk a few. Then I'm off to the bank to get an account set up."

"You'll like Bantry's. It's new. In fact, Madi can walk you there. Tracy's getting my lunch order ready. Madi, you'll pick it up. Bring it back here. Get yourself something while you're at it. My treat. Let me go get some scissors so that we can cut the tags off. That umbrella stroller is..."

"A disaster," Wyatt said, finishing for her. "But I had to leave the one I borrowed in Denver."

"We'll fix you right up." They watched her grandmother move toward the sales counter, then Madi scurried after her.

"Grandma," Madi hissed.

Her grandmother turned around. "What? Go tell him you're going to get his order together. He's a Larrabee. They're good for it."

"He's the guy from yesterday. The one I told you about."

"What guy?" It took a moment before her grandmother's eyes widened in comprehension. "Oh."

"I can't shop or deliver for him. It's awkward."

Her grandmother touched her arm. "You can and you will. Apologize if you need to, but this is a huge order. And he's not a bad dad. He adopted those boys to save them from the foster system. Maybe you misinterpreted things. I told you, this is Legacy Canyon. We do things differently."

This was worse than her male colleagues mansplaining medical procedures. She pressed a pair of scissors into Madi's hands. "Go help him before those boys get antsy. Don't keep him from meeting his grandmother. She'd have my hide if he's late."

"Fine." With a huff to show her displeasure, Madi headed back over to Wyatt. "My grandmother says to take this stroller and we'll settle up. Says you're good for it."

"Thanks, Madi. I appreciate the shopping and delivery." The way he said her name sounded like he was trying it on, tasting it. No wonder several women who'd wandered into the shop were unabashedly staring at him. "Your help is a godsend, believe me. I appreciate you greatly."

"Even if I yelled at you yesterday?"

"Even if. It simply means you cared."

Wyatt's minuscule shrug made her feel slightly less self-conscious. "Comes with the job. I'm a pediatrician. I'll be in private practice in March"

"Totally makes sense now. And no worries. It was a simple mistake to make. I would never endanger my sons."

Madi knew he believed that, but she'd seen far too many injured or sick children come through the ER with their well-intentioned parents. "Well, let's get your cute sons moved so you can go meet your grandmother. If she's anything like mine..." Madi paused. She'd met enough of the committee to know they had a type. But despite being a Larrabee, she didn't know Wyatt. Didn't want to be critical of his parenting, at least not more than she already had been.

"Yeah, exactly. You don't have to say it. Believe me, I know exactly how she is. And you've not met my mother, either."

"Lucky me?" Madi asked.

"One hundred percent. She's best avoided whenever possible." The cheeky grin crossing his face threatened to turn her into a gooey puddle, not that Legacy Canyon had seen any real rainfall in months. The lack of rain was a constant on everyone's minds, and the last snowfall had been pretty but not nearly enough. Madi's grandmother had told her that some ranches in the area were land-rich and cash-poor.

"My hat's off to you then, for having to endure," Madi said.

"You aren't wearing a hat."

"Exactly." Madi arched her eyebrows before dissolving into a laugh. "Not sure what's gotten into me." Especially since she was flirting, of all things.

"Legacy Canyon has that effect on people." Wyatt lifted one of his sons and used a burp cloth to wipe off some spittle. He turned the baby around so he faced Madi. "This is Ethan."

"Hello, Ethan." Big brown eyes started at her and Ethan gave her a razzing sound, the kind that made her biological clock immediately begin to tick. An anomaly, she decided, especially as no other infant she'd worked with had done the same. Despite this extended "vacation," she was still a pediatrician. She was around babies all the time, whether in a medical environment or the store. Babies were adorable, like kittens or puppies. That's all this heartstring tugging was. But for a woman whose biggest stressor was deciding where to work, she was certainly having weird pitter-patters.

"This is Noah. He's a little shyer." Wyatt pointed to the son still seated in the umbrella stroller.

"Which is fine. We don't all have to be extroverted." She checked the urge to slip into baby talk and coo at the cute Noah. She was a professional. When Wyatt grinned at his sons, though, she struggled to remain unaffected. But she refused to let herself long for something she didn't want to voice, much less acknowledge. Plenty of time for motherhood later.

A woman edged closer, her face peering at Wyatt's. "I know you," she said. She looked at Ethan. "And you. You've gotten bigger."

As if he was used to this type of intrusion, Wyatt gave the lady a patient yet pleasant smile. "I apologize in advance if I don't remember meeting you."

The middle-aged shopper waved aside his apology. "Oh, no, we've never met. You're that weatherman who adopted those kids. I live in Denver but I'm down here visiting my daughter. I saw the report your station did. My daughter and son-in-law saw the show. Because of your segment, they're now foster parents. Thanks for the good work."

"That's wonderful to hear. I'm glad they've done that.

It's so needed. Thank you for telling me." Wyatt appeared genuinely moved.

She held out her phone. "Do you mind if we take a selfie? My daughter is not going to believe I met you in Legacy Canyon, of all places."

"Uh, that's great." To Madi's eye, Wyatt didn't look too comfortable, but he played along. The woman took a picture and thanked Wyatt.

"Does that happen often?" Madi asked as the woman left the store, her fingers texting the photo. She'd also noticed Wyatt hadn't told the woman he was from here.

Wyatt appeared embarrassed. "It did in Denver. Hopefully less now that I moved back home yesterday. I wanted to be closer to family so I could raise the boys. I was driving into town when my grandmother asked me to pick up my grandfather's meds. That's why I stopped."

His saying that felt like a truce of sorts. "Ah. That makes sense. I'm sorry I judged."

"You've probably seen some things as a doctor," Wyatt acknowledged. "So, where are you from. Not here."

"No. Boston. But you are clearly from Legacy Canyon."

"Yep. But gone until I ended my exile." That sexy little dent in his chin dipped. "Needed a break from the noise. I'm hoping my being recognized won't happen as much as it did in Denver. What you saw is the result of me telling my story of fostering and adopting these two. Thankfully I'll be at the ranch most days when I'm not at the station."

Maybe he was more than a pretty face her fingers itched to touch. "That's admirable. I worked with some foster families when I was a pediatric resident. It's an important role and there's such a great need."

He arched an eyebrow. "And now you're in Legacy Canyon working here, at the store?"

"Just temporarily. You heard my grandmother. She broke her arm. I flew out before the holidays. You can see how she is. And I needed a break, too. In that, we might be kindred spirits."

Her grandmother chose that moment to reappear. "Why are the two of you still standing around? Get going. Hand me those." Marya took the tags Madi had cut. "I'll ring everything and call you with the total. You can pay me then."

"That's perfect. Appreciate it." Wyatt lowered Ethan into the front seat and put Noah in the back. Once he'd buckled them in, Wyatt glanced at his watch. "I'll look forward to getting the delivery. I should be home after three. Thanks for your help. Got to go. My grandmother's waiting."

Marya gave him a cheery wave. "Tell Clarissa I said hi. And, Madi, you're showing Wyatt the way, remember? So you can pick up my lunch order? You need to go get it."

Madi refrained from an eye roll and led Wyatt from the store. She shivered. She should have worn a coat like Wyatt and his boys. While the temperature was warmer than yesterday, it was still cold. "It's just three or four storefronts down this way."

Wyatt fell into step beside her. "You know, she didn't need to send you. Bantry's delivers."

"You don't think I know that?"

He laughed. "Feel free to say what you're thinking,

that you don't know why she's making such a fuss. Or that she's being incorrigible."

Madi stopped short and faced him. "Am I being that obvious?"

Lips any woman would want to kiss curled in a grin. "No, that was your grandmother. Which is why you don't need to worry. I'm used to it. I know how members of the committee are. Their machinations are legendary. Let me guess, you've been the subject of their matchmaking attempts since you arrived."

Madi sighed in relief. "Oh, yes, terribly. Let's see, there was her plumber. He was divorced and at least six years older than me, not that there's anything wrong with that. Her worst attempt was the package-delivery guy who brings the stock. She tried, anyway, even though I'm so not his type. I'm not sure who was more mortified, me or him. I wish the committee stuck with organizing events."

He had the type of grin that could suck someone in and never let go. "Well, since they have the event organizing down to an art form, that leaves them plenty of time for meddling, their true calling. They like to have their noses in everyone's business. Been doing it to me since I was as young as these guys. That's Legacy Canyon."

"Like yesterday's handoff outside the drugstore." Madi was beginning to understand.

"Exactly. We try to be helpful here, and Matt and I go way back."

"In Boston, most people pass each other and never speak."

"That is not the Texas way. In Legacy Canyon, you'll

be best friends with someone by the time you're at the end of the supermarket checkout line. That's one reason I came home. While I liked Denver, once that story aired, everyone suddenly wanted to be Mrs. Larrabee. And there's something about returning to my roots to raise my family. I want the best for them."

"That's a noble goal." Madi nodded at someone they passed. Realized that to any passersby, she and Wyatt probably looked like a family. She quickly brushed aside that image. While she still had to decide her future, staying in Legacy Canyon was not one of the choices. "Let's hope the committee doesn't turn their attention to you."

"That's my hope, too, but I'm not holding my breath."

"Well, I feel like I owe you another apology. This one for my grandmother. She can be pretty intense. Pushy. Which is why I'm escorting you."

His laugh was deep and rich, the kind that washed over a girl and made her insides gooey. "Just wait until you meet my grandmother. We're here."

"In fact, we are." Why was she disappointed? She held the door to Bantry's so Wyatt could push the stroller through. He glanced around and frowned. "Although, you might have met my grandmother if she was here."

"She's not?" Madi scanned the crowded room, not that she knew what Wyatt's grandmother looked like.

Wyatt pulled his cell phone from his pocket. Sent a text. A reply came quickly and he groaned. "But of course."

"What is it?" Madi had moved to the take-out counter, and she turned around so she could face him.

"She's canceled. She's a no-show." Wyatt held out

his phone, as if Madi could read the text from where she stood.

"That's awful. I'm sorry." Madi smiled at the girl behind the counter. "Order for Marya Brennan, please."

The girl glanced through the tickets before checking her computer. "Are you sure you called an order in? We don't have anything for Marya."

"How is that possible?" Madi stared, dumbfounded, as Wyatt pushed the stroller closer. Whatever aftershave he wore permeated her senses and made delicious goose bumps prickle. She really needed to get out of here. Not only had she misjudged him, but now, her hormones were also acting crazy.

Wyatt wore an odd expression. "Let me guess. Your grandmother doesn't have a lunch order?"

"I don't know what happened," Madi said. "There must be a mix-up."

"There's nothing for Marya? You're positive you didn't miss it?" Wyatt peered at the girl working behind the counter as she studied her computer screen.

She shook her head. "Sorry, but no. Nothing."

Wyatt turned to Madi. His lips puckered. "How convenient."

Madi frowned. "She must not have placed the order. It's a simple mistake. I know what she likes. I can do it."

He shook his head. "Oh, Madi, Madi, Madi."

"What?" She didn't like feeling naive, or his pitying expression.

"Hate to break it to you, but yours has no order and mine's a no-show. It means we've been set up."

Chapter Three

Wyatt would commiserate more with Madi if the situation wasn't already so awkward. Who could have predicted his grandmother would try to set him up with the woman who'd accused him of being a terrible father? Fate's sense of irony was strong today. Madi had apologized, and after speaking with her at the store, he understood her reasoning came from the fact she was a pediatrician. But he shrugged it off since he had to deal with the bigger problem, which was that he and Madi had been sideswiped by the committee. No matter how well-intentioned, his annoyance flared.

At least Madi seemed like a woman who could hold her own, which impressed him. It didn't hurt that she was easy on the eyes, either, as she craned what could only be described as a lovely neck to read the menu board above the counter. "I'll order her something and bring it back. She told me to grab something, so I will. And make her pay."

Madi's chest heaved and Wyatt yanked his gaze upward. "Pay for the sandwich or pay for trying to set you up with me?"

"Both." Madi didn't miss a beat. "It's the least I can do to return the favor."

A chuckle burst forth and he liked how she smiled back at him. "Smart woman. Now, let me take a minute to apologize for the situation. I'm sorry our grandparents put you on the spot. It was rude of them. The committee is merciless in their meddling and you being an outsider means you don't deserve this."

"I hate to be thought of as an outsider."

"Mea culpa. What I meant is that since you didn't grow up here, you don't know how terrible their good intentions can be. To survive, those of us who did grow up here learned how to run interference. It's a lifetime skill set. Sort of like tolerating the endless breeze."

"God's blow dryer."

Her mouth twisted wryly and he resisted the urge to smooth it. "Yep. You've already got the lingo down."

"How do you stand it? The meddling, I mean, not the wind. Like I said, they've been relentless with trying to fix me up with this person or that one since I arrived. Today, it was you. I keep telling them to stop but it does no good."

"Nope. Not one bit. *No* is not in their vocabulary." He checked on the boys. Done with their sippy cups and secure in their fancy new stroller, they'd fallen asleep. "I hate to tell you this, but their manipulations are ingrained. Like they're born with it. They couldn't stop if they tried. Haven't for decades. One generation just passes it down to the next."

Madi's mouth dropped. "You're kidding me." She stared at him with those beautiful bluebonnet-covered eyes. "Really?"

"Yes. It's because they don't have anything better to do. Events like the Lasso for Legacy rodeo basically run themselves, so what's left, besides interfering in other people's lives? It's like they took a master class in meddling or something and then they teach others. It's like a book club. Or worse."

"Definitely worse." Madi bit her lower lip and let it go with an audible pop. He felt the impact in his groin. "Then we just have to be brighter and bolder. Figure out a way to outsmart them and beat them at their own game."

Wyatt wished it was that easy. "If only." He adjusted the lapel of Ethan's puffer. His sleeping son didn't stir. "I wouldn't be surprised if they're concocting another scheme. It's what they do."

"Probably. My grandmother does what she wants, which is probably carrying as many boxes as she can right now, despite being told by her doctor not to lift things. She's insisting she's fine, which why it's taking longer than normal for her to heal. But that's how she is. Stubborn as a mule. She's Jo March but with a baby store."

Madi's Boston accent slipped out, and the word came out as *stubbahn.* A splash of pink stained her cheeks. "Sorry. My college professor once said the blue-blooded Boston Brahmin accent drops its *r*'s like social obligations, while elongating its vowels as if they were family lineages stretching back to the *Mayflower.* Which, if you meet my mother, she will ensure that you know how far ours stretches. It's ridiculous, really. Who cares?"

Wyatt couldn't help but smile. Despite his initial impression on the sidewalk yesterday, they were kindred spirits in having families notorious for both legacy and matchmaking. "No worries. I think it's rather cute." That made the pink stain spread farther. He tried to reassure her. "And your family has nothing on mine. I'm the fifth generation, as my dad likes to say. And believe me, he lets me know how I disappoint him daily. Career. Lack of wife. You name it. It's a long list." The café had started to get even more crowded and people were starting to stare.

"There has to be a way we can make them stop trying to ruin our lives."

Wyatt recentered his gaze, taking in the determined way Madi's eyebrows knit together. "If you can figure it out, I'd love to hear it. But do you mind if we sit down? The boys and I are starting to attract a bit of attention. If we get situated, then we won't be so exposed."

Madi glanced around. "Oh. Wow. You do get the looks, don't you? There are people staring with blatant interest. Does that happen a lot?"

"Yeah. It's annoying," Wyatt confirmed. "Especially since the news story went national. Then the clip went viral. At one point, it felt like the entire country was trying to find me a wife. There was commentary on Reddit. Not to mention the women who'd mail things to the studio, or show up."

"They did that? I can't imagine."

"Me, either. Until it became my life." As Wyatt's coworker had told him after Security had turned away yet another small crowd, a man with a cute dog was a chick magnet. A gorgeous, sexy single dad with infant twin boys was the kick start to every single woman's hormonal desires. Not that he considered himself gorgeous or sexy, but he'd been told he was handsome enough for TV, so there was that. He pointed toward the window. "Let's take that table over there. We can order something to go if you want."

"Let's brainstorm while we wait. We can't let them

do this to us." Madi's face colored. "I mean…you and me. There is no us."

"No," Wyatt said. Even if the idea held some appeal. Madi was beautiful. In addition to her eyes, she had those angular cheekbones the camera loved. He'd describe her as a ray of sunshine on an otherwise gray day. He gave her a reassuring smile. "Madi, seriously. When I say no worries, I mean it. While it's not okay they tried to play matchmaker, I'm not offended this happened, or the fact that our grandmothers thought to introduce us. It's been a while since I've met someone who has no interest in me or my sons. I'm not surprised they didn't even wait twenty-four hours. This town doesn't just have a grapevine—it's got an entire vineyard."

An idea struck him. "And since I've got an hour to kill before going to the bank, instead of doing a carryout order, how about we give the gossips some payback by giving them something to really talk about? How about you join me and the boys for lunch?"

He'd shocked her. Worse, the offer was tempting. How long had it been since she'd been on a date that wasn't one arranged by her parents? Then again, this wasn't a date. It was lunch with a guy she'd met yesterday in the weirdest way possible.

"I…" She paused. Was she accepting? His saying she wasn't interested in him or his sons felt like the furthest thing from the truth. Despite yesterday's lapse in judgment, Wyatt was the type of man dreams were made of. If she wasn't careful, he might become the stuff of fantasies, too. When standing next to Wyatt, her body hummed as if spring was arriving after a long winter, and since it was mid-January, spring was still officially two months away. By then, she would be in Boston.

"You do have to eat, don't you?" When he turned that megawatt smile in her direction, Madi felt its full impact in the marrow of her bones.

"Come on, Madi. Since we're here, at least let me buy you lunch. The committee is already plotting their next move. We should, too, if we want to have a hope of circumventing whatever they're doing next. If we have lunch, we can tell them we're not compatible. Who knows, maybe that'll take the target off our backs. And maybe we can figure out how to end their meddling before they move on to our next candidates. Because you know there will be others thrust upon us."

"Yeah, that's true. It's like they have an endless supply. And I am hungry." Her stomach rumbled its confirmation, so Madi settled down at the two-top table across from Wyatt. He moved the stroller so it wasn't blocking the aisle and turned it to face him. He kept the sun shade up and she studied the black waterproof fabric. Laminated menus were in a holder on the table, and she lifted one and gave it a brief study. "If you haven't eaten here, the French dip is quite good, as is the club sandwich."

"Good to know." Wyatt fingered his own menu as a server headed their way. A few minutes later, they'd ordered and Madi forced herself to relax. While this wasn't a date, it sort of felt like one. "I'm insisting on paying for my own meal," she told him.

She liked the way he smiled at her when he agreed. "And I'm man enough to let you do that. Don't worry, Madi, I'm not going to put any moves on you."

Problem was, part of her wished he would. She hadn't

been on a real date with a man who interested her in forever. She'd forgotten what it was like to sit across from a man in a nice restaurant, enjoy a delicious meal and make pleasant conversation. Those times in the hospital cafeteria discussing patients with other residents did not count. Neither did the blind dates with sons of her parents' friends and colleagues. "So you wanted to raise the boys on the ranch."

He nodded. "I did. Even though my father and I often butt heads, when I adopted the boys, there was a part of me that knew I wanted them to have the same slower way of life I enjoyed. Then, when my live-in nanny decided she didn't like my schedule and chose to work elsewhere, her resignation seemed like a sign. I'm moving to the evening shift and I'm working a reduced schedule of four or five days a week instead of five to seven. No early mornings or weekends."

"So you're a TV meteorologist, which is why you asked if I knew who you were." She'd finally put it all together.

"Yes, and thank you for calling it that. I hate the term *weatherman*. Meteorology is a science, and it was something I fell in love with and wanted to do. My sister's a vet in Chicago. My brother, Caleb, is the rancher. He's actually the operations manager, second only to my father. At least my dad got one son in the family business."

Madi sensed an underlying sense of bitterness but didn't pry. Wyatt seemed pretty straightforward. If he wanted her to know, he probably would say something. "I'm an only child. I understand family pressure. My father's a cardiac surgeon."

"But it's clear you wanted to be a doctor. You love medicine."

Madi waited until the server put down her drinks before answering. "I do. I'm returning to Boston as soon as I'm certain my grandmother won't reinjure herself. Until then, I'm weighing my options. Trying to find the best fit as to where I want to practice. If I take this one position, I'd start there the middle of March."

"I guess I never thought there were that many choices. My aunt, Kay Larrabee, is a pediatrician here in Legacy Canyon. Seemed straightforward."

"Oh, no. Some practices have doctors who are affiliated with the hospital, meaning part of your job is to staff the pediatric ER. Then there are full-time pediatric ER positions, doctors who work directly for the hospital system as hospital employees. Some physician groups are also owned by the hospitals, which means that the doctors in those groups are also employees. Then there are doctor-owned practices, those whose doctors run their own businesses and practices. Those doctors are often affiliated with a hospital and have visitation rights, but they'll only be at the hospital if they have admitted patients. Same goes for the specialists. Like there are pediatric cardiologists or pediatric neurologists. Pediatric psychologists. My dad wanted me to go into the cardiology field, but I didn't think it was my calling. I like general pediatrics. Wellness checks. Sick-kids visits. I have an offer and it's a foregone conclusion I'll take it. I need to give them my answer."

"I had no idea the medical field was that complicated."

"I haven't even gotten into insurance billing."

He sipped his soda. "I hope you get what you want."

"It's a big decision where I decide to work. It keeps me awake at night sometimes." Madi reached for her glass of water, plucked the lemon from the rim and set it on a napkin. She wasn't a garnish person. Either choose to drink lemonade or filter the tap water and serve that. "This time in Texas has allowed me some needed distance and perspective. I've used it to consider the correct decision, what's best for me."

"That's why I moved to Denver, because I wanted to be in a larger market and make more money. Be a bigger fish, so to speak. Was considering a move to LA, and an even larger market, but these two little guys changed my plans."

"Babies often do, not that I'd know except for being a pediatrician. I assume I'll have kids someday, but…"

He smiled. "That would require a man."

A tilt of her head acknowledged that statement. "Or there's artificial insemination, and neither option is on my radar. I'm focusing on my grandmother and my career. Whatever I choose to do practice-wise, I'm insisting on a positive work-life balance. It's important that good mental health is a priority." She couldn't go through another crash and burn. The one she'd recovered from had been brutal enough.

"I support that wholeheartedly," Wyatt said, his sexy chin dipping. "If you're not at your best, then no one around you is."

"Exactly." She was impressed he understood. "Not many people get that."

"Trust me, I do. Another reason I moved home. You and I have high-intensity jobs that demand our full attention. If there's a weather emergency, that takes precedence over everything else. Same for a patient in the ER, I guess."

"Oh, yes." Madi pushed her hair behind her left ear.

Unlike when she'd been at the hospital and had it in a tight French knot, in Legacy Canyon she could wear it down around her shoulders if she chose, so she often did, as it felt freeing. "You wouldn't believe the social events I missed because I wasn't able to go off shift as scheduled."

Their server brought their food, setting a Caesar salad with grilled chicken in front of Madi and a French dip and fries on the red-and-white-checkered tablecloth for Wyatt.

"This does look good." Wyatt lifted a section of his sandwich and dipped the light and crusty French roll into the au jus. Madi swore her legs clenched when he swiped his lips after taking a bite. To divert her attention, she stabbed her fork into her salad, spearing a piece of chicken, some lettuce and a sliver of Parmesan cheese.

"Don't look now, but a few of our grandmother's friends have just arrived," Wyatt said. "Looks like they called in the calvary."

Unable to help herself, the directive not to look made Madi instinctively glance over. "Those ladies at the counter? They seem far younger. Like my mom's age. Mid fifties at most."

"I told you not to look. And don't let their ages fool you. That's the mayor's wife, Jill Sears, and the president of the chamber of commerce, Michelle Woepke."

Jill was the taller of the two. "How many people are on this committee?" Madi asked. "They keep coming out of the woodwork."

"At least ten, no more than fifteen. It can fluctuate depending on the year."

Madi wasn't sure about that. She suspected the number to be far more. The two women were having an animated conversation, but they paused, as if sensing Madi's perusal. She sheepishly looked at Wyatt. "Sorry. They've spotted us and are coming this way."

"Which is why I told you not to look. It's like saying someone's name three times. That summonses them." He lifted his eyebrows, which let Madi know he was joking. Sort of. Part of him was totally serious.

"Shh. They'll hear you." She set down her fork as the two impeccably dressed women approached.

"Why, Wyatt Larrabee, it is you. I heard you were back in town," Jill said.

"The rumor is true." Wyatt rose and accepted their hugs. He swept his arm in Madi's direction. "Do you know Madi?"

"Of course, Marya's granddaughter," Michelle said, giving Madi a wide smile that did nothing to hide the speculative gleam in her eyes. "How is your grandmother doing? Better?"

"Much. She's at the store getting into everything even though the doctor told her to take it easy," Madi said.

"That sounds like Marya," Jill said. "She can't sit still. However, that means she's always the one we can depend on. She's helping me organize the Valentine's dance." That was news to Madi. "And you're having lunch with Wyatt."

"We ran into each other at Bundle and Bloom," Wyatt said, returning to his seat. "Madi helped me buy this stroller and then she'll fill and deliver the rest of my shopping list while I'm at the bank."

"How wonderful," Michelle said.

"So are these your precious bundles?" When Jill bent to see under the stroller canopy, Madi understood now why Wyatt had left it up. "Adorable. You must be so proud." She straightened and Madi didn't think Jill had gotten much of a peek. "Well, we don't want to keep you from your lunch, but we had to stop by say hello and tell you we're glad to have you back in town and on our local news. We'll have to hold a proper town welcome for you at a later date. Maybe at this weekend's Snowball Festival? How does that sound?"

Wyatt parried the offer easily. "We'll see. I want these two to get settled into their new routine before I can commit to anything. You know how raising children can be."

"Oh, I do," Jill said.

Madi admired the skill Wyatt had at turning the tables on them.

"Madi can help you with your children," Michelle volunteered. "Especially as she's shopping for you. She told you she's a doctor, right?"

Oops, maybe Madi had misjudged Wyatt's abilities. But he held his own.

"She's a pediatrician," Wyatt confirmed with a smile that never faltered. "It was great seeing you both. I'll tell my grandmother you said hello."

"Give her our love," Jill said.

Madi watched them pick up their carryout orders and leave the store. "Could they have been any more obvious?" she asked.

Wyatt gestured with one of his thick fries. "That's how they operate. Don't let them ruin your appetite. And if your salad isn't good, I'm happy to share my sandwich. Besides, we wanted them to see us together. Let them think their meddling worked."

"I can't believe our grandmothers sent them to check up on us."

"I do because the word *quit* is not in the committee's vocabulary. And stop stressing. Don't fuel their fire with your oxygen." He chewed his food for a moment before drinking some water. "We need more. Like some real form of revenge. We need to find a way to stop them before they figure out a way to trap us like spiders do their prey. Because that's what they're doing. They're weaving a web to ensnare us."

"That sounds harsh." Although accurate. She'd already been their victim, if the men they'd tossed in her path counted. "I don't live here. I'm leaving."

"That won't stop them. What do you say? Shall we try to turn the tables on the committee?" As if his sons wanted Madi to say yes, they began to babble. They were waking up. Wyatt reached and removed Ethan from the stroller. He bounced him on his lap. "Would you like to hold him? I have to get Noah."

Madi couldn't help herself. When she put out her hands, Wyatt passed over his son. Secure in her arms, Ethan's deep brown eyes stared at her with avid interest. "Aren't you the cutest thing?" Madi said as Ethan smiled at her. Wyatt passed her a teething ring and Ethan waved the clear circle in his chubby fist before putting it in his mouth.

"Be careful, he already knows how much of a lady killer he is, don't you, Mr. Charmer?" Wyatt called. He handed Madi a burp cloth.

"Is your Daddy calling you names?" Madi teased Ethan as she caught some of his drool. As he blinked at her, she swore she fell in love on the spot. “Then again, your daddy might be right. You are enchanting.”

Ethan pulled out the teether and showed it to her. “Da,” he said before beginning to chew again. Madi made another swipe as more drool arrived. “Da.”

“That’s right. He’s your dad,” Madi agreed. Having Ethan sitting secure in her lap felt as natural as breathing. No wonder Wyatt had adopted the boys. She had this overwhelming sense of protectiveness, something she didn’t necessarily experience when tending to her patients. She wanted to heal them, but this was something more. It went far deeper, as if Ethan had reached in and taken a piece of her soul. This was why women were tossing themselves at Wyatt. Madi would do the same if she wasn’t a professional and able to turn her feelings off. Besides, he’d said he wasn’t interested in her. And she’d told him she was leaving.

Already adept at using the stroller’s various features, Wyatt flattened the bottom and used it as a changing table. He tucked Noah’s used diaper into a special pouch and wiped his hands with a baby wipe. “There you go, buddy. Nice and dry.” He set Noah in his lap. When Noah noticed Madi, he tucked his blond head into Wyatt’s shirt. “Noah’s much shyer. Let’s see if we can swap.”

With a bit of maneuvering, Madi soon held Noah. He trained his wide-eyed gaze on her, and as if deciding he could tolerate her, began to suck his pacifier. “He likes you,” Wyatt said. “My mom tried to hold him and he started crying.”

“I’m honored you trust me,” Madi told Noah as a sense of maternal pride filled her. Even though he and Ethan were twins, she could see subtle differences, besides just the different puffer coats they wore. Ethan's lips were fuller, and he had one less tooth. Once Wyatt changed Ethan, he propped him in the stroller. He reached for Noah and strapped him in as well. "Do you mind watching them for a second while I wash my hands? There's only so much hand sanitizer can do and I've got to be at the bank in about twenty minutes."

"Happy to," Madi said.

"Thanks." He whipped the stroller around so the boys faced her and strode off.

"Don't worry, he'll be back," Madi told them. "Until then, you have me." She glanced at the server, who put two plastic to-go containers on the table, one empty and one filled. Wyatt had finished his food. "What's this?"

"That's your grandmother's lunch order. She called it in after you sat down. And that's an empty box for your salad."

"Thank you." Madi drew her lips under as she realized what her grandmother had done. Then she thinned her smile and leaned toward the twins. "My grandmother is a menace."

"What did she do?" Wyatt asked as he returned.

"Oh, that's her food order."

Wyatt threw some cash onto the table. "You can get next time. I have a feeling we're going to need to meet again and plan something. Maybe when you come out to the ranch and deliver everything I bought. We can talk then, say over dinner? The committee gave me enough casseroles to last a couple of months."

"Of course, they did." Her grandmother still had food in her freezer from when she'd broken her arm.

"I don't know how I'm supposed to eat it all, so help a guy out, will ya?"

Madi rose. "Fine. I'm in."

Wyatt's brow creased. "In for dinner?"

"I'm in for all of it," Madi said with more vehemence than necessary. But something inside her stirred, as if a spoon had found the ingredients of her soul. This matchmaking needed to end. "The committee deserves some comeuppance. The revenge you suggested? Count me in. I will not be played."

"Yah!" Ethan's noise sounded like approval.

"Exactly, little buddy. Exactly," Madi agreed.

Carrying the take-out boxes, she followed Wyatt from the store. She pointed toward the bank. "Go—even if it's warmed up compared to yesterday, it's cold out here. I'll see you later tonight, when I bring everything out. Because you know she's going to insist on me helping you get whatever it is set up."

Wyatt grinned. "Oh, that's a given." He handed her a business card. "My cell's on there. Text me your number. I'll see you tonight, Madi."

As he walked away, Madi realized she was looking forward to it. And that would not do at all.

"So how was your lunch?" Madi's grandmother asked when she returned to Bundle and Bloom.

"Lovely," Madi said. "Wyatt seems like a nice person but you really didn't have to send me. He knew the way. Here's your to-go order and my leftovers."

Her grandmother's disappointment lasted a split second, her expression so fleeting it was as if Madi might have imagined it. She took the carryout boxes from Madi's hand.

"Well, we have a bit of a lull so you can find everything on his list. His purchase will have made our sales quota for the month. Then I'll have you deliver it."

"He said he's headed to the bank, then bringing the boys back for a feeding. He said I can come after the store closes."

Her grandmother's eyes danced with barely contained excitement. "We close at five."

Madi deliberately baited the hook. "Yes, I know. I'll probably miss dinner. Wyatt said he has a bunch of casseroles. The committee made them."

"They did. I mean, I didn't make one because of my arm." Her grandmother set the boxes on the checkout counter. "But usually I send my lasagna."

Which was delicious. Madi had grown up on it on every visit but this one. "His loss."

"I'll make him one once the hubbub of his arrival dies down. You'll be able to take it to him."

"I'm sure he'll like that, but I have to admit, something about him rubbed me the wrong way." Nothing had, but Madi had groundwork to lay.

"You two had a bit of a rough start. You're getting along now, yes? You did eat lunch together."

"We understand each other more, but I can't say we're going to be the best of friends. He's busy. I'm busy." Madi lifted her shoulder in an uninterested, oh-well shrug.

"You're not too busy. The doctor did say I needed to do more and more on my own. Thirty is not old. You're young. Wyatt's young. Go have fun."

"Wyatt's a great guy. We'll have dinner. But I didn't sense any zing." There was a whole lot of zing, but Madi wouldn't give her grandmother the satisfaction of thinking she was right in trying to fix them up.

"Really? He seems the type who'd send the electrons flying."

And she'd be right. "Where's the list? I should start locating what he needs since that's the whole reason I'm having to go out there."

"It's so good of you to help me," her grandmother gushed, which made Madi realize she hadn't given up. So much for groundwork. "Take him the last two Valentine's Day bibs as a thank-you gift. We sold the rest but should get another shipment in tomorrow. I'll be in the back if you need me." After retrieving her lunch, Madi's grandmother headed toward the office.

By the time her phone rang hours later, Madi had found all the items on Wyatt's list. She added the last one to the ever-growing pile behind the counter. With her grandmother back on the sales floor, Madi accepted her mother's call and stepped into the hallway leading to the office. "Hi, Mom."

"Madi." Her mother's voice came through clear. "How are you? I expected you to call me earlier. You're to call me every day, but you've been slacking."

"I'm at work with Grandma," Madi replied. "Didn't you get my text?"

She could almost hear her mother clutching her pearls. "Please, tell me you're coming back soon."

Madi gazed heavenward, as if the universe would somehow answer her prayer. "Mom, we've been over this. I'll be here at least until the end of February."

A small pause stretched as if her mother was choosing the correct words. Then she dove right in. "Your father and I had dinner with Dr. Clermont and his wife last night. Dr. Clermont needs an answer, Madi. Your father has gone to bat for you, but enough is enough. Are you joining his practice or not? Marya is fine. My mother-in-law is made of sturdy stuff, and she can hire local help if the store is that busy. Is it?"

"Of course, it is," Madi said. "You should have seen it right before Christmas." That was the truth. "Why, today we sold several thousand dollars of merchandise, which makes for a solid profit." Mostly thanks to Wyatt.

"I'm always amazed at how much raising children costs these days," her mother said. "And all the new stuff we didn't have when you were growing up."

"Same. And as for Dr. Clermont, I'm considering all offers. I have until the end of February to make my decision and I don't want to rush things."

"I really don't see why this is even an issue." The silence stretched and Madi worried she might have dropped the call. Then she heard her mom's resigned sigh. "Okay, Madi. I have to trust that you know what's best for your life and that you know what you're doing. I don't want to see you mess things up and lose out."

Which meant she didn't trust her daughter's decision-making process. Madi's perfectionist nature, the one she'd tamped down once she arrived in Legacy Canyon, began to rear its head. "I've got this." She wished she sounded more confident, but her mother didn't appear to notice.

"Good. We're scheduled to attend the Johnson wedding February twenty-eighth. I added it to our family's shared calendar. We will expect you to join us. You'll be returning for the weekend at least, right?"

"Most likely. I'm planning on it," she amended.

"You *will* be back," her mom said with emphasis. "The Johnsons are old family friends and we are not going to humiliate them by not being there as a united family. Besides, that's probably a good weekend for you to simply move home. Marya will understand."

"Mom." Madi squashed her frustration. Some social standards had to be upheld, and this was one of them. And she had gone to school with Claire for fourteen years, when including pre-K to high school. While Madi was not close enough to be in the wedding party, she had received her own invitation to both the bridal shower and the wedding. She still needed to RSVP the latter, although it seemed her family had already done that for her. As for the bridal shower, she'd sent her regrets and a lovely present, one her mother had picked out and shipped for her.

"Ian Ellison has said he's happy to act as your escort, so when you do return your RSVP card, just put down one. I've already told them you're coming, and that Ian will escort you."

"Let me guess, Ian is thrilled." Madi gritted her teeth. Ian was the son of one of her mother's friends, and he'd already attended one function—this one a charity ball—as her mercy date. Unlike the sizzle she felt touching Wyatt, there were no fireworks. No sparks. If she had a brother, she'd assume she'd have the same sort of physical reaction of nada, zip, zilch. The one kiss he'd given her had been as chaste as a toddler putting on lip balm. Which was a shame, as on paper Ian was a perfect husband candidate. "Mom, I can find my own date. Please don't trouble poor Ian."

"Fine. I'll talk to his mother. Write down one plans to attend, pick your meal and send your card back. Mrs.

Johnson let me know they haven't heard from you and I told them you would at least be there. Who you're sitting by will be up to them."

"Some other single friend, I'm certain. It's okay if I'm at the singles' table."

Her mom gave a small, disapproving sniff. "It's what it is. Your dad is calling. Love you." Her mother ended the call before Madi could respond.

"I love you, too," she muttered.

"What did you say?" her grandmother called.

"Nothing," Madi said as she walked back to the register. "But I do love you."

Marya nodded. "Same. And I've rung up Wyatt's order and emailed him a receipt. We need to load everything into the van. Actually, since he took the stroller with him, this will fit in the back of your SUV if we put the back seats down. I know you don't like driving the delivery van."

"Not really." While she knew how to drive, she'd lived on the East Coast, with its fantastic public transportation, her entire life. Madi had driven more since arriving in Legacy Canyon than she had in all the years since getting her learner's permit at sixteen. Marya's full-size van made her nervous.

A few more customers straggled in, and once they left, her grandmother turned the sign from Open to Closed and locked the front door. They loaded Madi's car and set the alarm. Her grandmother plugged Wyatt's address into the GPS. "You shouldn't have any problems getting there. The way to the ranch is pretty well marked, and once you get onto the property, you'll drive past the main house and then the cabin is the next building. You can't miss it. It looks sort of like what you'd see set into the mountains or something, but bigger."

The map loaded onto Madi's infotainment screen. "Seems pretty straightforward."

"Remember to keep right at the fork before the main house. Text me when you get there so I know you're safe."

"Will do." Once she'd graduated college, Madi had drawn the line at using the find-my-friends function on her phone. Her family did not need to track her every move. "I'll see you when I get back."

She drove the speed limit out to the ranch, taking her time now that the sun was down. The land was dark and mysterious against the cloudy night sky, creating an indistinguishable horizon lit only by the bright headlight beams. She arrived, watched the huge ornate ranch gates open and made a right onto Larrabee Lane. Despite the flatness of the terrain, she couldn't see anything to either side of her. She assumed the forms on both sides of the road were trees. Once she thought she saw something dart across the road, but she hadn't gotten a good enough look to know if it was a living thing or some debris blowing in the constant wind.

The road forked, and Madi followed the blue line on her screen to the right. A large house with a huge front porch came into view, and Madi stayed on the road past the circular driveway. The house she passed certainly fit the bill for one of Legacy Canyon's founding families. Her headlights found another driveway, this one leading slightly behind and beyond the main house, and then she saw the cabin. In her mind, she'd pictured something small, but once she'd arrived from Boston, she'd learned that the saying Everything is Bigger in Texas was one-hundred-percent true. The cabin was easily the size of a sixteen-hundred-square-foot house. Her approach triggered the front floodlights, and she parked beside Wyatt's car.

She stepped out of the vehicle, onto the pavement. By the time she'd rounded to her SUV's liftgate, Wyatt had stepped onto the porch. "Hey, I see you found it okay."

"I did. Between my grandma and GPS I had no issues. Do you want me to start bringing this in?" She readied to open the trunk.

He walked toward her. "Nah, let's wait. We can get it after dinner. Come eat while the food's hot. It's chicken, broccoli and bacon casserole with a breadcrumb crust and no cheese. Looks good. I have to admit, I'm pretty good at popping things in the oven."

"Then how can I resist?" Madi followed Wyatt into the house. The cabin consisted of a huge, open-concept great room decorated in Western style, complete with a pair of longhorns over the fireplace.

Wyatt caught her stare and laughed. "I know. When my mom decides on a theme, she's commits to it. I can tell you this is not what I would have chosen. I'm much more contemporary in my decorating style."

"I guess the horns do fit the wood paneling." She glanced down. "And the cowskin rug on the floor."

"Welcome to the guesthouse. There's also a pool house across the way, but no one lives there. It's mainly changing rooms, a kitchen and bath, and a studio space."

"I'm not judging. My parents have a five-thousand-square-foot monstrosity in the Back Bay area of Boston on Marlborough Street. You know, one of those multistory, historic brick town houses that's completely renovated?" Which someone would have to put out at least nine or ten million to purchase? She didn't voice the last part. "It's quite ridiculous for three people."

"I've never been to Boston minus the movies. Let me guess, you used to run up and down the stairs."

"Are you kidding? That might scuff the hardwood. We used the elevator."

He laughed. "I had a condo in Denver on the twenty-second floor. That needed an elevator, too. Had a great view of the baseball stadium, though. I have to admit I'm going to miss seeing the Rockies play live."

"We could walk to the Boston Common." She glanced around. "Are the boys asleep?"

"Nope, they're this way."

She rounded the huge kitchen island to find both Noah and Ethan sitting in the play yard. Seeing her, Ethan tried to pull himself up but instead landed diaper down. He giggled and automatically Madi reached for him. Then she stopped.

Wyatt noticed. "It's okay. Feel free to pick him up. He won't mind. You don't even have to ask again. I trust you."

"Thank you. That means a lot."

Madi lifted Ethan, and once closer, Ethan began to babble. "Ah da. Ooh."

"Noah won't get jealous if I have Ethan?"

"Amazingly, not really. Noah knows he'll get his time. Don't ya, buddy?" Wyatt lifted Noah and put him in a nearby high chair, where Noah immediately grabbed a thinly sliced piece of strawberry from his tray.

Wyatt took Ethan from Madi and strapped him in. "I hope you don't mind that they're eating with us."

"Why would I?" Madi asked as Ethan also grabbed

some of the soft finger food. This wasn't a date. "They need to eat, too."

"Exactly. But I had a gir—" He let the word drop. "Never mind. Doesn't matter. Take a seat and let me get everything."

Madi took the kitchen table chair perpendicular to Wyatt. Noah's high chair was on Wyatt's left, and Ethan's was in between Madi and Wyatt. Ethan reached out, trying to hand Madi a piece of strawberry. "Thank you, but I'm good. You eat that," she told him. With a grin, he shoved his fist into his mouth. Gummed the food and showed Madi the results before banging his hands on the tray.

"You are funny," she told him as he reached for another berry. He waved it at her before shoving it into his mouth.

Wyatt passed her a plate filled with casserole. "You're probably a great pediatrician."

Surprised by the compliment, she blinked. "Why do you say that?"

Wyatt served himself. After sitting, he chopped some of the noodles into small pieces and put them onto the boys' trays.

"Just the way you deal with kids, like mine. I've become an expert in how they interact with people. You make them feel valued and comfortable. They took to you immediately. That's rare."

His words warmed her. "That's kind of you to say. I love being a pediatrician. I like healing those who can't really speak for themselves. I wasn't planning on this specialization, but when I did it during my rotation, I was like 'this is it.'"

"Not at all." Ignoring his own dinner plate, Wyatt began spooning cereal into Noah's mouth. "You looking at a guy who decided during high school he was going to be on TV telling people how to dress for the day. My dad was livid, but I just knew."

Madi liked that Wyatt understood. "My father didn't mind. Well, he did at first, as he wanted me to follow in his footsteps and have a father-daughter practice, but he eventually came around. As long as I had an *MD* behind my name, along with some form of board certification, I'd fulfilled his hopes and dreams. That was one expectation I knew I had to meet."

"Amazing how that happens," Wyatt said. "What is it about some parents that make them start grooming us from birth? I was supposed to take over the ranch, but I don't have it in me. Neither does my sister, Kristen. But my brother, Caleb, he's got the ranch in his blood. This is his land far more than mine."

"How many years separate you?"

Wyatt began to feed Ethan. "Let me think. I'm thirty-two. That makes Kristen thirty, as we're eighteen months apart. Caleb is twenty-five. Minus college, he's never left. My dad likes to brag that he's the youngest ranch manager in Larrabee history. He's a hard worker, and he's earned his position through dedication and innovation. Both are truly needed since we're in a long-term drought. You'll meet him at some point. Although I've been here over twenty-four hours and haven't seen him yet. He's also a single dad of a soon-to-be three-year-old. His wife died about a year ago."

"I'm so sorry to hear that." She was, even if the answer sounded perfunctory.

"Yeah. Me, too. I'd love to say we're close, but we're not. Luckily, these guys will get to grow up around their cousin Emma. They'll be a bit younger, but that's okay. And who knows why I'm sharing this with you."

She made light. "Perhaps I have one of those faces."

"It is a pretty face, that's for sure."

"Thanks." Heat bloomed across her cheeks. She had no idea if this banter meant anything. As for family, she didn't have any cousins. Her father had been an only child, as had her mother. Was that why her parents were always so standoffish? She brushed aside the thought. While Wyatt had been feeding the boys, he'd insisted she eat. Full, she reached forward and gestured toward the baby spoon. "Here, let me feed him. That way you can eat something. We've been talking for a while and your casserole is getting cold."

"Thanks." Relieved of duty, Wyatt reached for his fork. "Half the time I don't even eat on a regular schedule anymore. They do, but me not so much."

"Tonight, let me help. Really, I don't mind." Madi scooped some cereal and brought it to Ethan's mouth. As she fed Ethan, she ignored the pitter-patter of her heart and the clench of her biological clock as it wound tight. But how could she stop her body's instinctive reaction? Especially after Ethan's precious gaze fixed on hers, his mouth opening and closing as she slipped the tip of the spoon between his lips. "Now I can understand why you say he's a charmer and why people always say their baby is the most adorable."

Wyatt's chuckle was warm molasses. "In my case, it's true. My boys are the absolute best." He reached to wipe Noah's mouth. Some of the formula in his sippy cup had gone down the front of his face and onto his puppy-themed bib. Noah laughed and grabbed for a strawberry and squeezed it. Wyatt wiped Noah's hand, too. "However, I hope they haven't ruined your appetite. They are messy eaters."

"Not at all," Madi said. "I was finished, and anyway, my stomach's made of iron. Most babies this age are messy. Babies explore things through touch, and food is very tactile, which is why they put everything in their mouths."

"Don't I know that. I'm a babyproofing fiend."

Before she could reply, a knock sounded, and Wyatt frowned. Madi heard the sound of the front door opening. "Are you expecting someone?"

Wyatt's face darkened. "No. Will you excuse me?"

But before he could stand, a woman around Madi's grandmother's age and with the same full head of white hair entered. "You didn't call me," she accused. She stopped short as she saw Madi. "Oh, hello. Wait. I know you. You're Marya's granddaughter. I wondered whose car was out front."

She said it with such innocence, her brown eyes blinking behind those oversized black plastic frames, that Madi might have believed her if she didn't know better. And right then, Madi realized another thing, this one not involving beautiful babies or raging maternal hormones or even confusion over what she wanted to do with her life.

The committee would stop at nothing to get their way.

Nothing at all.

Chapter Four

The first thing Wyatt planned to do after Madi left was take away his grandmother's key. Tomorrow, if needed, he'd change the locks. She might be his elder, but his grandmother simply could not barge in here whenever she wanted, even if she'd seen a strange car out front. In fact, he was more than one-hundred-percent certain she'd been monitoring the security feeds for Madi's arrival as she'd probably had forewarning from Marya Brennan of Madi's having to make a delivery. Having gotten a full report from the committee, his grandmother planned to check on things personally. Social niceties dictated he let her—at least to an extent.

"Grandma, this is Madi. You know, the one you tried to fix me up today with at lunch when you no-showed."

His grandmother had perfected the art of innocence and the who-me? expression. "What are you talking about? I did no such thing. I simply sent you to the best baby store in all of Legacy Canyon. Is it my fault you chose to go get lunch afterward? I don't remember us having anything written down in ink."

"Uh-huh. Okay." Her grandmother also had gaslighting and deflection mastered.

She pointed to the kitchen table. "I see you're eating

another casserole. Good. I'll let Marlow know you like it." She peered at Madi. "I'm Clarissa. Finally, I get to meet you." Still seated as if frozen in place, Madi set down the spoon and shook her outstretched hand. "So where's everything?" his grandmother demanded pleasantly. "All the things you bought?"

"Still in the car," Wyatt said. "We ate dinner before unloading since the boys need to go to bed soon. A dinner you interrupted."

Clarissa waved off his subtle rebuke. "Can I help wanting to see my great-grandsons? You're lucky your mother's not with me, but she and your father went into town." She approached the high chairs. "But I can come back. Or Madi and I can get these guys changed while you unload her SUV. She does have to go home at some point. Unless she's spending the night."

That was laying it on far too thick. "Are you chaperoning?" Wyatt countered.

Clarissa wasn't known for missing a beat and she didn't now. "Simply stating the obvious, my boy. Nothing wrong with that, is there?"

Wyatt's jaw set. If he didn't love his grandmother…

Madi rose. "You and Wyatt go put the boys to bed. I'll unload the car."

"You're a guest," his grandmother pointed out with a fast shake of hair that had thinned over the past year. "Wyatt can do that."

"I loaded the car, I can unload it," Madi insisted. "I'll set the purchases inside the door. Does that work, Wyatt?"

"Perfect. Wherever you'd like to put them sounds good." After being set up today, he didn't want to have Madi experience any more awkwardness.

"Then it's settled. I'll get the stuff." Madi left the room.

He noted the disapproving pucker of his grandmother's lips, but she said nothing.

Instead, she'd removed the tray from the high chair and unbuckled Ethan. She lifted him. "How's my big boy?"

Yes, Wyatt decided, they would definitely have a clearly needed discussion on boundaries.

She glanced at Wyatt. "Don't just stand there. Help her unload the car. And while you're at it, ask her to the Snowball Festival." She narrowed her eyes. "Don't give me that look. It won't work. It's not like I haven't handled babies before. Shoo."

With a dip of his head in acknowledgement, Wyatt went after Madi. He caught up with her as she juggled two oversized paper bags through the front door. He took them from her hands. "Thanks. Appreciate it."

"What kind of a gentleman would I be if I didn't help?" He set the packages on the floor and followed her back outside. He peered into the car. "Wow. Didn't realize I'd ordered so much stuff."

"You are buying for two."

"True." They made several quick trips. When they returned to the kitchen, Wyatt's twins sat in the play yard. Wyatt's grandmother had changed the boys into their sleepers and straightened the kitchen. "And I changed their diapers," she told them. "You'll thank me for that one, especially for Noah. He dropped the motherlode. Phew. What is that child eating?"

"Thank you for taking one for the team," Wyatt said.

"Of course. Now, I'm out of here. Be good. Nice to meet you, Madi. You come around more often, you hear?" With that, she disappeared and Wyatt heard the four-by-four she'd driven over from her house start up.

Wyatt gazed at an expectant Madi. "And that," he told her, "is my Texas tornado of a grandmother, Clarissa Larrabee, ringleader…oh, pardon me—past president of the committee."

"I can now understand why they are so formidable. She's a tank."

"Understatement of the year. Enough to drive a man to drink. Speaking of, would you like a glass of wine? I usually don't drink when I'm by myself, but I need one to dull the temptation of throttling her. And we do need to discuss our current predicament."

"Then let me help." Carrying Ethan, Madi trailed Wyatt into the boys' bedroom. They placed the twins on their backs in their respective cribs and the boys were soon fast asleep. With the night-lights providing a glow, they stood gazing at them. "Like seeing heaven," Madi said.

He liked how she thought the same. "Agree. Come on. I have the baby monitor. We'll hear them." They stepped back into the living area. "What can I get you?"

"Red wine is fine. But not too much." She settled onto the couch.

"A small pour for each of us then." He uncorked one of his favorite bottles and handed her a glass before settling on the opposite end of the couch. "See what you think of this. It's a zinfandel from California." Madi sipped and he liked the way her eyes widened. "I know, right?"

Her smile was better than the wine. "This is delicious. Good choice."

"Thanks. I found the winery while on vacation. It's one of my favorites." He pushed away the memory. That he'd been on an overnight weekend with his then-girlfriend—the one who'd dumped him when he'd begun fostering the twins—hadn't dulled his enthusiasm for this particular vintage. Madi glanced at her phone. "Everything okay?" he asked.

She turned the phone back over. "I have a voice mail I'll have to deal with once I get home. I had my phone on silent." She took another sip.

"Must be serious if it's a voice mail."

"I have a job offer that I have to respond to and a few other things. Like I said, I put my life on hold when I came here, and now, that life is catching up." Her chest heaved as she sighed. "The real world sucks sometimes, doesn't it?"

"I'm sorry. The committee's meddling is just adding another layer of complexity, isn't it?"

Madi tapped the end of her nose with her forefinger before pointing it at Wyatt. "Yep. Nailed it."

He grinned. "Well, we have wine and some time, so let's plot some revenge."

She shifted. Gazed at him hesitantly. "I was thinking about that. What if we go along with it?"

Mid-sip, Wyatt coughed. "What? You want to date me?"

The shake of her head came as quickly as her denial, which he found oddly disappointing. "No. I suggest we fake date. It sounds like a wild idea, I know, but what if we pretended we're a couple? Would that get the committee off our case?"

Wyatt's frown was instantaneous. "Doesn't that trope always end badly for the couple?"

Madi's frown joined his. "I'm impressed you know the word *trope*."

"I'm sorry. I'm not trying to be offensive. But I'm not an ignorant heathen. I have a sister. I worked with a bunch of coworkers who loved romance novels and romantic movies. This never works out. It's too risky." After trying for almost a year to fend off women, pretending to date seemed counterproductive. Even if was the pretty woman in front of him.

Madi's lips twisted. "Of course, it will. This isn't a movie. It's our life, and in my case, only until March, at the most. I live in Boston. You'll be here forever. We pretend to date, I leave, you're heartbroken and they leave you alone. Simple and effective."

"Or they throw more people at me to try to help me over my heartbreak." The idea seemed ludicrous. Even if it meant spending time with Madi, which, he again reminded himself, he did not want.

"Well, you'll have time to figure it out. A month at most until Valentine's, we'd have to do something for that I guess, and then a few weeks after that depending on when I leave. Until then, we outwardly pretend we're falling for each other while inwardly we know the truth. We're friends. Well, at least sort of. Or whatever this is."

"You really haven't watched much television, have you?"

Those long full lashes blinked at him. "No, I've been doing long days during residency and before that med school. My parents demanded excellence, and I'm wired that way, anyway. If we do this, we'll set some ground rules. Number one, we know this has an exit date. Number two, we agree not to date others, not that I want to date anyone. Number three…" She paused. "Number three is that we be honest with each other at all times. We might be lying to the world, but we are honest with each other. If we don't, this subterfuge won't work."

"That's fair," Wyatt agreed. "You really have thought about this."

"My mind works that way, and as soon as I realized how the committee operated, I realized it's the most logical step. I've been using this time to figure out what my next step is career-wise. I have an offer that I'd be a fool not to take, but for some reason I haven't been able to commit. I'm also helping my grandmother get well. Your priority is your boys. We need space to do what we need to do, let our lives be our sole focus, so it serves we'd work together."

"I'm glad you recognize my priorities. Most women want to be number one."

"I'm not most women."

No, she was not. She was like a fresh, cool breeze on a long, hot day. He liked how she was a straight shooter, telling him her exact thoughts and her reasons. He'd met women who hid their true selves and played manipulative games, but so far that wasn't his experience with Madi. He hadn't known her long—didn't know her hopes and dreams besides her career—but he knew enough to know they didn't include him. And the boys were young enough they'd never remember her once she left for Boston. "As long as we're in perfect understanding, then yeah, we can do this," Wyatt agreed, pushing aside any misgivings, including that those good intentions never seemed to work out correctly in books or movies. "I'll handle any fallout after you go."

"There will be some bugs to work out, some things we haven't thought about," Madi said. "But we can figure those out as they come up."

Wyatt yanked his gaze away from her beautiful mouth. He'd been watching her speak, watching the way her lips with a hint of pink formed words. She had full, heart-shaped lips, the kind a man envisioned sampling, or feeling against his skin doing more decadent, desirous activities. He tamped down a part of him that began to stir. He was a dad. Madi's stay in Legacy Canyon was temporary. But his fixation did bring up an interesting conundrum. He rose and retrieved their empty wine-glasses. "We're going to need to kiss."

Her blue bluebonnet colored eyes widened. "What?"

"If we're dating, we're going to have to kiss." He tried to backpedal as she rose. "This isn't me trying to kiss you. But the committee won't believe we're in a relationship otherwise. People who date kiss. You heard my grandmother. She asked if you were spending the night."

"True." Her lower teeth tugged her bottom under. Her light nibble destroyed his concentration. "They do." She loosened her arms, straightened and drew herself up to her full height. "Well, let's do it. Get it out of the way."

Now, it was Wyatt's turn to be surprised. "What?"

She shrugged. "Let's kiss. We'll get the awkwardness over with now, while we're in private. Because as you said, as soon as we pretend to date, they'll be scrutinizing us through a microscope. We'll be feeding the grapevine and all eyes will be on us."

"I'm glad you realize that. They'll be hard to fool." He put the glasses on a kitchen counter and resisted the urge to cover his mouth and check his breath before walking back into the main area. She might as well get him at his worst. Especially if they had to kiss out in public and he didn't have time to floss. Better she get any revulsion out of her system so it didn't show on her face. Wyatt's grandmother wasn't the type who missed much. She could ferret the truth out of anyone.

"We'll approach this clinically," Madi decided. "I'm a doctor. I can see the human body as a person while also controlling my own body's reaction. I could tell you stories, but believe me, some are not fit for consumption. Suffice to say, I quickly learned to hide my shock, surprise or disgust when facing people."

"I hope kissing me doesn't fall into the latter category." Wyatt tried to keep his tone light, but she was starting to give him a complex. No woman had complained since he'd first kissed Nicole during middle school, something Madi's grandmother had thankfully missed, unlike his smoking attempt. Then again, why was Wyatt worried about his male pride? They were fake dating. It would be a fake kiss.

Madi's face had heated, but she boldly stepped forward like a defiant woman headed to the gallows. "Okay, I'm ready. You can kiss me."

Wyatt had never been in this situation before. Normally, there was some romance to get things going. Maybe low lighting. A zing of anticipation caused by eating a good dinner and enjoying great conversation. Then came that leaning in, that touch of his fingers against a woman's face, sliding them down her cheek and jawline. Perhaps he'd press a light fingertip to her lips. He'd hold her gaze and tilt his face to come closer until their exhales mingled. Then he'd offer the lightest touch of his lips to hers before letting nature take over.

Madi waited impatiently, as if she was about to miss a bus if he didn't hurry and get this over with. "Okay," he said, "but when in public you'll have to appear a little more excited."

"I will, when we're in public," she promised. She rose on her tiptoes and brought her lips quickly to his. One brief touch and that was that. "Not so bad."

"No, not if we're relatives in some European country." Wyatt tempered his exasperation. "Madi, we can't go with a quick peck. I'm seriously not trying to kiss you, but no one will believe that. We aren't siblings."

Madi's face fell. Then she squared her shoulders. "True. Alright, let's go again."

Wyatt sighed. Kissing wasn't a video game with a reset button. "Let's do it right this time. I'm going to touch you. Are you okay with that?"

"Yeah." She nodded and her brown hair fell over her shoulders. His fingers tangled in the silky strands as he slid his hand along the back of her neck. He swore he heard a small gasp. Good, since his fingers sizzled. Her reaction was a positive sign, right? He hoped so.

He lowered his head, paused at her deer-in-the-headlights stare. "You sure?"

"Yes." She closed her eyes, and Wyatt closed the distance.

He slanted his mouth over hers as if her lips were the sweetest of berries. This might be a clinical exercise, but he refused to be labeled a bad kisser. He might be out of practice, but muscle memory kicked in. Start with a light press. A gentle tug on her lower lip. Then a slide of his tongue to moisten what he'd caressed. Add another soft touch or two, and they'd be able to break apart.

Wyatt didn't know what shifted, but when Madi bloomed like a wildflower and kissed him back, his self-control slipped faster than wearing the wrong shoes on an icy Denver sidewalk. His tongue found hers. He traced her mouth, memorizing the taste and texture. His body responded eagerly, straining against his jeans. He deepened the kiss, and fought teenage detonation as her tongue slipped between his lips. This was better than ice cream on a hot day. Or the rush of downhill skiing. It was a slice of heaven. A prelude hinting at the wonders to come should they continue.

A cry coming from the baby monitor served as a welcome rain shower and he stepped back. "Go," she told him, pivoting too quickly for him to read her face.

"I'll be right back," Wyatt said. He went into the nursery to check on the twins. Whoever had made the noise—he suspected Ethan—had settled back to sleep. He checked diapers and no issues there. He pulled the door closed behind him, leaving it slightly ajar.

"They're fine," he said as he returned to the living room. But he discovered he was speaking to empty air. Madi was gone.

The next day, Madi couldn't believe she'd left Wyatt's like an escapee. Her hands trembled as she restocked the Valentine's Day onesies, a little shake that had been there since last night when Wyatt had kissed her. Thankfully, her grandmother wasn't working today. Minus another of the part-time employees, Madi was the only family member on duty since her grandmother had a committee meeting. At least that meeting had gotten her away from watching Madi too closely. Although, they were probably discussing her and Wyatt.

Madi gazed at the onesies, moving two to ensure the

entire set was perfectly in line. She raised her hand and then jerked it back before she dropped her arm. She'd touched her swollen lips enough last night, as if checking that Wyatt's kiss had been real and not some figment of an overactive, hormonal imagination, of a biological clock whose alarm had started to shrill that time to have her own children was running out. Although many women had children after thirty-five, meaning Madi still had several years. She had a career to build first.

But she'd felt Wyatt's kiss in her womb, as if her body had shouted, "Him! He's the one." Biology—pheromones and such—were cruel. As was the fact he knew how to kiss. He'd lit her up like a firecracker on the Fourth of July over the Boston Harbor. No other description fit. While she wasn't a sexual goddess like some of her cohorts, Madi wasn't a novice, either. She'd had enough bad kisses to be an expert, like that one guy who'd shoved his fat tongue in her mouth as if he was trying to stab her. And poor Ian, whose kiss had been as flat as day-old soda pop.

She'd had some good kisses, too, the kind that raised her temperature but didn't necessarily lead anywhere. *Pleasant* was a nice descriptor. Good, but nothing to write home about. Then there'd been some great kisses, few and far between, that were *ooh la la*. Wyatt's kiss had been akin to a knockout punch. She felt the sexual impact everywhere. Her skin had tingled. Her desire had built and spread, heated the place between her legs, making her core throb.

If Wyatt had scooped her into his arms and carried her to his bed, she would have been putty in his hands and a more than willing participant. Every neuron had been firing, and saying "take me now!" in a way that hadn't happened to her in years, had never happened if she was being honest. Sex was enjoyable but it wasn't passion personified. Wyatt had shown her there was more behind a magic door, one she'd never expected to find, much less open.

Which meant that this fake-dating idea had suddenly gotten problematic. That he'd been right in saying movies and TV shows proved this idea wouldn't work, that they might fall for each other. Overwhelmed, she'd left. Run out of his house like a child caught breaking a rule. Not one of her better moves. So much for being clinical, smooth and suave. She'd folded like a house of cards at first touch. It had been all she could do not to moan from the pleasure he'd invoked, and from the connection she'd felt that she didn't need or want.

Her phone buzzed and she winced as she read the caller ID. Seeing that the store associate had things under control, Madi answered. "Hello, this is Madi."

"Madi, I'm so glad I finally caught you. I was starting to think you were avoiding me."

"No, of course not. Just been busy with my grandmother. I'm helping at her store." Two truths and a lie. Madi didn't really want to talk to Belinda Hillyer, office manager for the most prestigious pediatric practice in Boston, for every time they talked, Belinda added another layer of pressure. Today, Madi discovered, was to be no different.

"That's noble of you." A brief pause and then the woman said, "Thank you for finally taking my call. I've been trying to reach you as we've had a small complication on our end."

This was the third or fourth one, and Madi's fingers tightened. "Oh."

"It's nothing too worrisome, simply a switch in the timeline. Dr. Clermont has moved forward his timetable. Instead of leaving at the end of March, he's retiring at the end of February. We'd need to on-board you no later than February twenty-third. Your grandmother will be healed by then, correct?"

"Yes. She should be," Madi confirmed, her brain reeling with the implications.

"Good. I know this is inconvenient, but the change means we'll need your signed contract by the end of this month. If not, we'll be moving on to our second choice. We hate doing that, but Dr. Clermont's wife needs more chemo and he wants to be home with her. I'm sure you understand. We have been really generous with you, but it's time to firm things up."

"I understand," Madi said. She already felt the pressure, and Belinda had upped the stakes even further, including pushing Madi to make a decision on her birthday. "A customer just walked in."

"We'll chat soon since I know we have a few more details to nail down. But I can't wait to have you join us, so let's get them settled soon, okay? 'Bye now." Belinda ended the call.

Madi loosened her grip. As a doctor in the ER, she'd learned how not to panic, how to control the spikes of adrenaline that came with being in emergency situations. But her pulse thumped and anxiety hummed. She thought she'd have more time to consider her options. What was it she wanted to do? Her parents wanted her to take over Dr. Clermont's patient load, and she'd liked the other doctors and the staff she'd met during the selection process. The office had fifteen pediatricians, with five of them being pediatric specialists. It was an ideal place to start her practice. As her father had told her, it wasn't often that someone got this lucky, and this was a lifetime gig.

She shouldn't be hesitating. Everyone knew she was going to say yes. While a few other things could come to fruition, accepting this offer was really the one and only choice, as it was the best option for her, for everyone. It would make her dad happy and proud. Madi's chest tightened. If Madi didn't want the job, which would be foolish of her, the practice was prepared to move to its second choice. What she should be doing was negotiating their offer, those details Belinda had mentioned, and customizing their offer to her satisfaction. Her father had said he would help, and that he'd ensure she got a great deal. So what was she waiting for? Why hadn't she jumped on this? Her parents wanted this for her.

"Madi? Can you come up front?" a coworker called.

"On my way." Shoving her phone into her pocket, Madi made her way to the front. As she passed through the opening to the sales floor, she stopped short.

"Hey," Wyatt said. He stood at the counter in a forest-green chambray shirt and pair of worn blue jeans that fit far too well. Only noon and he wore a deep five-o'clock shadow best described as sexy stubble. And was that a cowboy hat? She felt as if the air had escaped her lungs.

"Hi. How are you?" Madi asked.

His gaze searched her face. "I think I should be asking you that."

Thankfully, Madi's coworker scurried off to greet a group that was coming through the front door.

"Sorry I ran out," she said, once everyone but Wyatt was out of earshot. "I figured you'd be busy with the twins."

"Nope, they went right back to sleep. Stayed that way for about six hours."

"Good." She stood there awkwardly. Glanced at the shopping bag in his hand. "Do you have a return?"

"Just an exchange. I asked for the wrong size. Need it one bigger." He set the bag on the counter and sheepishly grinned. "And this return gives me a reason to come talk to you. See if you still wanted to stick to the plan, or if that kiss messed things up."

That kiss had messed with her head only because she'd wanted more. Much more. She gazed down but didn't see a stroller. "Do you have the boys with you? They're not out in the car are they?"

"And risk your wrath? No. My mother and grandmother are babysitting. They insisted, and since they'll be helping out when I go to work, I figured I'd do a test run during this short errand. So far, no one's texted. I'm actually on a solo outing."

"Ah. Good for you." Madi had heard some of her patients' parents talking about how they considered even shopping by themselves at a superstore to be needed *me* time. She reached for the package and removed the contents. He'd brought back two matching sleepers, tags still on. She stepped out from behind the counter. "Let me go find the correct size. I'll be right back."

He followed her, anyway. "If it helps, they can be a different color."

"No, we have them." She went to the clothing rack and found the correct ones. "See? I'll just run the exchange and…"

"Madi." His voice stopped her in her tracks. "It's okay."

"What do you mean?" Finding her footing, she hightailed behind the counter and logged into the computer terminal.

"I wanted you to know that kiss affected me, too."

"Oh." She gazed at him. "I see."

That sexy dent in his chin lowered as he nodded. "Uh-huh. I was as into it as I believe you were."

She could lie and say she was acting, but Madi instead exhaled her relief. "I was into it, too. And it freaked me out a little. A lot actually."

"Same," Wyatt admitted.

Madi placed the correct sleepers into the shopping bag. "As long as we don't do that again, we can manage our..." She lowered her voice. "Fake dating."

"Good. Because my grandmother told me I should ask you to the Snowball Festival."

They were going out so soon? Her brain shouted danger while her body grew excited by the prospect. "That's Saturday."

"Yes. Tomorrow," Wyatt confirmed. "The whole town will be there. It'll be a good time to put our plan into motion and show everyone how we feel about each other."

Trouble was, that kiss had her feeling all sorts of things she shouldn't. "I'm surprised your grandmother isn't at the committee meeting. That's where my grandmother is."

"Oh, today's meeting is bunco, or bridge or rummy, or something like that. Socializing with games. I don't know and really don't want to know."

That made Madi smile. "I have no idea. We're definitely a topic of conversation, though."

"Of that I have no doubt." A cheeky grin full of mischief lit Wyatt's face. The gold flecks in his eyes accented a wicked glint, and unable to stop herself, Madi preened under his attention. She snapped herself out of it. Reminded herself to get it together. They were coconspirators, nothing more. Even if that kiss had been earth-shaking.

Wyatt's smile widened. "In fact, assume they know I'm here talking to you."

She frowned. "How? No one's in here but me and the high-school helper."

"Madi, Madi. You have so much to learn. The moment I drove into town triggered the grapevine. Wait five minutes after I leave and someone will be in here saying 'Was that Wyatt Larrabee I just saw?' Mark my words."

"People really need to find better things to do with their time." As a customer approached the counter, Madi passed Wyatt the shopping bag. "How about you text me the details later?" Following their lunch, they'd exchanged phone numbers.

"I'll do that. I have to run up to Amarillo and visit the station for a bit. I'll do it around dinner."

She ignored the fluttering of her heart. "Sounds perfect."

Madi waited until the part-time worker and the customer were almost at the counter. No time better than the present to dive in and give the gossips something to celebrate. "In that case, Wyatt Larrabee, it's a date."

Chapter Five

It had been a good solo outing, Wyatt decided as he turned onto Larrabee Lane. Not only had he spent an hour visiting his new TV station and acclimating himself to his office, but he also had a date for tomorrow's festival.

He found himself whistling to the country song playing on the radio. One of the few things he and his father did agree on was the merits of Merle Haggard, Johnny Cash and Loretta Lynn. Wyatt also liked rock, but unless the song was from the seventies or early eighties, his father called most of what Wyatt liked trash. Lately, though, Wyatt wasn't listening to anything that wasn't kid-themed. He'd learned not to mind. Whatever stimulated his sons' brains came first.

Speaking of stimulation, his blood pressure spiked when he reached the main house and saw his father standing on the front porch. It was almost 4:00 p.m., so why his dad was waiting was beyond Wyatt. But before he could drive past, his dad stepped onto the sidewalk and gestured for him to stop. Wyatt schooled his face into neutral, put the car in Park and rolled down the window. He kept his tone light. "Hey, Dad."

"Wondered if you could help me move a few calves.

Caleb's gone to Amarillo and he's running late. Got caught up in something."

"Just came from there. You need my help now?" He'd been hoping to spend some time with the boys.

"Buyer's coming for 'em in an hour. Know it's late notice, but this is the time we had and we gotta get 'em loaded. Got to do it before dark."

"Of course, I'd be happy to help." Glad the TV station manager had told him to dress casual, Wyatt was in jeans and a chambray shirt. He climbed out of the SUV and followed his father to the four-by-four.

"Got some gloves in the back," his dad told him as he fired up the engine and drove away from the main house toward the barns. The journey gave Wyatt a chance to look at land he hadn't seen in a year. The effects of the long-term drought were evident everywhere. The grass was browner than it should be in winter. Bare spots showed where the soil had cracked, creating lines across the earth. A few years back, his father had had to thin out the herd since the grassland wasn't enough to support the animals. Hay already had to be brought in to supplement their diet.

"How's the fire risk?"

His father grunted noncommittally. "Caleb's working on some things to help. We've been lucky so far."

"That's good." A few years ago, Wyatt's news station had covered what had become known as the Smokehouse Creek Fire, which had swept through counties farther to the northeast after being started by downed power lines. Fueled by warm temperatures and gusty winds, the wildfire had burned over one million acres, and over sixty counties in Texas and Oklahoma had been effected.

The Larrabee Ranch was a good seventy-five miles away from what had burned, but any dry pastureland was a powder keg waiting for a spark. And the Larrabee land, minus what was irrigated, had plenty of fuel ready for ignition.

"Caleb takes his role as ranch manager seriously." Was this a subtle dig at Wyatt's defection? If so, his father followed it with a statement of fact, as if designed to temper his jab. "What we really need is rain."

"Yeah. Everyone does," Wyatt agreed in an attempt to keep the peace. While Legacy Canyon had been spared some of the severest droughts on record, the ranch hadn't come through unscathed. But where some counties had seen layers of topsoil blow away, crops die in the dirt and wells run dry, so far his family had escaped that fate. However, normally this region saw eighteen to twenty inches of rain a year. Last year, ranchers had seen nine. It wasn't enough. The only thing keeping conditions from being like the dust bowl was savvy land conservation, spearheaded by his brother. Wyatt hoped it would be enough. While he didn't want to work the ranch like his father and brother, he loved the land.

"We're here." His dad parked besides the barns.

Glad he'd had the foresight to wear his boots today, Wyatt stepped out and retrieved the extra set of gloves. He gazed over various pastures filled with herds of cattle. "How many head are we moving?"

"Taking ten," his father answered. He pointed. "Those heifers over in that pen are the ones going. We just need to move them into the loading chute and onto the trailer. Clem Randall's buying them for breeding stock."

Thanks to the melted snow, a thin layer of mud stuck

to the underside of Wyatt's boots. But the mud didn't mean that water has seeped deep. If one dug into the ground, the earth grew dry at four inches deep. Go down six feet, and even the subsoil moisture was missing. The drought was an ecological disaster happening in real time.

Wyatt followed his father. They greeted two ranch hands, and soon they'd moved the heifers onto the trailer. His father had a way with cattle, as they ambled along calmly and in single file under his direction. They were off to another ranch about fifty miles down the road.

"Thanks for your help," his father said once they were finished and Clem had driven off. "Appreciate you stepping in."

Wyatt hadn't done much, aside from latching and unlatching gates. But he played along, recognizing this was his father's version of a test, a way of trying to reintroduce him to ranch life. Even without Caleb, his father had had enough help. "You're welcome, but now I need to get back to my boys. Mom will be wondering where I am."

"She won't mind. Already texted her. Come see the changes we've made." He didn't say "spend some time with me," but Wyatt heard the directive, anyway. Hoped it might be an olive branch of sorts.

"Okay." For the next hour, until it got too dark, Wyatt rode in the side-by-side as his father took him over the main portion of the ranch. He had to admit he was impressed at the conservation techniques his dad and his brother had implemented. He'd watched as the ranch hands used machinery to unroll hay bales, which the cattle immediately found and began eating. Because of the constant wind and dry conditions, the Larrabees had added both natural and man-made windbreaks to the land. Drought-resistant native trees grew along the edges of pastures. His father and Caleb had built V-shaped open-to-the sky structures using foot-thick posts that went four feet below the frost line. At eight foot tall, the walls redirected the wind that blew in a straight line, giving the cattle shelter.

"You and Caleb have done great," Wyatt said, complimenting his dad as they returned to the main house.

"Yeah, he's got a magic touch. That agriculture degree is getting good use. He's considered a pioneer and he's been teaching others."

As if the man himself had heard his name, Caleb appeared on the front porch when they pulled up. "Wyatt," he greeted as Wyatt climbed the stairs.

"Uncle Wy!" Emma came out onto the porch, and after peering around her dad's leg, held out her arms. Wyatt scooped her up. She'd almost left her terrible twos behind. Her pigtails bobbed as she held out her arms.

"How are you, Em?" Wyatt asked, lifting her.

"I help Grandma. I'm a big girl."

"You are a big girl since I've seen you last! You're heavy." It was amazing how much children grew and how fast they changed in such a short time. Emma, being both precocious and gifted, had developed an entire vocabulary since he'd last seen her.

"She couldn't wait to visit with her cousins," Caleb said. "So we came over after I grabbed her from preschool."

"I like school." Emma's head bobbed and those blond ponytails shook. She fingered the strap on her mint-green overalls. "Babies. Noah. Ethan."

"That's right." Wyatt lowered her to the porch. "My sons. Can you take me to them?"

Emma laced her tiny hand in his, and Wyatt held the door open. She let go the moment she ran inside. But before she could race to the nursery, Wyatt's mom had scooped her up. "Dinnertime," she told Emma. "And they're sleeping."

"They're sleeping," Emma told Wyatt, using her most serious expression. She held her forefinger in front of her lips. "Shh."

"Shh," Wyatt said, mimicking her and watching as his mother led his niece into the kitchen. "She's changed so much."

"Every day." Caleb grinned. Then he sobered. "Not been easy without her mom."

Wyatt clapped his brother on the shoulder. "You've got this," he told him. "You're doing great."

"Yeah," Caleb said, although he didn't appear convinced. If anything, he appeared older than his twenty-five years. "Trying, anyway."

"That's all we can do," Wyatt encouraged. "I'm in the same boat."

"Let's go eat," their father said. He led the way into the kitchen. Dinner was a rather quiet affair, with Caleb and his father mostly discussing the ranch.

Wyatt listened as his mother told him about the boys' day. "Your grandmother loved babysitting. That's where the casserole came from."

Dinner was an enchilada casserole containing layers of ground beef, corn tortillas, cheese and refried beans along with a host of other things. "More from the committee?"

"Of course. They mean well. They sent it for your grandfather and your grandmother brought it over. Gave the cook the night off from prepping our meal." Usually his mom had something sent from the bunkhouse cook. When Wyatt had discussed moving back, she'd offered to hire someone full-time for the main house, but Wyatt had nixed that idea. Hence the casseroles filling his freezer.

"So I hear you have a date," his mom said, her fingers primly using a knife and fork to cut a bite of the casserole on her plate.

"What?" Caleb choked a sip of sweet tea and somehow managed to set down the glass without spilling. "I'm not dating anyone."

"Daddy date," Emma said from her booster seat.

"I meant Wyatt," his mother clarified.

"Thank god," Caleb said. He wiped his mouth. "Don't blindside me like that."

"Wait, Wyatt has a date?" His father's eyes widened. "Already?"

"That's moving fast," Caleb agreed now that the heat was off him. "Even for Wyatt."

"What's a date?" Emma asked.

"Nothing you need to worry about until you're like twenty," Caleb said. He reached over and replaced her napkin in her lap. Emma frowned and stuck her lips out in an exaggerated pout before lifting her spoon.

"A date means Wyatt's going to the Snowball Festival," his mother told her granddaughter. "Unless I heard wrong?"

The town grapevine moved at the speed of light. Clearly, Madi had told her grandmother, who'd told Wyatt's, who'd told his mother. Probably told half the town, too. “No, you heard right,” Wyatt said. “I asked Madi Brennan. Marya’s granddaughter.”

“I met her in Marya’s shop. She’s very nice.”

“She’s a shopkeeper?” his father asked, not impressed.

Wyatt’s feathers ruffled. “She’s a pediatrician. She’s helping her grandmother because she broke her arm. I believe I told you this.”

“I’m sure you did.” Wyatt’s dad’s face didn’t change its confused expression. His eyebrows remained knitted together as if he was solving a complicated equation. “Was busy with the stock. But if your mother approves…”

Working and passing the buck to his wife was Wyatt’s dad’s answer for everything. If it dealt with the livestock or the ranch, or if it was a slight on his honor, Wyatt’s dad could recall the details as if he’d been told ten minutes ago. Anything else? Not so much. Well, minus his anniversary and his wife’s birthday. Those he’d learned not to forget, or the fresh bouquet of flowers he’d arranged to be delivered every Monday without fail.

Wyatt tried for a casual tone. “It’s not a big deal. People suggested we attend, so last night when she delivered my purchases, she agreed to go with me. I mean, why not? Neither of us had dates.”

Caleb nodded and his lower lip jutted out. “Ahh. I get it. The committee suggested you go.”

The best way to survive this gauntlet was to stick close to the truth. “Not in those exact words, but they did sort of force us to have lunch together. I was to meet our grandmother and she canceled last minute. And Madi’s discovered her grandmother hadn’t placed a carryout order.”

Caleb snickered. “Well, I’m all for it as you’ll take the heat off me. I’m rather tired of the matchmaking. At least they didn't try to fix her up with me. That might have been awkward."

Wyatt tamped down the flair of jealousy. "Yeah, we've never dated the same women and I'd hate to start now. But, yeah, we figured we'd go together. She likes the boys and I like her. Besides, she's a pediatrician. A doctor," Wyatt added for emphasis. "Boston education and everything."

"Way to sell an outsider," Caleb teased.

"Her grandmother's here and her father grew up here," Wyatt retorted.

"Until he moved away," Caleb pointed out. "So she's an outsider."

"I think she's lovely," his mother said, ending the debate. She shot Wyatt's dad a glance, and he gave a short grunt before helping himself to another serving. Finished eating, Wyatt pushed his plate forward an inch.

"What time did the boys fall asleep?" When his mom named a time, Wyatt knew they'd be awake soon.

"Wyatt, Caleb and I could use some help after supper," his father said. "Your mother's got the kids." The doorbell rang, setting his dad's edict in stone.

"I'll get it." Wyatt's mom rose and exited. Wyatt heard some muted conversation, and then she returned with a visitor.

"Madi." Wyatt threw his napkin on top of his plate and rose to greet her.

"Hi." She gave him a hesitant smile and held up a shopping bag. "Sorry to drop by unannounced, but my grandmother said to deliver this. Somehow it didn't get loaded yesterday so I brought it out to save you the trip."

Which meant her grandmother had purposefully hidden the items to facilitate this meet-cute.

"You didn't have to bring it out, but I appreciate it. Have you eaten?"

"She hasn't and we have plenty. That's why I invited her in," his mother said. "Wyatt, grab her a plate from the sideboard, will you? Madi, you can sit by Wyatt."

There was one empty chair since Caleb had Emma next to him. "Pretty," Emma said.

"She is," Wyatt confirmed. He put his fingers lightly on Madi's lower back and guided her to her seat. "Madi, this is my brother, Caleb, and his daughter, Emma."

"Nice to meet you," Madi said. As she settled into her seat, Wyatt grabbed her a plate. "I don't mean to intrude, Mrs. Larrabee."

"Oh, we're delighted," his mother said as Wyatt handed Madi a plate. "And call me Jane. Mrs. Larrabee is far too formal. We don't stand on ceremony. Eat up."

"Thank you, Jane."

"And this is my husband, Joe. If your ears were ringing, we were just talking about how Wyatt's taking you to the Snowball Festival."

"It's very kind of him," Madi said. "And nice to meet you, Joe." Wyatt's dad wiped his mouth on a napkin and returned the greeting.

Wyatt's mom gestured to the plate she'd set in front of Madi, the set of tableware magically appearing as further proof of another committee setup, one his mother had approved. "I was about to get dessert, but we'll wait."

Wyatt leaned over to Madi. "They are relentless, aren't they?"

"Let's hope I pass the vetting process or this will never

work," she whispered back. "And, yeah, was sprung on me, too."

"So, Madi, Wyatt says you're a pediatrician," Joe said. Wyatt arched an eyebrow and Joe shrugged. "I was listening," he said. "And you're helping your grandmother."

"Yes." As Madi explained, Wyatt observed the way she interacted with his family. By the time dessert arrived, even Wyatt's dad was smiling. Emma laughed and made silly faces, which Madi returned. His mother leaned back in her chair, satisfied by the "impromptu" dinner party she'd arranged.

While she might not be an official member of the committee, his mother had no problem being fully committed to some of their schemes, on the right occasion. "I really should be getting back," Madi said as the meal ended.

"You must come back another time," his mom said. "We loved getting to know you."

"I'll walk you out." Wyatt accompanied Madi to her car. "I told you they were relentless."

Madi's brow furrowed. She appeared slightly overwhelmed. "That doesn't begin to describe it. We may have to step up our game. What's the protocol for tomorrow? I'm not familiar with the Snowball Festival."

"It starts with kids' activities around one, but we won't be attending. The boys are too young."

"I don't get off until five, when the store closes, so I couldn't attend that, anyway."

"Five is when the community chicken dinner opens. It's followed by the dance, which starts at seven thirty. It's a given we have to attend that, but it's casual. Think more dress blue jeans and fancy cowboy shirts than suit jacket and tie. It's not a prom."

"So don't overdress." Madi nodded. Her forehead had smoothed and her eyes had lost some of the shell-shocked look.

"Some women will wear dresses, but they won't be club attire. More hoedown, but winter-themed. Lots of cowboy boots."

"Which I do not have." She placed a hand on his arm. "By the way, they're watching. I saw the blinds flicker."

"Of course, they are." He lifted a strand of hair and tucked it behind her ear. Leaned to give her a quick kiss on the cheek. "I'll text you tonight and we'll work out the details. Dance? Dinner? You tell me."

"Sounds good." She slid into her car. "Chat soon."

With that, she closed the door and Wyatt stood in the driveway until she'd driven out of sight. He went back inside and stepped into the foyer, where everyone tried to appear innocent.

"The boys are still sleeping," his mother told him. "And she seems very nice. I liked her."

"Nice," Emma echoed. "Like her." She dove from her dad's arms into Wyatt's. This would be the size of his boys in about two years, give or take. "Unca Wy nice. Madi nice."

"She is nice," Wyatt agreed. "But don't get your hopes up."

"Why not?" Caleb asked. "She handled being thrust on us. That's pretty impressive."

"Because she's due back in Boston in March. My life's here. I can't see this relationship going anywhere."

His mother's face fell and she frowned her disappointment. "That's a shame. Maybe she'll change her mind."

"I doubt it. She has a job. A life," Wyatt said. Her leaving was part of their deal to fake date. They had an exit strategy. She wanted to build her career. He wanted to raise his boys. Falling in love was not in either of their plans.

Even if part of him wanted to change his mind.

Chapter Six

Madi knew she shouldn't be nervous, but darned if she wasn't. Even if this wasn't a date in the traditional sense, Wyatt was still picking her up from her grandmother's house as if it was more than two friends with the common goal of getting the matchmakers off their backs.

They'd texted back and forth, discussing the details of the Snowball Festival. If they'd spoken on the phone and she'd heard his voice, her anxiety might have gone off the charts. As had been ingrained by her mother, Madi had dressed with care. She'd chosen a dark green denim ankle skirt and a flowy, gauzy long-sleeve white top with drawstrings that dangled on each side of the curved collar. She'd topped the shirt with a blue jean jacket she'd found and purchased on her lunch break in the resale shop located on the square.

Since December, she'd become a frequent visitor to Canyon Classics. Alyssa Hernandez was a second-generation store owner, and she'd come into Bundle and Bloom to buy a baby-shower gift. Almost the same age, she and Madi had hit it off immediately. Madi, much to her mother's disappointment, had no sense of fashionable style—it really wasn't needed when she wore a lab coat—and once she'd left the Larrabee Ranch, she'd texted Alyssa and begged for help.

Madi gave herself a once-over in the mirror of her bedroom before snapping a picture. She sent it to Alyssa, who immediately sent her back a thumbs-up and a "see you soon."

The fact Alyssa liked her outfit and would be at the festival made Madi feel better. She slid her feet into brown cowboy boots that hit right above her ankle. They'd been another one of Alyssa's suggestions that she'd purchased today. Madi slid her hair behind her ear and applied one more layer of lipstick to ensure it stayed put. This was as a good as it got, and it wasn't like she was trying to please Wyatt, anyway. Right?

Of course, you are, an inner voice whispered.

"Madi!" her grandmother yelled from the main level. "He's here."

"Coming!" Madi shoved the lipstick and her phone into her brown leather saddlebag purse—the designer one that had a horseshoe motif—and double-timed it down the stairs. Wyatt did not need to endure any sort of grilling from her grandmother. Bad enough she would accompany them to the festival. However, she'd already told Madi that she had a ride home from one of her friends. Madi wondered if her grandmother had wanted to attend the festival more to see Madi with Wyatt than to see her friends. It was a toss-up.

"Ah, here she is," her grandmother said as Madi came down the stairs.

"I'm here..." The rest of whatever Madi was about to say died on her tongue the moment her gaze landed on Wyatt, who turned to face her.

Immediately, she noticed his smile. It was expectant, and upon seeing her, it morphed into a wide, welcoming grin before his lips rounded. He gave a low whistle. "I'm going to be the luckiest man there tonight," he said. "You look fantastic."

Even though she knew he was playacting, Madi swore she blushed. The words felt real enough that she wanted to believe them. "You don't look half bad yourself," she answered, proud of maintaining the right mixture of a teasing tone and sounding impressed.

"Only half?" It was impossible, but Wyatt's grin split wider. "You wound me."

"Hardly." Madi's denial came out on a flirty undercurrent. "You know how handsome you are. If it was more than half no one would be able be in the same room as we'd be so awed by your beauty that we wouldn't be able to do anything but stare."

"Well, I'd be staring at you."

Madi came off the last step. While on it, she'd been at eye level with Wyatt. Now, she looked up at him and the sexy dimple that was dead center in his chin. The dimple her finger longed to touch. He raised his eyebrows at her, and her breath caught. She shouldn't have this physical reaction, but rampant desire meant she wanted to run her fingers through the jet-black curls at his nape. Those deep dark brown eyes with gold flecks seemed to see into her soul, as if knowing she fought the urge to trace his Roman nose, or run the back of her hand over those granite cheekbones and down a sexy jawline that had been shaved smooth.

"Are we going to stand here all day?" her grandmother

asked, breaking the spell. “Time’s a wasting and it’s not like I got endless years.”

“Oh, please.” Madi rolled her eyes. “Minus your arm you’ll live forever.”

“If I can have one more moment,” Wyatt said. Arms covered in deep crimson flannel moved, bringing forth a white paperboard box. “Madi, I know it’s not that type of a dance, but my mom taught me you don’t ask a girl out without bringing her flowers. I thought you might like this.”

He opened the lid to reveal a beautiful corsage. A pale blue ribbon decorated with silver snowflakes wove between white roses. “It’s gorgeous.” Madi couldn’t believe he’d bought her a corsage.

“May I?” He appeared hesitant and she thrust her left arm forward and inched up her sleeve.

She tamped down her giddiness. “Please.”

Wyatt removed the corsage, widened the elastic band and slid it onto Madi’s wrist. She swore fireworks went off as the simple touch of his hand on hers was akin to flint creating a million sparks. She lifted her arm and studied the flowers. “Thank you. I love it.” Impulsively, she kissed his cheek.

“That was worth us not leaving on time. Well done, Wyatt,” her grandmother said, praising him. “I’m going to take some pictures. Stand over there.”

“Oh, we don’t need to,” Madi protested. Then again, why wouldn’t she want a picture with Wyatt? Someday she’d look back at this moment and remember the way they’d helped each other out. That shouldn’t be a sad memory. Why was she afraid it might be?

“Move closer,” her grandmother said, waving her hand

in the direction she wanted Madi to go. "Put your arm around her, Wyatt. You're not plastic figures on top of a wedding cake. Stop being so stiff and get in there."

"Yes, ma'am," Wyatt said, settling one of those muscular forearms around Madi's waist. Her hip connected with his, and Madi felt the heat through the layers of her clothing. She slid her arm around his lower back, the gesture more intimate than when she posed with her friends.

"One, two, three, smile," her grandmother ordered. She began snapping photos, turning her cell phone both vertical and horizontal until, after checking the screen, she declared herself satisfied with the results. "I'll text them to you later," she said.

No doubt after she showed her friends, Madi thought, but by unspoken agreement, everyone was moving toward the door.

Fifteen minutes later, they were at the Legacy Canyon Civic Center on the far edge of town or, as the residents called it, "the saloon" because of the throwback design of the exterior.

"Fun fact," Wyatt told Madi as he helped her from the SUV. "Several TV Westerns have used this building in their shows. Both inside and out."

"I did not know that." Madi watched Wyatt help her grandmother from the vehicle.

"He's right," his grandmother said. "The most recent wrapped before you arrived." Her grandmother named the show and then her favorite actor who was in it. Madi had heard of the series, but because she worked so much, she hadn't seen it.

"We should find out if we get another season next week," her grandma said. They walked through the doors into the huge, open space. White-and-silver snowflakes hung from the rafters. Crepe paper had been wrapped around vertical support beams. Foam snowballs of all sizes added to the decorations. Round tables had either white or blue tablecloths. The centerpieces contained flowers and snowmen.

"Oh, I see Louise," her grandmother said. With that, she hustled off.

"Alone at last," Wyatt said as he and Madi surveyed the crowd. "Can I get you some wine or anything?"

"I would love that. A glass of Riesling if they have it. If not, pinot grigio or chardonnay."

His grin was teasing and infectious, the kind that warmed rather than belittled. "Not a beer person, I take it?"

She arched an eyebrow she'd taken the time to shape during her beauty routine. "In my parents' social circle? Beer is for Sunday barbeques, at best. And in med school I opted for wine—that was when I had time to go out. I was more the studier than the partier." Because if she hadn't been, her grades might have suffered. And that would have been unacceptable. She'd never had less than an A.

"Let me see what they have. But I'll warn you, I'm a beer guy."

Wyatt wove his way into the crowd. While children weren't normally at any wedding reception Madi had attended, the Snowball Festival dance was best described using that term, minus a bride and groom. Kids dashed around, watched by parents and townsfolk who didn't seem to mind. Some elderly couples danced like they could be professionals on TV, while in another corner a group performed a line dance. Groups of friends sat laughing at round tables, and some families had young children sleeping in car seats or in their arms, their ears covered by noise-canceling headphones.

"Madi, you made it!" Alyssa's squeal easily cut through the noise as the band went on break. "This is Trent. He's actually on leave this weekend. I'm excited you two get to meet."

"Hi." Madi shook Alyssa's boyfriend's hand and noted his strong grip. "Nice to meet you."

"Same," Trent said.

"Is Wyatt here?" Alyssa craned her neck.

Madi pointed in the direction Wyatt had gone. "He's at the bar."

Alyssa turned to Trent. "You should head there and grab us some beer. You know Wyatt, right?"

Trent shrugged. "Just from watching him do the weather."

"Well, he looks the same as on TV." Alyssa waited until Trent moved out of earshot before lifting Madi's wrist. "So you have to tell me everything, especially about this. And I'm loving this jacket on you. Glad you bit the bullet and bought it. Same with the boots. Spill. You and Wyatt. I didn't think you two were already this serious."

"Wyatt said his mom raised him to bring a woman flowers, so he got me this. That's all."

Alyssa lifted Madi's wrist and sniffed. "Smells good, too. And you don't see Trent bringing me flowers, do you? The man doesn't see me for three months and all he wants to do is fall asleep. Well, after...you know."

Madi did know, not that she'd been with anyone in

ages. Sex had not been on her radar—exhaustion had a way of doing that to a person. But Wyatt was a man who certainly tempted, making him a complication she didn't need. "Sorry to hear that," she said, which seemed to be something safe.

She'd answered correctly, as Alyssa nodded. She'd worn her hair in a ponytail, whereas Madi had let hers fall around her shoulders. "I agree. I haven't seen him and it's like over and he's out. We've been together for so long, but still. I miss him when he's gone. I might wear this ring on my finger—" she flashed her small but pretty diamond "—but it's been a year and we don't even have a wedding date. Or an idea of one." After a sigh, she brightened. "But listen to me! I'm being morbid and I try to never wallow. So let's have fun. Let's dance and get drunk and make the boys drive us home. Do you hear that, honey?" she called as Trent approached. "You're the DD tonight. So that's it for you."

"What's it?"

Alyssa grabbed the clear plastic cup filled with foaming, golden liquid. "That's your one and only beer. Madi and I are the ones drinking tonight."

"You are?" Wyatt's breath in her ear made Madi jump. She whirled and he handed her a short plastic cup filled with white wine. "Pinot grigio."

"Perfect." Madi stepped to the side as two other couples passed by. "And, no, this is it for me. I'm not much of a drinker."

"Same," Wyatt said. "The boys will wake early, and my mom's had them all day and tonight. I need to be up with them."

"So an early night then. Cheers." She lifted her glass and took a sip.

"Cheers." Wyatt took a quick sip from the taller clear plastic cup and brushed the foam from his lip. "And I didn't say an early night or that we had to leave early. Just that my head doesn't need to be in hangover hell tomorrow morning. And I'm driving. Come on, I saw some seats over there."

"Alyssa, we'll be this way," Madi called. Alyssa, who was in a heated conversation with Trent, waved over her shoulder.

Each table sat eight comfortably, and Madi and Wyatt found an empty table near the back wall, far enough away from the dance floor and the band to hold a conversation. "Don't look now, but there are some of the committee," Wyatt said.

Madi glanced over and saw Jill Sears and Michelle Woepke. When they waved, she did the same. "I told you not to look," Wyatt said as he pushed her chair in.

"Oops. Well, then stop telling me to not look," she teased him. "I can't help but be curious."

"So this is all my fault, huh?" One corner of his lips inched upward.

"Just like a man, think it's all about you."

He laughed at that. Saluted her with his beer. "Touché."

She could drown in his grin and die happily, but instead she reached for her wine. It wasn't the greatest vintage, but one certainly passable enough, even though the sip lingered on her tongue longer than necessary. But taking a sip allowed her to find some much-needed composure.

They'd been flirting, and it had felt far more real than simply performing a show for the committee members, who were watching them like hawks. Madi focused. She could not misread things. Wyatt had made it perfectly clear where he stood on the whole idea of dating.

Alyssa dropped into the seat to Madi's right. "Am I the you-know-what if I expect more from him? And you and Wyatt should go dance. This is a good song."

The band had returned and people were moving toward the dance floor as an upbeat country number started. "We just sat down," Madi said. "We'll dance later, right?" She pivoted to her left to glance at Wyatt.

"Whatever you wish." He shoved his phone into his pocket. "Sorry. Was texting my mom and checking in on the boys. They're all good, which means I'm all yours."

Her heart gave a leap as he covered her hand with his. Then, seeing Trent on his way over, Madi broke the connection and stood. She didn't know Alyssa well enough to tell her friend that something about Trent rubbed Madi the wrong way. He gave off a self-absorbed, self-important vibe that Madi recognized. The wavelength was universal—whether from a snobby boy from upper-crust Boston or an entitled fiancé from Legacy Canyon. Trent radiated superiority, and it irked Madi the way Alyssa immediately began to fawn over him. "I'm ready to dance," Madi said. "Who's with me?"

Wyatt stood. "Me, of course."

Alyssa rose. "Babe? You coming?"

Trent didn't glance up from this phone. "Be there in a minute. Go ahead."

A short eye roll and a little shake of her head—one Trent didn't see with his own gaze on his phone—told

Madi her friend wasn't happy. But Alyssa threw on a smile, placed one hand on Wyatt's back and the other on Madi's, and began to propel them toward the dance floor.

Having had ballroom-dance lessons and a debut at a charity cotillion that raised money for cancer research, Madi could waltz and foxtrot. She'd also thrown her arms in the air, dancing in darkened clubs after the semester ended. But as soon as she stepped on the dance floor, the crowd divided into parallel lines, everyone facing the same way. Madi froze. She didn't know how to country line dance, much less recognize the song playing.

"Come here." Wyatt reached for her hand and led her to the back line. "Let me show you."

He put his hands on her hips and guided her through learning the steps. By the time the band finished and everyone clapped, Madi had mastered the choreography. When the band finished, she collapsed into Wyatt's arms. "You did great!" he proclaimed.

Adrenaline raced through her. But her flush wasn't from the exertion but rather Wyatt's instructive touch. Her chest heaved as she caught her breath. "Thanks! I can't believe I've never done that! So much fun!"

"Trust me, there will be more and I'll help you figure out the steps to each song. We'll dance to whatever ones you want. Choice is yours." The band suddenly started a slow number. "Ah, but on one condition. Dance with me to this song. If you're game. But know the committee's watching."

That took some of the wind out of her sails, that he wanted to slow-dance because of the committee. But she went into his arms willingly despite the dance being for show.

"You good?" he asked as they began to sway.

She could only nod, for when he put his arms around her waist, she had to tamp down the fireworks. If the fireworks he brought forth were this dazzling when they were faking it, what would they be like if they were created for real? What if they detonated and turned into spectacular displays of light? What would that be like? Perfection.

Without a second thought and moving on instinct, her arms tightened around his waist. His hands moved up her lower back, urging her closer. Her cheek moved to rest on his chest, where it fit as if preordained. They moved in sync, the beat of the slow song acting as a catalyst or a prelude. Madi wouldn't let herself question to what. For once, she let herself simply enjoy the moment. Didn't matter that said moment contained a life-altering quandary. Didn't matter that it contained unrealized potential or a longing for that elusive more. If she ignored the part of her that analyzed, that worried, that nitpicked and that cared too much, being in Wyatt's arms was perfection in itself, a chance to let herself simply be. The moment was enough exactly as it was.

Except the buzzing in his pants pocket wasn't from desire, or the fact he was already backing away. Madi followed him off the dance floor. Wyatt withdrew his cell phone, frowned at it and pressed a button. "Mom, what's going on?" He listened, pausing every so often to add an "uh-huh," "okay" or "yeah." Whatever was happening, their time on the dance floor had come to an end. That fact was evident in the tight grip of his fingers on the phone, the frown he wore and the deep river crevassing his brow.

"Is everything okay?" Madi asked as he lowered his arm.

"Yeah, what's up?" Alyssa asked as she came over, dragging Trent behind her.

"Noah's throwing up and my mom said he has a low-grade fever. I need to go home."

"That's terrible," Alyssa said before Madi could. "I hope he's okay."

"Me, too. I'm sorry," Wyatt told Madi. "Do you want to stay?"

"We could drive you home," Alyssa added.

She didn't want to be a third wheel. "No, thank you. I'll go with Wyatt."

As the overhead lighting shifted, splashing some colors on the dance floor, Madi wasn't certain what expression crossed Wyatt's face. Relief? Disappointment? She thought of something. "You drove me. You'll waste precious minutes taking me home. I can stay. I can go find my grandmother."

Wyatt's lower lip popped as his teeth let it go. "It's okay. I was hoping…would you mind checking on Noah? It's a big ask, I know. No worries. I'll call Kay."

"You think Noah needs a doctor?" That made Madi worry. "Of course, I'll take a look at him."

She could check on him. She had the confidence to do that. She'd at least be able to tell Wyatt what to look for, and whether Noah would need to go into the ER. "We should go."

"I don't want to take you away from the party."

"I'd feel better if I examined Noah. Let's touch base tomorrow," she told Alyssa. Madi gave her friend a quick hug before following Wyatt from the venue. She caught the curious glances from some of the committee but ignored them.

Even without speeding, they reached the ranch in record time. Before Wyatt could round the SUV to open her door, Madi had climbed out. "Go," she urged, then watched him take the steps two at a time. Her low boot heels made her move slower. She shut the front door behind her and began to shed her coat. The sleeve caught the corsage and several petals ripped off. She made to reach for them, but Jane stepped into the great room.

"Hi, Madi. Thanks for coming."

Madi slid the corsage off her wrist and set it a nearby table. She entered the nursey. Wyatt sat in a rocking chair with Noah. "Hey, buddy," he said. Ethan, oblivious to the commotion, slept soundly in his crib.

"What's his temperature?" Madi asked.

"It's ninety-nine-point-nine," Jane said.

"And what did the vomit look like? How wet were his diapers?" Madi listened as his grandmother described Noah's symptoms.

"Okay, let me see him." She took Noah from Wyatt's arms and lay him on the changing table. "Let's take a look at you. Aww, you feel like you have a tiny temp."

While she examined Noah, she spoke to Wyatt and his mother. "Most likely this is a virus. Those typically resolve themselves in seven to ten days. I don't have any of my equipment with me, but I don't see any discharge in his nose or signs of mucus." She gently pried his lips apart and, using her cell phone's flashlight, looked inside. "I see he has a tooth breaking through. That could have caused him to throw up, especially if he swallowed a lot of saliva and it made his stomach upset. That's rare, but it happens. His throat is a bit red, but that's to be expected following vomiting. His lymph nodes aren't that swollen."

She checked his pulse and then pressed gently on his abdomen. "Pulse is good and I don't feel anything in his GI tract. As long as he doesn't keep vomiting and stays hydrated, and his diapers are wet like normal and he sleeps, this isn't an emergency. I'd suggest a follow up phone call to his pediatrician on Monday, though. His fever is considered low-grade. Tonight you can give whatever sized dose of baby acetaminophen you've used before. Of course, if he gets worse, go in immediately."

"I will. Thank you." Wyatt's obvious relief warmed her heart. "He's had a cold before, so I know the signs."

Madi lifted Noah and passed him to Wyatt, who cradled him tightly. Safe in his dad's arms, Noah's eyes closed.

"That's right," she encouraged. "He needs sleep. Viruses are tricky things and the body has to fight them off. We can treat the symptoms, but doctors don't like to give antibiotics until there are signs of an ear infection. Antibiotics don't treat viruses. Would make my job easier if they did, as parents would be much happier. But really, for now, pain reliever, rest and monitoring."

"I can do that," Wyatt said. He gave his mom a one-armed hug and kissed her forehead. Let her kiss Noah's forehead. "Thanks for calling me."

"I feel bad that I ruined your date."

Madi bit the inside of her lower lip so she didn't blurt out that it wasn't an actual date, that she and Wyatt had attended to throw off the committee. "It's fine," she said instead, hating the lie and that it made Wyatt's mom feel bad for ruining their evening. "I'm glad Noah's okay. As a doctor I'd rather get the calls that turn out to be nothing than have family wait until things take a real turn for the worse and then we're playing catch-up with the care." As had happened with the young girl and her appendicitis.

"It has been a while since mine were this young," Jane admitted. "I'm out of practice."

Madi nodded. "And Wyatt's a new dad. But you both did great. Noah vomited, so it's better to be safe than sorry."

"And now we know what to watch for," Wyatt said as he placed Noah in the crib.

"Exactly," Madi confirmed. "No need for the ER or urgent care tonight."

"Thank goodness." Wyatt's mom touched her pearls. "Do you still need me?"

Wyatt checked that the baby monitor was working and handed his mother the receiver. "Can you stay until I get back? I need to take Madi home," Wyatt said.

His mom nodded, dropping the pearls as they all left the nursery. "Of course. Happy to. You should go back to the dance."

"Oh, I'm good," Madi said. "I have to be up early. I'm the opening shift at the store tomorrow."

"It's kind of you to help your grandmother," Jane said. She set the baby monitor on the kitchen counter. "I'll make myself some tea while you're gone."

"Thanks. Madi? You ready?"

"Let me get my coat," she said. She retrieved the corsage from the counter and slid it back on. She glanced at Wyatt, and saw that he noticed the petals on the floor.

"I'll have to get you more flowers to make up for the fact those are falling apart."

"I'm good, really. No need." She buttoned her coat and followed him through the door.

"I don't mind," Wyatt said. "Did you see the flowers on the front table of the main house the other day? My dad gets my mom a new bouquet every week. He's been doing it since they were married. The other night you might have noticed they aren't the most affectionate people, so it's his way of showing her."

"It's a sweet gesture. I'm a rare-occasion flower girl. And when I finally get settled, I want a cat, and I heard cats often eat flowers."

"I know cats eat grass. We had an indoor-outdoor cat once when I was growing up. Moses. He was a giant yellow-striped cat. Moses would eat grass, come inside and promptly regurgitate it on my mother's floors. Moses moved to the barn shortly after. I think both Moses and my mom were both much happier with that arrangement. And he lived a long and happy life until a few years ago. Died at age eighteen."

"I'm sorry." She slid into the SUV.

"It's okay," Wyatt said before he closed her door. He finished the conversation once he was buckled into his own seat. "Eighteen is a good long life for a cat."

"We never had pets. My mother didn't have time for them. She also said they leave fur everywhere."

"Shame. My siblings and I grew up around animals. In addition to Moses, a few of our wranglers have dogs. We've got several barn cats, and there are plenty of horses and cows. So while we didn't have any pets in our house, we had plenty on the ranch."

Shortly, they reached Madi's grandmother's house. Wyatt's electric car made no noise as it idled at the curb, but Madi saw the curtain flicker before falling back into place. "She beat us home. She's watching us. She knows I'm back. I also texted her. She'd worry otherwise. I drew the line at letting her or my parents track me."

"Smart move. So..." Wyatt paused and his gaze searched her face. "Do we need to put on a show for her?"

"She'd find it odd if we didn't." Madi hoped the darkened interior hid her desire. She'd liked Wyatt's previous kiss far too well. She wasn't opposed to another one. She wanted another taste, if only to verify that the most powerful, knee-weakening kiss of her life hadn't been a one-off fluke.

"Then come here." Wyatt leaned over the center console and slid his arm around the top of her shoulder. He angled his face and brought his mouth to hers. The moment their lips touched, fireworks flared and stars sparkled, proving their first kiss hadn't been an aberration. If kissing could brand a person, bind them to another, then Wyatt's lips were superglue, a special magic sending desire racing through her.

And what might have started as a performance for her grandmother took on a life of its own. When he deepened the kiss, she swore parts of her melted. She slid her left hand between the seat and his back. Sent her fingers into his hair before breaking her mouth from his to plant kisses along his smooth jawline. She moved her lips over the sexy dimple in his chin until she found his mouth again like a cat finding the cream. His hand went into her hair, supporting the nape of her neck, which allowed him to tilt her neck so he could trail kisses down to her collarbones. Heat built. Need throbbed. She wanted him to touch her, to cup her breast and run his hands everywhere until she lost herself. As if knowing that, his hand slid lower. Went around the breast straining against the flowy shirt, a thumb flicking lightly against the fabric enough that it sent tingles to her toes.

As their tongues once again mated, Madi knew if they weren't in a car, she'd launch himself at him. Maybe even slide down his zipper and…

Wait. They were in a car—in front her grandmother's house—making out like randy teenagers.

What the heck was she doing? Common sense shocked her system, jolting her as if she'd jumped into an icy river.

"Madi?" he asked as she backed away from him.

"We got carried away," she said, her breath and tone shaky. "That's good enough, I think."

"Yeah." He drew his hand back and through his hair. "Wasn't expecting that but can't regret it."

At least he was honest. They'd promised each other that. "Same."

"Guess we're compatible this way."

"Clearly." Not that she could see his face in the darkened SUV. What was his expression? Even though he'd said he didn't regret it, maybe he'd been being kind? No, that wasn't Wyatt's way. But after having endured some head games from a few men, Madi worried and second-guessed, anyway.

"Let me at least walk you to the door," Wyatt offered.

"It would be the gentlemanly thing to do." And her grandmother would be expecting that.

"I am a gentleman."

"Yes." She had no doubts on that score. "And you didn't do anything I wasn't into."

"Good. Same. I'm finding that I'm into you, Madi. We didn't intend this, but…"

"It's the truth all the same," she said, then reached for the car door handle. Wyatt held her hand and helped her from the SUV. He handed her the mangled corsage. "Maybe we can sleep on it and pick up the discussion tomorrow," she suggested. "Decide next steps."

"I'll text you."

How many times had she heard those words from a guy?

"Please. I want to know how Noah is."

"I will text you," he promised, and Madi knew he meant it.

Wyatt held the screen door as Madi opened the front door. "Night, Wyatt."

"Good night, Madi." He gave her a quick kiss on the lips before stepping back as if to ward off temptation. "Sleep well."

"You, too." She entered the house and locked the door. Before she'd gone five steps, her grandmother rounded a corner.

Her grandmother peered at her. "How was the dance? How's Noah?"

"It's most likely a virus. And the dance was great. We had fun."

"I'm glad. And look at you, putting your medical skills to good use."

"Yes. And I learned to line dance."

"I saw. He seems to like you."

"We'll see," Madi hedged. "We've only known each other a few days. Far too soon." But she did like him.

Her grandmother must have seen Madi's faraway expression, as she shook her head. "Oh, Madi, you got to admit it. You have it bad for him already. Piece of advice. You gotta lock that man down and soon."

Madi's eyebrows knitted together. "You're sounding like you've been watching some teenager talk on social media or something. I don't need to lock anything down. I'm leaving, remember?"

"Oh, then in that case you won't mind that Annabeth Center is back in town. She arrived at the dance after you and Wyatt left."

"Who?" Madi had no idea where this conversation was going. "I have no idea what you are talking about. Why do I care about her?"

"Because she was Wyatt's high-school girlfriend. Everyone thought they were perfect for each other. And if you think the committee is bad with you, just wait until they push you out of the way so that she can go after him. There's nothing this town loves more than a good reunion."

"Great, I appreciate the heads-up." And she'd let Wyatt know. Because maybe he did want Annabeth Center. No matter how real the heat in their kisses, desire was fleeting, like a candle that burned until extinguished. City girls didn't stay forever with country boys, even if said country boy felt perfect in her arms and had the most adorable twins.

If Wyatt wanted Annabeth, Madi would step aside. Even if that meant the committee turned to other matchmaking attempts for Madi.

And if it meant her heart felt the sting of rejection.

Sadness mixed with horror and dread. She did have it bad for Wyatt. She'd done the unthinkable, the thing she'd promised she wouldn't do when she'd agreed to this fake dating scheme. She'd started to fall for Wyatt. His kisses had branded her as his. And she wanted to be his, even if it meant upending everything.

These burgeoning feelings were bad. Very bad indeed. Scarily bad.

And Madi had no idea what to do about it.

Chapter Seven

Wyatt woke to better weather than the day before, a sunny day with highs in the fifties. In even better news, he found Noah's temperature had returned to normal, his color had returned and his diapers had been wet. Whatever had made his son throw up had left his system. Still unaffected, Ethan waved a teething ring at Wyatt while uttering a series of incoherent noises.

"I'm going as fast as I can," he grumbled good-naturedly as he prepped the twins' breakfasts.

"Da da," Ethan said before thunking the teething ring on the high-chair tray. Wyatt's son didn't associate the noise with his father yet, but that would come in time.

"Demanding, aren't you?" Wyatt handed him a sippy cup before giving Noah his. "But I guess you can't get it yourself."

In acknowledgement, Ethan blinked at him over the top of the cup as he drank. Noah fingered a slice of banana into his mouth. Wyatt had learned about the BRAT diet, so today's meal for both boys included bananas, rice cereal, applesauce and softened toast. He'd almost finished feeding them by the time his front door banged.

His grandmother entered, brandishing something in her hands. "Good morning!"

"Good morning." He really needed to take away her key. He wiped Noah's face.

"Brought you some of the cinnamon streusel coffee cake I made. Couldn't attend the dance so I baked instead. Figured after last night you'd be hungry. How's he doing?"

"Noah's much better. Thanks for the food. I'll give them some later." As Wyatt's stomach growled, he decided he'd forgive her this time for barging in. "Thanks. The committee gave me everything but breakfast stuff."

She set the cake pan on the counter. "Surely, there's one breakfast casserole in there."

"Went through them all. Not a one."

She peered at him. "Really? Huh. I'll have to let them know they're slacking."

Wyatt shook his head and held up his hands, palms facing her. "Oh, no. Don't even. I have at least ten casseroles in the freezer and three in the refrigerator. Last thing I need is for you to say something and they send over even more food. I'm good."

"Because it's an easy phone call. Well, a message. We have a group chain going on one of those apps."

Of course, they did. The committee was nothing if not progressive in its embrace of technology. He wouldn't put it past them to have installed hidden cameras. Which reminded him, he should probably check. Nah. They wouldn't go that far. Would they? Then again, his grandmother had fortuitous timing. She was either that intuitive or had insider info.

The woman in question shed her coat and placed it over the back of a chair. She leaned over the boys. "How are my precious grandsons today? Noah, have you barfed today?"

"He has not. Last night only. And he doesn't have a fever or anything and his diapers were fine. Nice and wet. And a regular bowel movement on top of everything."

"Your mother always did overreact. Probably nothing. She shouldn't have interrupted your date."

"I'm glad she called me, though. Better to be safe than sorry."

"True, but she didn't need to grab you from the dance. You were having fun with Madi."

"I was, but the boys are my priority."

"Doesn't mean you two couldn't have stayed a little while longer. Heard you had one slow dance. Shame you couldn't have had more."

"Madi was happy to come with me. We'd had enough dancing."

"Doubtful. Is there such a thing as too much dancing? Men are so silly. Are you going to grow up to be silly, Ethan?" His grandmother made faces at the twin, who laughed and spewed bananas down his chin. "No? Of course, you won't. You'll be smarter than your daddy."

His grandmother picked up an intact slice of banana from his tray and popped the bite in her mouth, then wiped Ethan's face. "See, yummy," she told Ethan. His smile grew even wider, but no more food fell out.

"You are too much," Wyatt said, but he couldn't help but laugh.

"Yep," his grandmother agreed. "And you wouldn't have it any other way."

"True." Aluminum foil crinkled as Wyatt removed the covering from the disposable cake pan. At least he had some compensation for the disturbance. "Would you like a piece?"

"Thank you, but I'm full. Had some cinnamon-raisin oatmeal with your grandfather. What are your plans today?"

He cut a slice and put it on a plate. "More unpacking. Trying to get everything in place and then see what I need. I start working at the station tomorrow, so my time is about to become even more limited."

"Your first day in the p.m. slots. Are you excited?"

He retrieved a fork. "I am, actually. And it's a regular shift at five and six. Need to be there around one. Should be home by seven."

"That's not eight hours."

"No, not on day one. Tomorrow is mostly paperwork and then doing the prewritten weather broadcasts. But I'll have much longer hours by the end of the week. We do a lot of forecasts throughout the day that go out on both social media and the station's website, and those can take a lot of time to write and record."

"Well, I'm looking forward to watching you on my local station. And watching these little goobers."

"You better be referring to the chocolate-covered peanut candy and not be saying that my sons are foolish."

"Goobers schmoobers. Your boys are perfect. As I just told Ethan, they'll be far smarter than you when they grow up, and you're pretty smart. Well, in most ways. You're lacking in finding a good woman and settling down. You sort of dropped the ball in that arena."

"Now, you sound like my dad." Which wasn't a compliment.

Since she was fiddling with Ethan's bib, Wyatt's grandmother had her back to him. "Well, he's right in some aspects. And he only wants what's best for you." She tossed a glance over his shoulder. "We all do."

"Which is why I took Madi to the dance. She seems very nice. And she gave Noah a checkup to ensure he was okay. What more do you want?" He wondered if that's why she'd made an early morning appearance, to see if Madi had stayed over. His grandmother must not have talked to his mom yet.

"That Madi is a good one. You should ask her out again."

"I'll see her again. I told her I'd text her today."

"Flowers might be appropriate, too."

"I gave her a corsage." Even if it had gotten beaten up. "But I can send her something else." That idea, once it took root, quickly grew. He'd told Madi he wanted to replace the flowers that had gotten damaged.

"Excellent. You should do that today. I like Madi." His grandmother took off Noah's bib. "She'd make a perfect girlfriend. Maybe even more if you were smart."

Before Wyatt could comment, his grandmother pushed on. "She has my vote. Speaking of girlfriends, your ex is in town. She showed at the dance, but after you and Madi had left."

While he'd dated frequently before and after moving to Denver, there was only one ex who was known to his family: Annabeth Center.

"What's she doing back?" His heart gave a slight leap, but Wyatt didn't think it was in a good way.

"Heard she got a divorce and hightailed it back to Legacy Canyon like you did."

He finished his breakfast. The coffee cake had been delicious. "I didn't get a divorce."

"You know what I mean. Stop twisting my words around. She's living and working in Amarillo. You both have the foster-family thing in common. She's a social worker at the foster-and-adoption agency—you know, child and family services. She'll probably be the one you'd be meeting with to do your segments. You are still doing those, right?"

"The station and I agreed we'd restart those segments." It had been one of the things he'd insisted on. While he craved more privacy, he wasn't giving up his passion project.

"Excellent, because putting the spotlight on those kids will help them find homes, and drive ratings."

He ignored that she'd made the kids sound like homeless cats and dogs, as the fact was, many foster kids often had no real or permanent homes. While the goal of the foster system was to reunite kids with their parents, and it happened in under half of the cases, the truth was that, at any one time, over one hundred thousand kids were eligible for adoption nationwide. The average number of placements for a child in foster care was two.

Even worse was the statistic that nine percent of the kids in foster care aged out of the system. If he hadn't stepped in to adopt Ethan and Noah, might they have become a number on a bureaucratic chart? The average child spent twenty-two months in foster care. Thankfully, Ethan and Noah had spent less than three weeks in between the death of their mother and his taking over as a foster parent.

"Annabeth and I might run into each other," Wyatt told his grandmother. "If you see her before I do, you are free to tell her I wish her well. But don't say anything else. She doesn't need to hear about my boys or my job. Can you promise me that?"

"I can promise you that, but I can't control the committee. You know how they are."

"I do, which is why you need to tell them it wouldn't be fair to Madi. They wanted to fix me up with Madi, and I'd like to see her again. So let's let me have a chance with her."

He did want to see her again. They'd had a fantastic time until his mother's call had interrupted them. He'd liked slow dancing with her, and she'd been a good sport when she'd learned to do a country line dance. And that kiss had been sizzling. Sensual and mind-blowing. He pushed aside that memory. If he thought any more about how her lips had felt on his, part of him would rise to the occasion, and he'd embarrass himself in front of his grandmother. "Let me sort out my own love life. I don't want to be seen as some player. Never have been one and I'm a father of two. It looks bad and reeks of dishonesty."

She considered his words. "True. You aren't a player. I can let them know that they need to leave you be. Don't know if it will help, but I'll see what I can do."

"The last thing I need is more interference. I've got a lot on my plate right now, including the casseroles I'm working my way through. And I should send Madi some flowers, so if you want to hang with the boys while I do that…"

"Happy to." She lifted Ethan and her face scrunched. "I'll even change him. Take another one for the team. Only because you're going after the girl. You know your grandpa would love to see his firstborn grandson walk down the aisle. While he loves Caleb and Kristen as much as he does you, he's seen them wed. It's you he's worried about. And we're not certain how much time he has left."

Nothing like adding some strong, arm-twisting pressure. Wyatt held out his phone. "Needing to order."

"Send them to her work." She carried Ethan out of the room. "She's there today."

"I know. Opening shift. I can handle my own love life," he called after her. Bad enough the phone call to the local florist would give the committee something to talk about. But he liked the idea of sending her flowers. The corsage had made her smile, and he'd liked the impact that smile had had on him. He liked Madi.

But he was smart enough to know they'd made a deal. She was leaving. When she did, he could pretend to have a broken heart.

As long as he played things safe, so no one actually got their heart broken. "I'll be fine. Right, buddy?"

"Ooh ooh," Noah said. He gave a toothy grin that said he was definitely feeling better.

He did a quick online search and found the local florist. He pressed the number. "Exactly. No one needs to get hurt. What we are doing is just a means to an end that's best for everyone."

But for some reason, as he made the call to send her a bouquet, the ever-present voice inside his head whispered one word: liar.

The bouquet arrived at Bundle and Bloom around 1:00 p.m. Since her grandmother signed for it, Madi didn't give the delivery a second thought, not until her grandmother called, "Madi, this is for you."

"What?" Her heart fluttered and she calmed herself. She'd had flowers delivered five times in her life, with the four previous being gifts from her parents to celebrate various academic milestones. They'd often sent white roses or white lilies, or sometimes hydrangeas.

Madi tore into the paper from the top and lifted out the arrangement. This bouquet was full of color, an eye-popping mixture of orange, yellow, green, red and blue blooms. She wasn't a flower expert, but even she could tell there were daisies, roses, lilies and sunflowers arranged in the blue-and-white abstract ceramic vase. The floral arrangement stood a compact foot high, with the width being a little less.

"That's gorgeous," her grandmother said. She fingered a petal. "Excellent choice."

Madi fingered one of the three orange roses, the petal silky, then reached for the card and read the typed message aloud. "'Madi, thanks for last night. I had a great time. Can't wait to see you again. Wyatt.'"

Her grandmother peered over her arm. "That is so sweet of him. Good job, Wyatt."

Madi agreed. "It really is sweet." And also so unnecessary, like the corsage.

But that didn't mean she didn't like the flowers, or that she regretted the warm fuzzies flowing through her. Wyatt was considerate and thoughtful, which was one reason she'd agreed to this scheme. The thought he might have sent the flowers to cement his affections for the committee dimmed her excitement, but the heady floral aroma of the beautiful bouquet made her push aside the melancholy. She could enjoy the gift if she didn't think too deeply into his motives, so that's what she'd do. Flowers were meant to be enjoyed, no matter what.

"I'll set them in the office so they don't get in the way."

Her grandmother quickly protested. "Oh, leave them on the counter over here so that everyone can enjoy them. They'll be fine. Then you can take them home at the end of the day. They're too pretty to be put away."

Madi pocketed the card and placed the bouquet on the front counter, in a visible yet safe space where no one would place any items they wished to purchase. For a Sunday, the store was abnormally busy, perhaps because of the previous day's Snowball Festival.

"Beautiful flowers," a female voice said.

"Oh, thank you." Madi glanced up to accept a set of 3T-sized toddler clothing from a woman about her age. Madi scanned the item.

"Your flowers or your grandmother's?" the woman asked.

Madi didn't think much of the question, as people had been asking all day. "Mine. From a friend."

"That's a great friend to have."

"I like to think so." Madi reached for the woman's credit card, which allowed her to take a long look at the customer. Blond hair. Blue eyes. Cute, pert nose, the kind Madi wished she'd been born with. Late twenties or early thirties, it was so hard to tell. "For your daughter? And you know my grandmother?"

The customer took her credit card back and watched as Madi began to wrap the clothes in tissue paper. "The outfit is for a child in need, one of my charges. I'm a social worker. And my mother and grandmother know yours. You know, the committee."

"So you live here," Madi said, making the friendly conversation that was so indicative of Legacy Canyon.

"Actually, I'm in Amarillo. I'm visiting for the weekend but I stop by this store when I do. Your grandmother stocks the cutest things." She put a hand with perfectly manicured nails forward. "Annabeth Center."

Madi shook it, highly aware that her dry cuticles needed moisture. So this was Wyatt's high-school ex. How convenient and what a coincidence after what her grandmother had said last night. "Madi Brennan."

Annabeth's friendly smile was offset by a speculative gaze. "Oh, I know who you are. The town's abuzz with your arrival."

"I've been here since December and I'm not that interesting." Madi passed over the paper bag with her purchase. "It was great meeting you. Thank you for shopping with us and have a great day."

She watched as Annabeth stopped on the way out to chat with her grandmother. The two hugged before she left. Madi tamped down the jealousy. Annabeth had that Texas girl-next-door fresh-faced look. A smile no one could help but return. She and Wyatt would look adorable together. Probably had.

"Snap out of it," her grandmother said as she approached, fingers clicking. "I've locked the doors, and we've got a bit of cleanup to do before we open tomorrow. Unless you want to come in early?"

"No, I'm good." Madi wasn't scheduled to work until the afternoon. "I've got some career stuff to take care of, and I promised my mom I'd call her."

"Then let's get to it."

About an hour later, they left via the back door and Madi drove them home. "You're not going to ask?" her grandmother said as they stepped into the kitchen. Madi set the flowers on the counter and her grandmother's calico cat gave them a sniff. Madi shooed the kitty away.

"Ask about what?" Madi gave an innocent blink.

Her grandmother didn't buy it. "About Wyatt's high-school girlfriend. That was her."

"Was it?" Madi feigned ignorance. "I didn't realize. She seemed very nice."

Her grandmother shook her head. "I'm disappointed in you."

Madi huffed out a breath, pretense lost. "You shouldn't be. I like Wyatt, but I've just met him."

"You know love can happen in an instant. You've heard my story."

"Yes, how you met Grandpa in a dance club in Dallas. You were in one of the cages up on the ceiling and he saw you and knew he had to meet you." It was hard to even think of her grandmother in a dance club, much less dancing in a wire cage she'd had to climb a ladder to reach.

"You had to be really good to go up there," her grandma confirmed, striking a pose that probably looked far better when voguing was a thing. "And he was waiting for me at the bottom, and he asked if he could buy me a drink. I was starstruck, so I agreed, and the rest is history. So don't think you can't meet someone and fall for them quickly. Happens all the time."

"My generation is different," Madi said. "We meet online, in the apps. We don't really date." In fact, saying

"Oh, we're just talking" about a guy could cover anything from a few words upon meeting them to having hung out for five months.

Her grandmother's lips puckered in distaste. "Your generation needs to get more. Put the phones down. My time was much simpler."

"You might be right." If there still were such things as modern-day dance clubs like the ones her grandmother had frequented, Madi hadn't been in many, if any. Certainly none since undergrad. Back in Boston, those of her med-school crowd either went to sports bars with dozens of TVs to watch the Celtics or the Bruins, or they went to speakeasies and had high-end, crafted cocktails with names like Lifeaholic, Talking Too Much or 100 Hour Work Week. Her doctor friends had always joked about that one, which was made of gin, lemon juice, simple syrup and some type of bitters with a name Madi couldn't remember.

"There's a Valentine's Day dance next month. Maybe you and Wyatt can go to that since your dance was interrupted. But you should see each other before that, too."

"Maybe. I'll ask him." Madi hedged. She still hadn't figured out when she was leaving and she had to attend the wedding in Boston. She also needed to start the negotiations for the job.

Working for her father's friend was a foregone conclusion. It was an excellent practice and an excellent offer. She was a fool to be wavering. She needed to send her dad the latest offer and have him review it and tell her what to change.

"Have you texted Wyatt to thank him for the flowers?"

"I did." He'd sent back a smile emoji, the kind with

mouth open and showing top teeth. She'd smiled when she'd received it.

"And have you called him as well?"

Madi blinked. "No."

"Madi." Her grandmother's disappointed tone accompanied a slight frown. "When a man sends you flowers, you call him. It means he wants to hear your voice."

"Wyatt's busy. He's working tomorrow. His first day. I didn't want to bother him," Madi said defensively as her grandmother set a pot of water on the stove. Dinner would be spaghetti with a tomato basil sauce, the latter coming from a glass jar purchased at the supermarket. Sunday dinners were nothing special.

"Call him," she persisted. "Set a time to see him again."

Madi's heart leaped when her phone vibrated, but it was Alyssa, not Wyatt. "Hey," she said. "How are things?"

"Terrible," Alyssa wailed.

As her grandmother broke the dry noodles in half and began to add them to the pot, Madi headed to her bedroom. "What happened?"

"Trent was such a jerk last night. He was horrible. We had the worst fight and now he's headed back to the base and…"

Madi settled onto her bed and listened as Alyssa launched into the story…

"I feel so much better," Alyssa said after Madi had commiserated with her for almost an hour. "Let's hope this doesn't happen to you and Wyatt. I liked seeing the two of you together."

"Why would it happen to me?"

"Because Annabeth is back in town. She came by my

store today and bought some clothes. She asked about you. You know she wants Wyatt back."

Even though Madi had no real claim, it felt as if someone had twisted a knife into her heart. "We don't know that for certain."

"Well, she does. You have to be careful, Madi. Wyatt's a great guy. You don't want to lose him."

"Well, Wyatt did give me flowers." Madi read her the card.

"That's a positive sign. He must really like you."

"I guess." Madi felt terrible for deceiving Alyssa, but she couldn't tell anyone that she and Wyatt were fake dating. Worse, Madi didn't like how everyone was making Annabeth out to be a wicked witch, or that doing so made Madi feel as if she should protect Wyatt at all costs. He was a grown man who could make his own decisions—decisions she would have to respect. Madi couldn't let her instinctive jealousy ruin his chances for happiness. Since she was leaving, she had no business standing in his way or fighting for his affections.

"Madi! Food's been ready for a while," her grandmother called.

"I've got to go." Madi tried to hide her relief as she hung up with Alyssa. The stress of maintaining the fake-dating lie was already starting to get to her, increasing her stress levels and her anxiety. The entire reason, aside from her grandmother, that she'd chosen to come to Legacy Canyon was to reduce her burnout and depression and to alleviate her stress. She'd needed a mental reset.

Whatever happened next, she couldn't backslide now.

Chapter Eight

It was a week before Madi saw Wyatt again. During the workday, he'd spend time with the boys on the ranch, and then he'd head into the station by noon and not return home until around seven thirty. But she wasn't worried. After her run-in with Annabeth, the week had given Madi time to think. Wyatt had also sent her a text Tuesday morning inviting her to dinner Saturday night.

He'd also called her to discuss the details, and hearing his deep, sexy voice had made her feel warm and fuzzy. They'd had a lovely, long conversation about this and that, ending when Madi's break had ended. After confirming the time, before he'd hung up, he'd said, "Besides, we probably need to come up with a game plan." That had put what they were doing back in perspective. The great conversation they'd had was between friends, nothing more. She'd be wise to remember that.

Which was hard, as throughout the week they'd texted. He'd sent her pictures of Noah and Ethan and the cute things they were doing. A selfie of him standing by the green screen at the TV station. A photo of the Larrabee land—because Wyatt was also working with his father and brother. Down a ranch hand, Wyatt had been recruited. Guilted into it, more like it, but Madi kept those thoughts to herself. She knew the guilt well, since her mother was a master of it.

Speaking of her mother, it seemed her parents were coming into town soon to check on Marya themselves. They'd been on a cruise over Christmas, one Madi's grandmother had insisted her son and daughter-in-law not reschedule, especially not with Madi in Legacy Canyon to help.

"Do you know when they're arriving?" Madi asked her grandmother. Wyatt had had a meeting in town, so he was picking her up from the store for their dinner "date."

"You know their plans will be last-minute. Something always comes up," her grandmother said.

"Yes, but you know Dad will want to discuss the negotiations." Which would add more pressure if they were doing it in person.

"Will you gain anything by worrying about that now? Go have fun with Wyatt. The only time you've seen him is when you watch his videos. That's not enough."

"He's an excellent weather forecaster." Madi defended her actions and his. While he wasn't like that one guy who on occasion worked song lyrics into his weather forecasts and posted the videos on social media, Wyatt had a natural charisma, one she'd experienced firsthand. He was also highly accurate.

Today was another dry day with nary a raindrop in sight. Even the committee was discussing the impacts of the drought; one of their newest members was married to an agriculture professor at nearby West Texas A&M. While at the store, Madi had overheard the conversation, with two members relaying that this year would be like the last, with less rainfall than needed.

That meant more dangers than cracked earth. During his forecasts, Wyatt had warned viewers of wildfires and reminded them the county had a burn ban in place. The snow of the previous week hadn't been enough to abate the risks.

Madi went into the back office and took a moment to check her appearance. She dabbed on some lipstick, and by the time she'd returned to the sales floor, Wyatt stood at the counter chatting with her grandmother. "Hey," he said. For a moment he was watchful, as if awaiting her reaction, and he seemed nervous. Then Wyatt smiled and Madi's own nerves fled.

"Hi." Aware of her grandmother, Madi tried to play things cool. But she was too aware of the way Wyatt's jeans emphasized a muscular physique. His burnished gold flannel shirt showed the broadness of his chest and the gold flecks dancing in his brown eyes.

"Nice chatting with you, Mrs. Brennan. This is for you, Madi." Wyatt held out a single pink rose. When she took it, he offered her the crook of his arm. "Shall we?"

"You two have fun," her grandmother called as they left the store.

Wyatt opened the passenger door, and soon they were on their way. Madi sniffed the flower. "You don't have to keep bringing me these. But I'm not complaining. Thank you. How was work yesterday? I've been watching some of your clips."

He didn't fish for compliments, which was yet another thing she liked about him. "Work went well. I started my career with the station, so while most of the anchors have changed, I knew the producers, so that made the transition easier. When I was first in Denver, I realized it's not only getting to know the routine of those around you, but it's also introducing yourself to the viewers. If they don't like you, if you don't get the ratings, your tenure anywhere will be short-lived. Coming back here, though, was a reintroduction, so that makes it easier. The station manager said he's pleased with the responses."

"That's great. I saw where you showed pictures of the boys."

"Because of my story, people feel like they know them. There's a connection to Ethan and Noah. While I'm going to keep my life as private as possible, an occasional picture or a reference to their age milestones simply reminds the viewers, I'm a family man now. Let them build more of a rapport with me, a trust. People like to work with people they have a relationship with. Viewers watch my forecasts because they know I'll tell it to them straight and keep them safe."

Madi studied his profile. "I never looked at weather forecasting that way."

"Don't your patients relate better when they feel you understand them?" He risked a glance at her before continuing to watch the road.

"Yes, but..."

Wyatt looked both ways before making a turn. "It's not like you're becoming best friends. But every evening they invite me into their living room to tell them what their weather is going to be. Even more important, if I tell them there's severe weather approaching and that they need to take shelter, I need them to move when I say move. They don't do that unless they trust me, that they feel I have their best interests at heart. It's the personal touch that does that, creates that bond. I'm human and not some talking head. If not, why tune into those minute-long clips I put out on the web?"

"It's an interesting philosophy," Madi admitted. "When I enter a patient room, it's like we know each other, but the things we talk about are similar to the same things you might talk about to some stranger in the supermarket. You know, that idea of becoming friends by the end of the checkout line you mentioned on our way to Bantry's. But even so, you go your separate ways until next time."

"I'm with them night after night, and day after day. Even if I never see them in person, they comment on the posts. They send in feedback. They complain when I mess up. So I go into their living room, and they let me know if they don't like me. And sometimes, if I'm lucky, they let me know they do like me in ways beyond the ratings."

"The doctors' practice where I'm going to be working—I guess that's the foregone conclusion anyway—hangs their patients' Christmas cards on the wall. Like I didn't know you were to send your doctor a Christmas card. My mother used to send my teachers gift cards for the holidays, and I continued the practice in college, but I didn't realize doctors sometimes got plates of cookies and such."

"People send things to the station. Or they'll bring items to station-sponsored events, like the cancer walk. Again, they feel this connection, like we're friends. There is a wall, though, and that's one reason I was glad to leave Denver. In Legacy Canyon, people respect boundaries more."

He'd told her about that, how women had kept dropping by to volunteer for the role of Mrs. Larrabee.

"I met Annabeth," Madi said. Well, blurted was more

like it. Her face flamed, but thankfully, his gaze was on the road ahead.

"Yeah, she's working in Amarillo," Wyatt said. "Doing social work. I ran into her as well at the station this week. We caught up for a minute."

He hadn't told her that. Would he if she hadn't brought it up? "She seems very nice."

They'd reached Larrabee Lane, and Wyatt drove through the gates and onto the ranch. "She is nice. She's working with foster kids, so we'll bring that focus to the station. When I negotiated my contract, that was one of the things I requested. Shining a light on needy kids is a passion of mine and I didn't want to lose that."

"It's a noble goal and a necessary one," Madi said, ignoring the odd sensation clenching her heart, and felt as if it was being squeezed in a vise. "Where are we going?"

Wyatt had turned left instead of right when the road forked. Before she could contemplate if a strange silence had fallen, he parked in front of a two-story Spanish Revival–style home complete with iron railings, a white stucco exterior, a wide hacienda-style front porch and arched doorways.

"This is where my grandparents live. We call it the original homestead and it sits on twenty thousand acres," Wyatt said. He glanced at the cars. "Looks like we're the last to arrive. Sorry for the last-minute change of plans, but welcome to Clarissa's house. Our date got co-opted. I've been so busy today that I forgot to tell you."

Madi glanced at her outfit. She wore linen slacks and a silk shirt. Perfectly acceptable attire since Wyatt was in jeans. While her mother might call Wyatt's forgetfulness rude, if he had told her, she would have stressed for a week. "It's okay. We made a deal and this is part of it. Let's go in."

"Thanks for being so understanding."

Family dinner, Madi soon discovered, meant lots of family. Wyatt's parents were there, along with his brother and Emma. She met Wyatt's uncle, Silas Larrabee, and his wife, Kay, along with their just-out-of-college-aged twins, Jacob and Joshua. Kay was holding Ethan while Wyatt's mother had Noah. Both boys seemed interested in the chaos. "I think I mentioned before that Kay's a pediatrician," Wyatt whispered. "You should find things in common with her."

"I didn't realize your family was so big. I hope I remember everyone's name."

He chuckled. "I have complete confidence in you. And there's actually more of us, but they're not here. Kay and Silas also have two daughters, Ava and Ashley. They're in college so you won't meet them. They had the boys and then eighteen months later Ava came along, and then sixteen months along, hello, Ashley. And my aunt kept working."

"Impressive."

"And my sister isn't here. Kristen and her daughter, Kate, live in Chicago. I think I told you that as well. I can't remember." He gave her hand a reassuring squeeze. "And that's my grandfather, John. Let me introduce you."

With his fingers interlaced with hers, Wyatt led her over to where his grandfather rested in a recliner. Madi noticed the oxygen threaded into his nose and the marks on his arm from blood draws and other things. His plaid shirt probably hid a chemo port that would have been place on his chest.

"Granddad, this is Madi," Wyatt said, not letting her hand go until Madi stepped forward.

Brown eyes like Wyatt's focused. "Madi."

"Mr. Larrabee." Madi clasped his right hand in both of hers, taking care to hold gently. His age-spotted skin was loose over the frail bones, which protruded slightly. "Wyatt's told me about you."

"Madi," he replied.

"Short for Madison," she added helpfully.

"And you're with Wyatt." He glanced at his grandson then back at Madi, telling her that while his grandfather might be trapped in a body ravaged by fighting cancer, his mind remained sharp, even if it was having difficulty verbalizing.

"I came with Wyatt," she confirmed.

"'Bout time you got yourself a wife," his grandfather said, his inflection stronger. "Sit down, Madi. Tell me about yourself."

But then, as if the conversation had drained him, he started coughing, and Madi glanced at Wyatt. However, Mr. Larrabee's nurse assisted him and the coughing fit stopped. "Sit," John said once he caught his breath. "I'm fine. Leave me be."

Madi slid into the chair next to the recliner. Wyatt rested his hands on her shoulders before his grandfather shooed him off. "I won't scare her. So, they say you're from Boston," he said. "Long way from home."

"Yes. Harvard the entire way, including undergrad and medical school. My family lives there and I wanted to stay close to them. My dad grew up in Legacy Canyon."

He nodded his agreement. "Family is important. You want kids?"

Madi was prepared because it was a question strangers asked her all the time. Seemed that the moment she'd hit twenty-eight, everyone had become worried about her biological clock. "I'm not opposed to having kids, but until I came here, I didn't have anyone special in my life."

He shifted to get comfortable and to see her better. "What you do think of my great-grandsons?"

"I adore them and I'm glad you claim them as yours," Madi said before she could stop herself. "Family can be blood, yes, but family is also a choice, and Wyatt chose to open his heart and he's a better man for it."

His eyes widened. "You got some gumption. My son would disagree."

She'd stuck her foot in it now. "I haven't spent much time with your son, but Wyatt's dad seems like a caring man." For once, Madi was grateful her mother had taught her the art of diplomacy and how to recover when she waded into something she shouldn't.

Wyatt's grandfather coughed once. "He and Silas are like complete opposites. Silas left the ranch. Did you know he played pro baseball?"

"I did not." Madi knew little about Wyatt's family, except for the small portions he'd shared.

"Made it to the World Series with St. Louis but he was injured and had to sit out. Still has the ring, though. Nineteen eighty-two was a great year."

"That's wonderful," Madi said. "I'm a Red Sox fan, and my team broke their World Series curse in St. Louis."

"The second born usually gets the freedom. And Joe loves the ranch. That's why he was so angry Wyatt left. You'll need to understand that."

"Okay. Thank you for telling me." Madi had no idea

why Wyatt's grandfather was oversharing. "I'll keep that in mind."

"You can help them heal the rift. Fix their bad blood and hold your wedding soon, okay?" He gave her a lopsided grin. "Not getting any younger."

"None of us are," Madi added, smiling to lighten the moment, and to her relief, John's nurse returned to check on him, allowing her to rejoin Wyatt.

"How'd it go?" he asked. "He talk your ear off?"

"Fine. Told me about you and your dad and about Silas playing ball. Said to have the wedding soon. That's he's not getting any younger."

Wyatt gazed across the room. Noah and Ethan sat in the play yard, where their great-grandfather could see them. "He's not. The cancer took a huge toll."

Madi placed her hand on Wyatt's arm. "I feel bad deceiving him, for lying to everyone."

Wyatt covered her hand. "We're not. We're dating. Just because we've put an expiration date on our relationship doesn't mean it's a lie. People get together and have fun all the time. Even if we said it was fake, how is it different? It's not."

"It just is," Madi said, but the words were lost as Wyatt's grandmother called for everyone to take a seat in the dining room. Madi discovered she was nowhere near Wyatt, but was seated with Caleb on her right and Kay on her left.

Caleb spent most of his time chatting with one of his cousins—unlike Ethan and Noah, Madi couldn't tell Jacob and Joshua apart, so Madi listened as Kay told her about her medical practice. "It's a general practice. There's about fifteen of us, each with different specialties, although some of us do overlap. We take some rotations at the Legacy Canyon General. We're fortunate to have a full-service facility. Most towns in the area have urgent cares instead, and those needing hospitalization have to go to Amarillo."

"Let me guess. The committee."

"They do a huge fundraiser every year. I know what you're thinking. What don't they do? But the rodeo is for charity. Other events fund various civic programs, like our library's reading program and ensuring our town has a hospital that can hold its own."

"The committee is how Wyatt and I met, actually. My grandmother told me to go pick up an order and Wyatt's stood him up. So we had lunch together."

"They are meddlers but they mean well. Luckily, I'd met Silas in college, long before they could decide to interfere in his life."

"So you followed his baseball career?"

"I did. And when he retired, he came back here to work on the ranch and I came, too. Left it all behind for the man I love. Now, he coaches the pitchers for the high-school team. Not head coaching, mind you. He's too busy for that. But he likes to keep his foot in the door, so he helps out. One of our daughters is on her college basketball team, and like her brother, we'll see if it leads to anything." She saw Madi's expression. "Jacob is here until spring training."

"He plays baseball, too?"

"He hopes to. He was drafted, and now, we see if he can work his way into the starting lineup. He's a fantastic hitter, but there's always someone better, and he might have to stay in the minors for a season and make his mark there."

Madi found Kay's positive attitude fascinating. "So your children aren't returning to Legacy Canyon?"

"Like I said, Jacob is back for now, but Joshua is moving to San Diego for a position. As for the girls?" Kay gave a tiny shrug. "We'll see. It might sound strange, but despite the nonstop wind, you'll be grateful for when the dry summer heat gets here. The ranch has this pull. There's something about the land, that once you fall in love with it, whatever that something is seeps into your veins. It becomes a lifeblood. I can't imagine living anywhere else. My children…well, we'll see. I'd hate to have them not living close by, but I have to support their decision when they decide to leave the nest and fly. But I have a feeling that once the lure of whatever they are doing next loosens, they'll come home to roost."

"My parents expect me to return to Boston. I'm an only child." Might as well lay the groundwork for her eventual leaving. As Wyatt had said, they weren't really lying. They'd simply established an exit date. But the truthful words left a sour taste on Madi's tongue, anyway.

"Parental expectations are hard, aren't they?" Kay's smile was sympathetic. "But I'm a firm believer it always works out exactly the way it's supposed to, and that you have to do what makes you happy." She glanced down the table. "Looks like someone is going to get changed." Wyatt had unhooked Ethan from his high chair and he carried his son from the room. "I'm assuming you know how my brother-in-law feels about Wyatt's choices."

"I do. I also know your mother-in-law is not happy with it."

"Nope. We love those boys already, which is why you'll see most of us give Joe a wide berth. He's being stubborn. But in the end, it's going to be fine. You'll see. Joe will come around. This is a bump in the road, a mere blip. My boys were babies yesterday, and now, they're college grads starting the rest of their lives. It goes by so fast. Too fast."

"Wyatt said that already about his boys. They've more than doubled in weight."

"Growth happens whether we want it to or not. As pediatricians, you and I see the proof every time we see someone a year later and see how they've grown."

"True," Madi said.

"The secret? Enjoy every minute. Never let the sun go down on anger. Each day is a gift, and when I look at pictures of my boys, it's hard to even remember them that young. It's like the memory exists only in the photo. Video's helpful. In a photo, I can see the laughter but not hear the laugh. The memories become like spider filaments. Wispy and at the edge of being accessible, but not quite able to be fully grasped. But the moment was golden, and that's what you remember. That feeling never vanishes."

"I'll remember that," Madi said, taking Kay's words to heart. She tracked Wyatt as he returned to the dining room and secured Ethan into his high chair. As if sensing her, Wyatt caught her gaze and smiled before taking his seat.

Kay had watched the entire exchange. "He's got it bad for you. I don't think he's ever brought a woman home. Well, there was one in college, but she didn't last long so we never saw her but once. Then there was the one he dated in high school…"

"Annabeth."

"That's right. We might have seen her. But otherwise, you're it. Third time's the charm, they always say."

At that moment, Clarissa tapped her knife onto her water goblet, and everyone paused. "Thank you," she said, standing when conversation ceased. "John and I are delighted that we could host everyone tonight." Wyatt's grandfather lifted his hand and attempted to wave. "We are so grateful you could be with us. We're especially glad we could spend time with Madi, Wyatt's girlfriend. Madi, welcome."

Madi managed to nod, turning her head left to right as she caught everyone's gaze. "Thank you. I'm happy to join you."

"We're glad you did. And, Wyatt, welcome home. You don't know what it means that we get to see you, and your precious sons, more often. Great-grandchildren. We are truly blessed."

Wyatt dipped his head as the compliment hit home. Madi gave him an encouraging smile.

Clarissa paused. "But we do need to share some news. We saw the oncologist last week and there's another spot."

Along with everyone else at the table, Madi stilled.

"A new one," Clarissa continued, fighting to keep the quaver from her voice. "We'll have more information later this week once the pathology comes back, but we didn't want to keep it from you. When we know more, we'll tell you." With that, she sat with a thump and the table erupted in questions.

Upon hearing the noise, Noah started to cry, and as if he didn't want to be left out, and so did Ethan. Madi set her linen napkin on the table and went to retrieve Noah. Wide-eyed, he gazed at her before tucking his head into her chest. Following Wyatt, who had Ethan, she carried Noah from the dining room and upstairs into a quieter part of the house.

Wyatt opened a door. "There's a nursery in here. My grandma hasn't used it for almost eighteen years, but she's refused to change a thing. This house is so big she didn't need to, so she didn't."

"Oh, Wyatt, I'm so sorry about your grandfather," Madi said. She placed Noah on the changing table. His legs kicked as she began to unsnap his pants for a diaper change. "You must be reeling."

"It's not good news. Damn. I thought he had more time." Still holding Ethan, Wyatt began to pace. "This was not how I wanted tonight to go."

Madi finished changing Noah and settled him onto her hip. Women after birth often had more around their middle, forming a shelf perfect for infant bottoms and legs. Madi didn't have that extra padding, and she shifted Noah again as his bones dug into hers. "I'm sorry," Madi repeated.

"Me, too. When I left for Denver five years ago, he told me not to forget about the ranch, about family. Maybe I should let the committee work their matchmaking magic. Seeing me married would make him so happy. And if he doesn't have much time…"

"You don't know how much time he has," Madi soothed. She'd contemplate the repercussions of this later, when she was alone. "Don't think worst-case scenario until you get confirmation from the doctor. It could be a minor thing."

"But what if it's not?" Wyatt's distraught expression made Madi wish she could hug him. Instead, she adjusted Noah and placed her hand on Wyatt's forearm.

"Then you and your family will deal with it like you've been doing. Adopting the boys and bringing them home to Legacy Canyon means you're around to help. That's a good thing."

"I know. And I know none of us are leaving this place alive. But I wanted him to have more time. His eightieth birthday is in April, right after the boys'. He's young."

"He is," Madi confirmed as Wyatt spit out an expletive of "F cancer."

He gave a violent shake of his head. "My grandmother, she's five years younger. What will she do? What will we do?"

"I don't know," Madi said. She had a suspicion that Wyatt's grandmother knew more than she'd revealed tonight, and that everyone else thought the same. "We should go back down there and see what's going on. If it's too noisy, I'll help you get the boys home."

"They need to be in bed, anyway. I'm trying to keep them on their schedule as much as possible."

They went back out into the living room, where they found Silas, Kay and Wyatt's parents in deep discussion. Most of Wyatt's cousins had left, as had his brother. "I'll take you home," Wyatt said. "I wanted my mom to watch them for a brief moment later tonight, but looks like they'll be busy for a while."

Madi's grandmother usually didn't drive this late, especially after dark. "I can call for a ride. The town does have Uber and Lyft."

Wyatt nixed that idea. "It's not that far. I can drop you off. The boys will be fine with a car ride."

Jane saw them and broke away. "Wyatt, take the boys home. Madi, if you don't mind waiting for me, I'll come by the cabin later so that Wyatt can drive you home. That was the original plan, right?"

"Yes, thank you." Wyatt kissed his mom on the cheek. "We'll see you later."

"Perfect. It'll also give me an excuse to get your father out of here." With that, she waded back into the fray.

Not even ten minutes later, Madi and Wyatt entered the cabin. "It's bath night," Wyatt told her. "You can stay out here."

"Absolutely not," Madi said. "Let's do this."

The cabin had two bathrooms, and Wyatt used the one with the standard-sized tub to bathe the boys. Wyatt turned on the overhead heat lamp and filled the tub with about five inches of warm water—he'd tested it with his hand. He lowered Ethan into a bath seat suctioned to the bottom of the tub. Then he did the same with Noah.

Because the toilet was located in another part of the bathroom, both Madi and Wyatt could be lean over the side of the tub at the same time without being on top of each other. Wyatt got out the baby shampoo and soaped Ethan's hair before passing Madi the bottle. She used a tiny amount and washed Noah's hair. He splashed his hands and grinned at her.

"Be careful," Wyatt warned as he used the hand wand to gently rinse Ethan's head. "He likes to splash. But it's better than pooping the tub, which he used to do. Almost an automatic reflex he thankfully grew out of. Imagine how fun that was."

"No, thank you. I'm okay without doing that." Laughing, Madi took the wand from Wyatt and, keeping her hand over his forehead, made it softly rain over Noah's hair. Then she began to wash him. Bath time ended when Wyatt supported Ethan and stood him upright to give him a final rinse. Then he bundled Ethan in a towel. "Be right back."

"Just you and me, buddy," Madi said. "How hard can this be?" She unhooked the front and moved Noah to a standing position. She rinsed him fine, but when he wiggled to get free, she almost lost her grip because he was so wet and slippery. She dropped the shower wand and let out a squeal as the spray doused the entire front of her shirt. But she had Noah well in hand.

"Are you okay? I heard a…" Wyatt came in to find Madi holding Noah against her chest. Assessing the situation, Wyatt turned off the water and popped the drain. Then he grabbed a towel and wrapped his son.

"At least he didn't pee on me, too," Madi said, flicking away some of the water still clinging to her hands.

Wyatt's face cracked into a grin. "No, but you're drenched, anyway. And I do like what I see."

She glanced at her white shirt, the one that was now see-through and gave Wyatt a peek at the lacy bra she had underneath. "Yep. Soaked." She couldn't help but shake her head. "Babies, right?" A small resigned grin formed. "Adorable menaces." Noah made a raspberry at her. "Rub it in, why don't you?" she teased him, making a raspberry sound back.

Wyatt bit back his chuckle. "Give me a minute to get

him dressed and I'll get you one of my shirts. Until then, that towel's clean."

"Thank you." As Wyatt carried Noah from the room, Madi used the towel to dry the ends of her hair. She took off her shirt and bra and wrapped the towel around her.

Wyatt returned with a blue button-up dress shirt. "Change into this and I'll put your clothes in the dryer."

"Where are the boys?"

"In the play yard. They'll have some formula, brush teeth and go to bed. By then, hopefully your shirt will be dry and my mom will be over."

"I'm not in a rush. The only thing I'd be doing is reading a book. Tell her to take her time." Madi closed the bathroom door and changed. It felt a bit strange not to be wearing a bra—her breasts rubbed against the oxford fabric, the feeling not only freeing, but also somewhat erotic. She found Wyatt in the kitchen, where the boys sat in their high chairs, sippy cups in hand.

He rose. "Let me take those. And I poured us some red wine. Figured we deserved it after the night we had."

She saw two glasses on the kitchen table and found the gesture touching. "Thank you." Ethan lifted his sippy cup and waved it at her before taking another drink.

"You have a sweet dad," she told the twins. She chose a glass. "What am I going to do about him?"

"Ah," Ethan said before taking another sip.

Madi heard the muted sounds of a dryer running and the man in question returned a moment later. "Almost bedtime," he told the twins. To Madi, he said, "My mom might be a little bit longer. She texted that my grandfather, Dad and Silas are arguing about something. Most likely to do with the ranch."

"That doesn't sound good."

"It's not. Everything is in a trust, but my grandfather also has his own land that's not in the ranch trust, but rather in his own trust. When my grandfather started treatment, they urged him to add it to the ranch trust, but he's refused. Said he gets to do what he wants with it. The fact that he won't tell anyone what that means has created tons of contention."

"I can imagine. One benefit of being an only child, I guess."

Wyatt reached for the remaining wineglass. "The Larrabee Ranch is approximately a hundred thousand acres. My grandfather's parcel, the one that's his alone, is twenty thousand. We run them together, but they are separate entities. The houses sit on their own dedicated acreage."

"It's a bit hard to comprehend for this Boston townhouse girl," Madi admitted.

"It's hard for me too. Okay boys, bedtime," Wyatt told them. After he and Madi put the twins in their cribs, she followed Wyatt into the living room. He lifted the play yard and put it off to the side.

"Movie?"

"That would be nice." Since the fireplace was made of stone and was woodburning, the television was mounted on the wall to the right of it.

"Any preferences?"

"There's a new comedy I wanted to see." Madi named the film and the streaming service. "Do you have that?"

"I do." Wyatt found the flick and cued it up. He set the remotes on the side table next to his glass of wine.

"Lights on or off? And feel free to kick your feet up onto the coffee table. Won't hurt it."

"Off is fine," Madi said. She removed her shoes. "And thanks for doing this."

Wyatt flipped off the lights, plunging the room into semidarkness, illuminated only by the lights coming from the kitchen and the tiny red beacon on the baby monitor that let them know it was working. When he sat to her left, what was a long leather couch suddenly felt extremely cozy, especially after he handed her a fuzzy blanket. Madi covered herself and the movie started.

"Do you want popcorn?" he asked.

She demurred, since the wine was making her warm, as was the long-sleeved shirt and the throw. The movie was funny, and Wyatt wasn't one of those who didn't talk during it after a good part. He rose once when he heard a noise via the monitor.

"Feel free to pause it," Madi said. "I'll see if my clothes are done and use the bathroom while you check on the boys."

Wyatt turned on the lamp next to the sofa, filling the room with a soft glow. Madi found Wyatt waiting for her in the hall when she stepped out after drying her hands. "Your clothes," he said, pressing the warm shirt and bra he'd folded into her hands.

"Thank you." Her face flushed. "I'll change out of your shirt."

"Keep it if you want until later. My mom said they're still talking but she can come by anytime. I told her I'd text her once we finish the movie."

"It feels strange that you've seen my bra," Madi admitted. "And handled it."

"It's a piece of clothing, nothing more. Though I do like how my shirt looks on you." He fingered the collar. "You wear it better than me."

Madi's breath caught. "Be careful or I might not ever give it back then."

"An easy sacrifice." He caught her hand and tugged her after him. "Movie to finish."

But this time, as they returned to the couch, Madi snuggled into his arms and put her head on his chest. Twenty minutes later, she shifted. "What are we doing, Wyatt?"

"What do you mean?" He was giving her a chance to opt out, but Madi was already all in.

"You know. This desire. Don't tell me it's one-sided."

"It's not," Wyatt admitted. He shifted so he could face her. "And since we promised we'd be honest, I must tell you that I want you. But you and I both know that whatever we'd share can't lead to anything. It would be purely physical. Like friends with benefits. Somehow that feels beneath us."

"Part of me wants the benefits," Madi said. "Would it change anything?"

"Not on my end," Wyatt said, the back of his fingers moving to slide along her jaw. "I've had women throwing themselves at me for months, and not one of them has interested me. Except for you. Maybe we should take it slow, though. I don't want to rush things, get anything wrong."

"Slow sounds nice," Madi agreed. "I don't need to be a wild child or anything like that."

"Have you ever let go?" His fingers worked their magic.

She thought for a second. "I'm too much of a perfectionist. I overanalyze everything."

"Then let me see if I can make you forget things. Ready for me to kiss you?"

She'd been ready since the last kiss ended. Wyatt's lips found hers, sweeping Madi away. He branded her mouth, claiming her lips and tongue as his. Thoughts derailed. Desire flew. Analyzation took a back seat. Perfection in a kiss tended to do that.

"May I?"

Lost in the sensations, it took a second for Madi to realize what he asked. "Yes." The word was husky, breathless. Wyatt was quick, and nibbled as he undid the shirt buttons, freeing her bare chest to his roving touch. Desire rippled over her skin as Wyatt blazed a path and explored uncharted territory. The fire he created heated Madi, making her a steaming pot ready to boil. She needed release, and if sensing that, his fingers moved lower, undoing the drawstring and sliding beneath the elastic waistband of the wide-leg linen pants she'd chosen. When his finger curled into that most sensitive part of her, Madi gasped. When his mouth lowered to her breast, she detonated, and seconds later Wyatt swept her into his arms and carried her into his bedroom.

"You sure about this?" he asked.

"Never more so."

"I'll stop whenever you say."

Madi planted kisses along Wyatt's face before his lips captured hers. "I want you."

"And I want you right back." He lavished attention on her breasts. His fingers danced between her legs, until his mouth replaced them. Madi's hands gripped the comforter, and she held on for dear life as she tipped over the edge on life's best roller-coaster ride.

Ambient light streamed in the windows, enough so she could watch him shed his clothes and protect them both. "Ready?"

She'd lost the ability to speak so she nodded instead, and then Wyatt filled her, and it was marvelous. What was that term? Infinity and beyond? That didn't come close to describing their lovemaking. It was tender and gentle, yet hard and fast. A contradiction in terms—an oxymoron that somehow worked. Like he was the right medicine to heal whatever had ached inside of her, the cure she hadn't known she needed to become whole. But would one dose of his lovemaking be enough? Especially when it came with an expiration date?

But as she soared and flew, none of that mattered. She clung to Wyatt, her gaze locked to his as she met him thrust for thrust until her head went back and her body quaked until she floated down, spent. She lightly stroked his back as he planted kisses along her neck before dropping one on her lips. "That was incredible," he said, shifting to lie on her side.

Overwhelmed, Madi nodded. "My limbs are like jelly."

"I'll be right back. Would you like water or anything while I'm up?"

As the reality of what they'd done hit her, Madi panicked. "I should probably be going. We don't want your mom to have to wait up, and you still need to drive me home."

"Okay." As he went into the bathroom, she wasn't certain if he was relieved or disappointed. She rolled out of bed, found her clothes and slid into them before he returned. He'd donned his boxers, and seeing that she was dressed, he retrieved his jeans and put them on. Madi had set the shirt she'd borrowed on the bed. "Thanks for that."

"You're welcome." He cupped her chin and planted a kiss on her lips. Leaned back and studied her. "This is not going to change anything between us."

"No. Of course not." But it already had. The connection, the wavelength they were on, was unlike any other. She didn't have a lot of sexual experience, but even she knew their lovemaking had been transcendent, like an experimental rewiring of neurons. Madi didn't know if the resulting connection was real or not, or if she could trust her reaction.

Wyatt rubbed his chin. "I texted my mom. She should be over in five minutes."

"Okay." Madi darted into the bathroom. She finger-combed her hair and rinsed her hands before coating her forefinger with toothpaste and brushing her teeth and tongue. She sniffed her skin, found Wyatt's woodsy scent lingering. Hopefully, her grandmother would be asleep when she returned.

At about the same time Madi returned to the great room, she heard a knock and saw the door swing open. Wyatt had already turned on the lights, removed the wineglasses, folded the blanket and turned off the television. "Sorry to make you wait," his mom said. If she suspected anything, she gave no indication. Instead, she took the baby monitor out of Wyatt's hand.

"Everything okay?" Wyatt asked.

Jane sighed, but remained stoic. "No, but when is it? Your grandmother will tell us what's happening on her own timetable." She gave Madi a warm but tired smile.

"I'm sorry you had to see that. But I'm glad you met Wyatt's grandfather. It meant a lot to him."

"It meant a lot to me, too." Not a lie. Madi meant the words. "I hope he gets good news from the oncologist."

"Thank you. We all do. Now, be safe driving home. See you soon."

With that, Wyatt walked Madi to his SUV and drove her home. They rode mainly in silence until he parked in front of her house. "I'll call you tomorrow," Wyatt said once they'd reached her front door. He leaned to kiss her. "I have no regrets. None."

Madi searched his face. "Me, either. I had a wonderful time."

"Same." He gave her another kiss. "Sleep well."

Madi unlocked the door, and after another kiss, stepped inside. She locked the door and leaned against it until she heard Wyatt's footsteps recede. Then she peered through the front-window blinds until she saw the SUV pull away.

As she readied for bed, the doubts she'd pushed aside returned with a vengeance. The lovemaking had been fantastic. But had it lived up to Wyatt's standards? He'd described it as incredible, but compared to what? Had he and Annabeth had incredible sex? Would they again, once Madi left?

She was getting into her head, her worst flaw. His reaction wasn't something she could control. She had to concentrate on how wonderful her body had felt. They'd changed the rules to become friends with benefits, and the benefits had given her the best orgasm of her life. She was a doctor, and she was used to looking at bodily functions from a clinical, detached perspective. Surely, she could do that in this case, and same for any future occurrence, if the opportunity presented itself.

Madi's mind warred with her heart. She had never been a friend-with-benefits type of girl. She'd never had casual sex or made love to anyone she didn't have a deeper connection with. Sex was the next step in the relationship. With Wyatt, they'd enjoyed each other intimately as a time filler, for some mutual physical reasons. However, it had felt far deeper than some slaking of lust.

Madi set her alarm. Normally, she showered at night, but her body wanted rest and her brain fought the melancholy creeping in, so waking an hour earlier it was. She'd told Wyatt she had no regrets, and she chided herself for wanting more. She'd promised both of them that nothing would change, that she wouldn't be that type of girl who read something into nothing, or made more of a situation than it ever would be.

She was having her first fling, one destined to end, as if she was on holiday. She and Wyatt could be nothing more than they were. She was going to Boston. In fact, she didn't even know why she was hesitating. Madi gripped her phone, opened her email and reread the offer from her dad's friend. She'd be a fool to turn this down, but there were still things to negotiate. She hit Reply and typed quickly. Hit Send before she could second-guess herself.

Her phone pinged with a text from Wyatt: Thank you for tonight. I had a great time. I can't wait to see you again. Sleep well.

She sent back: Me, too. Sleep well.

Then put her phone on silent and turned it over. She'd made her decision.

But the assertion she'd made to Wyatt about having no regrets rang hollow, and as Madi closed her eyes, she didn't know if she did regret their lovemaking or her decision to accept the job once they'd reached terms. Or maybe it was a little of both. But it didn't matter. She'd chosen to accept the job. All that was left was to negotiate a few things and to sign the contract.

Her parents would be thrilled. As soon as she signed, her end date in Legacy Canyon was secured.

Exactly as promised.

Chapter Nine

For a Monday, Wyatt wasn't feeling too shabby. Making love to Madi had a lot to do with it. He hadn't ever been so connected to someone in bed before. The sex had been incredible. But even more was how he felt when he was around Madi. Like she could be the one.

With the exception of her leaving. Wyatt frowned. He couldn't ask her to stay.

"You had some pep in your step," Jason said. The 5:00 p.m. lead anchor adjusted the cuff of a starched white dress shirt that stood in direct contrast to his dark skin. He slid into a navy sport coat similar to the one Wyatt wore. "But looks like you just lost it."

"Nah, I'm fine. Was a good weekend." Minus these confusing feelings. And minus his grandfather's cancer returning. But that fact didn't need to be aired publicly and he trusted Madi not to say anything. They'd had a short conversation yesterday, but since her grandmother was at a committee meeting, she'd been the lead manager at the store and the place was busy. "How was yours?"

"My youngest son started walking, so there's that. Life will never be the same."

"No, it won't. I'm not quite there, but soon." A half

hour later, Wyatt turned as Caroline, their producer, entered, along with the station manager.

"Hey, Wyatt. Jason," she said. "How are the promos you're filming looking?"

"Great. Wyatt here's a real pro," Jason said enthusiastically.

"Would hope so. We're lucky to have grabbed him from Denver," Caroline said. She was a no-nonsense straight shooter whose forehead wore a permanent concentration crease. "Mike and I wanted to discuss the ideas we had for the Find a New Sweetheart campaign we're doing for February and your involvement."

"That sounds ominous," Jason said. "I'm not going to regret this, am I?"

Caroline gave him a teacher stare before continuing. "It's three parts. First, Jason, you're focusing on homeless pets and pet overpopulation—the spin is 'find a new friend.' We'll film a spot focusing on the no-kill animal shelter. Thanks to our sponsors, we'll also cover the adoption fee for the first twenty-five adoptions. While our focus on clearing the shelters isn't usually until August, we'll try to do it, anyway. Marlene will focus on the dating, romance angle, as she's newly engaged. The angle is find you and your sweetheart new spots to eat, stay and shop." Marlene was the noon news anchor. "And, Wyatt, we want you to focus on fostering and adoption. Kids are sweethearts, too. The angle is to make your family even sweeter. Can you work with that?"

"There's a lot of potential tie-ins there," Wyatt said.

Caroline gave a brisk nod. "We'll also host a two-hour special the night before Valentine's Day. A telethon of sorts, to raise money for our causes."

"That's Friday the thirteenth," Wyatt pointed out.

"And?" Caroline arched a pencil-thin eyebrow. "We have the entire evening of Friday night in prime time for a station programming, and I'd rather fill it with a community event that raises money for charitable organizations than show some random rom-com or horror movie. We haven't done a fundraiser like this recently, and we can live stream the event online. Our community liaison has been lining up sponsors who will donate prizes, donation matches, et cetera."

"It'll be fantastic exposure for us," Mike said. "Corporate thinks it's a great idea so I want all hands on deck."

"Of course," Wyatt said, ignoring the fact that he'd miss spending time with the boys. "No problems."

Jason didn't necessarily appear happy, but since it was in his contract as the lead anchor, he said, "I'm fine with hosting with Marlene and Wyatt. My wife's been wanting to get another dog, so I'll work that into the pet segments."

"A great idea. You both can film your personal journeys," Mike said. "That's the teamwork and big-picture ideas I like to see. We'll start recording the background segments immediately. Wyatt, that woman who stopped by. She's a local contact, right?"

He meant Annabeth. "Yes. I'll contact her. I'll do that now."

"Perfect." With that, Mike and Caroline left and Wyatt returned to his office, which, unlike in Denver, was an actual room with a door. While the eight-by-ten space wasn't large, it had a window, an adjustable desk and a comfortable chair. He had dual monitors and a computer loaded with the latest software so he could edit his recordings. Now, he took out his phone and texted a number that hadn't changed since high school. Within a few minutes, Annabeth called him.

"This is a nice surprise," she said. "Didn't think I'd hear from you so soon after bumping into you."

He fingered the photo of the boys he had on his desk. "Your pitch to the station manager worked. We received a prime time slot so we're doing a Find a New Sweetheart campaign and a live TV special on the thirteenth. I'm covering the fostering and adopting segments."

"Of course, my agency and I would be happy to participate. Shall we meet to discuss it? I've actually got a little bit of free time today, in about an hour. Shall we do a late lunch?"

Wyatt glanced at the agenda on his computer. He had a window between now and the 5:00 p.m. news broadcast. As long as he was back by four, he'd be fine. "Sure."

"Perfect." She named the place.

Wyatt ignored the way his gut clenched. It had been a long time since high school. "I'll meet you there."

During her residency, Madi had worked long hours, often catching sleep in the doctors' break room at the hospital. She should have been prepared for working seven days a week, but retail was its own beast. Her grandmother had been absent from the store on Monday, which was a hectic day because it was delivery day. Trucks had kept arriving with more and more boxes. Tuesday morning, Madi was in the middle of unpacking and inventorying. When she finished, she'd restock the floor displays.

"Have you heard from Wyatt?" her grandmother asked as Madi flattened the cardboard boxes.

"Not since yesterday. He's working." Madi placed the empty boxes next to the back door. She'd move them to the outside recycle bin once they were finished unloading.

"Would he like to come to your birthday dinner?"

"I don't know. He's often working. He often doesn't get home until late, and then he puts the boys to sleep."

"That boy always did work too hard."

"He loves what he does."

Her grandmother paused. "You sound like you really like him."

"I do." Madi could admit that. "He's a great guy. But I'm not going to do long distance, and I told you I've accepted the job as long as the practice meets certain conditions. My dad needs to review the contract, see if there's anything left to ask, and then I'll sign."

While at the time indicating her acceptance had been an impulsive decision, it was the right one and had been a forgone conclusion.

Her grandmother didn't appear too concerned. "How about we do your birthday celebration and combine it with a party for accepting your first big-girl job?"

Since she'd been working in one form or another since medical school, that idea of it being her first job was debatable, but Madi let the big-girl comment slide. "You know I don't like birthday parties." She hadn't even told Wyatt it was this Friday.

"Madi!" Upon hearing her name, Madi glanced up. "We've been looking for you. We need your help."

"Uh…" Madi stared at Jill and Michelle. Who'd let them back here?

"You'd be perfect," Michelle continued as if not noticing Madi's stare.

"You and Alyssa," Jill added helpfully.

"We need someone to help with Sweetheart Day. Someone younger than us," Michelle said with a sharp glance at Jill. "Although we're still pretty young, and we certainly don't look our age, you and Alyssa are far closer to the younger crowd that we want to attract to the dance. Therefore, we're adding you to the organizing committee."

"Um, th-thank you?" Madi stammered.

"Oh, don't get too excited. It's not the *committee* committee, just a subcommittee for the Valentine's Day events," Jill clarified.

"Still, what an honor," her grandmother said, as if trying to seal the deal. "You'll have the time. It can be your parting gift to Legacy Canyon."

While Jill arched her right eyebrow, she said nothing, and Madi figured the committee already knew that Madi was leaving not later than March. Her grandmother had probably told them yesterday.

"Okay, I can help." Serving on some dance committee was not going to make her change her mind and stay. "What do you need me to do?"

"Like the Snowball Festival, we make a day out of it," Jill said. "It's American Heart month, so the day's events focus on wellness. We figured you and Kay Larrabee, that's Wyatt's aunt, could run the pediatric booth. We'll have brochures on nutrition and preventive care. Growth charts and literature on prevention strategies for common childhood illnesses."

"I thought this was a dance."

"That, too. But that comes after the fair," Jill said.

"You could have a height-and-weight station, maybe a

vision-screening corner. Maybe games involving healthy foods," Michelle added. "The fire department will be doing car-seat safety, bike-helmet demonstrations and home-safety checklists. Kids and families first, dance later."

"Okay. I understand the concept." Madi was always into community health initiatives. "I assume you'll have a dental booth with free toothbrushes and toothpaste, so for the pediatric booth, what about child-friendly water bottles or lunch containers, or stickers or temporary tattoos? Even healthy snack samples?"

Jill's admiration seemed to grow. "Love those ideas. That's why you're so perfect for this role. See?" She turned to Michelle. "Told you." Then she faced Madi. "I'll tell Kay you're in and she'll be in touch. You two can meet and discuss what you need and send us a list. We'll make it happen. Our businesses always step up. We're fortunate in that aspect. We're off to talk to Alyssa."

With that, Michelle and Jill left. Madi turned to her grandmother, who wore a large smile. "Seriously? Did you do this yesterday? What just happened besides me being blindsided?"

"You won their approval. They asked you to help with something. That's rare. Congrats."

"I can't believe you volunteered me."

Her grandmother shrugged. "Since you're leaving, it's not worth worrying about. You'll work with Kay, get your swag and do your doctor thing at a booth. It'll be great for your résumé. Then you and Wyatt can attend the dance together."

Her grandmother blinked innocently before bustling off to the front of the store. Madi trailed her. "And don't forget that we're attending dinner Wednesday night at the nondenominational church," her grandmother said. "It's a fundraiser to purchase new benches for the town square."

"How many activities does this town have?" Incredulous, Madi shook her head, then used her hands to shake out her hair. She'd never worn it this long, and she needed to have it cut. "I assume we're going to that."

Her grandmother appeared aghast, as if she couldn't believe Madi had dared to ask the question. "Of course, we will be there. We need new benches. Besides, it'll be fun."

Wednesday night, Madi discovered she knew most of the people in attendance, which meant that when she walked into the church fellowship hall around five thirty, multiple people greeted her by name. Alyssa was there, and quickly pulled Madi aside. "Did you hear about Wyatt? When did you talk to him last?"

Madi's anxiety spiked and she scanned the room. "Why? Is he here? Is something wrong?" He should be doing the 6:00 p.m. news broadcast soon.

"No, he's not here. None of the Larrabees are here, except for Kay and Silas."

"I need to talk with her about the health fair. Did Jill and Michelle talk to you?"

"You need to focus. I'm asking about Wyatt because he was seen in Amarillo the other day having lunch with Annabeth."

She hadn't talked to Wyatt yesterday, minus exchanging a text or two. Madi relied on her doctor training to keep her face neutral and her tone calm and casual. She had no claim on him. She had been the one to suggest a friends-with-benefits relationship. She hadn't specified how many friends. "He can have lunch with whomever he wants. He and I are not exclusive."

Alyssa's frown told revealed she thought Madi had lost it. "Are you serious? Madi, this is Annabeth. If you like Wyatt, you should be worried."

Madi sighed. Dating sucked, real or fake. And she shouldn't care, but she did. "If I don't trust him now, when will I ever?"

Alyssa didn't appear convinced. "If that's what you believe."

"Let's get some food," Madi suggested, trying to uproot the seed of jealousy Alyssa had planted. Madi had no reason to water it. She hadn't told Wyatt she'd accepted the job. He hadn't told her he was having lunch with his high-school sweetheart. Minus Wyatt saying he was looking forward to seeing her again, they hadn't made plans. Why should they? The town matchmakers seemed to be laying off, with the exception being recruiting Madi for the Valentine's Day activities. Wasn't getting the committee to leave them alone the whole reason they'd entered into this ruse? To give them their lives back? She assumed he had better things to do, like care for the boys and settle in at his new job.

She wasn't perfect for him, anyway, and deep down she knew that. Tried not to let it bother her. Once she'd served herself, Madi brought her plate back to the table, where her grandmother sat with two friends. Since her family was out of town, Alyssa plopped next to Madi. Three chairs remained open at their round table for eight.

"How's the store doing?" Madi's grandma asked Alyssa. When the two of them began discussing the store's recent sales, Madi tuned them out. She surveyed the crowd that had turned out for smoked brisket and ribs, baked beans, potato salad, coleslaw, green beans and sweet creamed corn, along with that one-inch-thick buttered toast synonymous with Texas. The buffet was all-you-could-eat, and the fellowship hall served all ages. Families came with children, who raced around until their parents settled them. An older crowd grouped together—seniors who used the time to socialize. Young singles like Alyssa were far fewer, but enough of them filled a few tables near the back, and Madi wondered if they'd known each other from high school. A low hum of conversation surrounded her, voices chattering and laughing.

"Madi?" Alyssa elbowed her and Madi jolted. "Sorry, but you weren't paying attention. I was telling your grandmother I found you the perfect dress for the dance. She said you're going to be helping with the day's events along with helping me decorate."

"Uh, yeah. I'm staffing a health fair booth. I need to meet with Kay. Hasn't happened yet. After the fair, I'll go to the dance."

"With Wyatt? Then you need this dress."

Madi tried to listen as Alyssa described the dress. She really did try. But she couldn't focus. Found herself distracted by thoughts of Wyatt. What was he doing tonight? How were the boys? She liked Ethan and Noah. Felt a strong attachment to them. Weird to think the next time she might see them, whenever she finally made it to Legacy Canyon again, they could be in preschool.

Alyssa waved her hand in front of Madi's face. "You are really out of it today."

"Sorry." Busy thinking of her relationship with Wyatt, she hadn't even noticed that her grandmother had gotten up and headed somewhere. Madi really needed to get it together. “There’s so much on my mind lately. Will you excuse me for a minute? I’m going to touch base with Kay.” Madi headed over to the table where Kay sat.

“Madi! I’m thrilled to see you again!” Kay gave Madi a hug, which, had she been in Boston, never would have happened. “I’m so excited you’re joining me in the booth. I was going to reach out tomorrow. When shall we get together?”

“I’m pretty flexible. I need to clear the time off with my grandmother to ensure she has the correct amount of help, but otherwise I can work around your schedule.”

Kay opened her phone’s calendar app. “How about Friday around noon? I have patients in the morning and paperwork in the afternoon. If we do noon, I can have a true excuse to get lunch delivered for us and my staff. Will that work? That way you can also see the practice.”

They swapped phone numbers. “Of course. Let me ask my grandmother and I’ll text you, but it should be fine.”

“Perfect.” Kay gripped Madi’s hands gently. “I’m so excited to have someone working the booth with me who knows pediatrics. Silas is great at setup and breaking down.”

“But I’m useless at the rest of it.” Silas wrapped his arm around his wife and Kay planted a kiss on his cheek and her palm on his chest. Madi had seen their affection at Wyatt’s grandparents’ house, and it was clear they loved each other. Her own parents were more reserved in public displays.

“See you Friday. I can’t wait,” Kay said.

“Friday,” Madi confirmed. With a smile, she left Silas and Kay to their own devices. The doors had opened at five, and now that it was almost seven, dinner service was winding down. She paused as she saw one of her grandmother's friends but not her grandmother. "Have you seen Clarissa?"

"Not lately. Have you checked the kitchen?"

Madi hadn't, so she headed that direction. She ran into Alyssa on the way. Feeling a bit bad for leaving her earlier, Madi said, "I'm meeting Kay on Friday for lunch. What are you doing Saturday? Shall we do a girls' wine night or something?"

Perhaps if she already had plans, she wouldn't feel so bad about not knowing what was going on with Wyatt.

"Actually, there's this great local band playing out at Wiley's, which is this laid-back honky-tonk out on Dry Gulch Road. We can work on your line dancing. Besides, some of my friends will be there, and it'll be fun. When have you let loose?"

Madi squelched her immediate horror at visiting a honky-tonk. "Uh, okay. Let's do that." She grew more determined. About a year ago, she'd made a resolution to try new things and she'd failed miserably. Perhaps this year she could try again. "I'm in. We'll do it." The more she spoke, the more determined she grew.

"Yay. Perfect! We'll have a blast." Alyssa gave her an impulsive hug. What was it with this town and everyone's tendency to hug? "I'll text you tomorrow once I get to work. Maybe we can time our lunch breaks." With that, Alyssa was gone.

Okay, Madi thought. She'd filled both lunches for the rest of the work week and Saturday night. Friday was her birthday, so she knew she'd have to spend time with her grandmother for that.

Madi went to the kitchen and found her grandmother there, packaging the extra food that would be distributed to needy shut-ins. Legacy Canyon might be a small town compared to others in Texas, but it was big on heart.

"Jump in," her grandmother said.

Madi took an industrial-sized box of plastic wrap and began wrapping it around the take-out containers. By the time she'd placed her stack of containers into the reusable delivery bags, her grandmother was ready to leave. Well, that was after she spoke with a few more people.

Madi's phone pinged: Hope you had a great night. Kay texted me she ran into you. Shall we connect over the weekend?

Madi failed to stop her heart from jumping. Wyatt's text created a giddiness that raced through her, an excitement even greater than when Madi had learned she'd matched with her first choice of medical school.

She calmed her fingers, but it still took two times to type a reply: I've been coerced into visiting the honky-tonk Saturday with Alyssa.

A laughing emoji came back, along with Wyatt's response: I'll call you tomorrow. Maybe Saturday lunch then.

That could work, but Madi didn't know if it was a smart idea. She was falling for him, and she'd promised herself—and him—she wouldn't. She liked his message as three dots appeared, meaning he was still typing.

Her grandmother arrived and noticed. "The way you youngsters talk these days. Or don't talk. Seriously. I'm starting to worry about you."

The rest of his text arrived. Would seem strange if

we don't see each other. And we should probably discuss what happened and our next steps.

Madi's heart stopped racing. Wyatt had put things in perspective. If she wasn't leaving, she'd lose her heart to a man who wasn't interested in hers. The benefits might be fantastic, but they didn't mean anything beyond the physical.

"What's he saying?" her grandmother asked, trying to peer over Madi's arm.

"Nothing much." Madi shoved the phone in her purse and they walked to the car.

When they arrived to the house, her grandmother turned to her the moment they stepped inside. "We're celebrating your birthday Friday night. Be sure to tell Wyatt."

"He's working. The news doesn't end until six thirty."

"We're having a late dinner. Around seven thirty. If he leaves the station right away, he'll make it. Tell him we'll be at Henderson's."

"I'll let him know, see if he can make it. He does have the boys." And Henderson's was not the place for infants in high chairs. Not when it had white-linen tablecloths and subdued lighting, and served foie gras, tenderloins and gelato. Ideal for a date, an anniversary, or an adult birthday party. Not for sticky fingers holding sippy cups.

"If he cares for you, he'll be there. Ask him. Do it for me."

"Fine." This was going to be awkward, so she delayed the inevitable until she'd climbed into bed.

My grandmother wants you to come to my birthday party.

His reply came instantly. That's this weekend? Why didn't you tell me sooner?

Madi had to protect her heart. I didn't think it mattered since we've put an expiration limit on things. It's just another day. I'm turning thirty-two. That's not some milestone.

His reply came quickly. A birthday always matters. Send me the details and I'll see what I can do.

With a swish, she sent him the details. But instead of replying, the three dots faded. For the best, Madi reminded herself as she fought disappointment. Then she tossed her phone on the side table. She was being ridiculous. She shouldn't be this worked up over a man. Her stomach was in knots. Her heart pounded. She was letting her growing feelings for Wyatt get in the way.

She punched her pillow but couldn't make it comfortable. "Ridiculous," she muttered as she tossed and turned. "I am being ridiculous."

Frustrated, she grabbed her phone and swiped. Pulled up her email and reread Belinda Hillyer's response to the list of concessions Madi had requested. Belinda had met each and every one and repeated how excited they were to have her join the practice. Instead of replying, Madi closed her phone. She could answer tomorrow. This job was her future, and the pediatric practice would be a perfect fit. Her parents would be pleased.

Time to stick to the plan and leave Legacy Canyon behind.

Chapter Ten

She didn't think her birthday mattered. As Wyatt strode away from the TV set Friday night, he gave a quick shake of his head. He celebrated his sons when they aged another month. Every birthday mattered. She mattered, more than he wanted to admit.

How had this scheme of theirs gotten so out of control? Minus some text messages, what he'd wanted to say to her had had to wait. They'd never connected in person after their lovemaking, and he was afraid what he wanted to say wouldn't translate through text messages containing shoddy punctuation and too many emojis. Their lovemaking had been so explosive and life-altering, he worried that anything he might say might cheapen or degrade what had happened between them. That was the last thing he wanted. He wanted her to realize how much he cared for her. He'd told her at the start of their "fake dating" that the couple always fell for each other, and Wyatt hadn't been lying. He'd sent her another bouquet of flowers, and he'd bought a single long-stemmed rose to give her tonight. He wished she was staying. He wanted to be with her, could envision a future. But he couldn't keep her from her dreams. Which meant he'd have to deal with the eventual heartbreak.

Long distance didn't work. Caleb had loved his high-school girlfriend, Liv, but once he'd gone away to college after a long hot summer, she'd ghosted him and moved to California without telling him. To this day, Caleb didn't know what had happened between them. But Wyatt's brother had moved on. Married. Had Emma. Lost his wife. But the hurt lingered.

Wyatt didn't want Madi to ghost him once she left. It ate him up that he'd lose track of her, not see her smile again. They'd go their separate ways. So if these feelings were falling in love, they sucked.

Nothing about this was simple. Everything about her lived large in his mind. Once he'd taken the boys in, and his girlfriend had dumped him, he'd gone without a woman's touch and found he hadn't missed it. Dating, much less sex, was not something on a single dad's mind when juggling twin boys and a full-time career.

He hadn't been slaking some lust with Madi. She was under his skin, had been from the moment he met her. The connection he had with her had been the deciding factor, the reason he'd yielded to his desires and made love to her. He wanted to know her on an even deeper level. He hoped he hadn't messed things up, or that she was second-guessing. When she went back to Boston, he hoped they'd find a way to remain friends. Hard to think he wouldn't see or hold her again, much less talk with her. When she visited because her grandmother lived here, he hope it wouldn't be awkward if they weren't at least friendly acquaintances.

"Wyatt?" Mike, the station manager, approached. "How are things going on your segment?"

"I met with Annabeth this past Monday, and I'll be

filming with her next Monday morning. The crew is coming to my house this Sunday to meet the boys."

His boss nodded. "Perfect. Your viewers will love the update on your sons."

The original story—the one that had gone nationwide—had run months ago, when they'd been a little over three months old. "As long as we don't spend too much time on me. The focus should be on fostering and adopting. And that I get final review."

Mike checked his phone. Made a swipe. "It's your story. You cover it the way you want."

Wyatt planned on doing that. He checked the time. He hated not being home to put the boys to bed, but he wanted to be at Madi's birthday dinner. And the boys were thriving under his mother's care, along with that of Angelina, the bunkhouse cook. She'd been thrilled to have young children back at the ranch and had agreed to resume her role as a part-time nanny. With his grandfather's cancer returning, his grandmother had other things she needed to focus on.

Wyatt arrived at Henderson's with five minutes to spare. "Sorry I'm late," he murmured into Madi's ear as he slid his arm around her. "And this is for you."

"You're on time," she reassured him as she took the pink rose. "And this is lovely. Thank you, and thank you for the flowers."

"You're welcome. And on time is late in my business. I've learned how to move quickly when I've thirty seconds to spare." He reached into his suit-coat pocket and withdrew a small, thin box. "I had to stop for this. Happy birthday, Madi."

Madi's fingers trembled as she reached for the wrapped box. "You didn't have to come, or bring this."

"But I did." He reached for her, pulling her closer to his hip and liking the way she fit snug against him. She was delicate and feminine in his arms, the cashmere sweater dress she wore accenting her figure and soft against his palm. He brought his lips closer to her ear. "And it's just a small thing."

"What is that?" her grandmother asked, reaching for the long-stemmed rose. "Let me hold that. Open it. We've got a minute before they seat us."

Wyatt missed the connection when Madi stepped away. He held his breath as she slid off the ribbon and removed the lid. He hoped she liked what he'd found. Madi lifted the silver chain with a horseshoe charm from the bed of tufted white cotton.

"It's beautiful!" She turned to Wyatt, her eyes wide with surprise. She tossed her arms around him and gave him a kiss. "This is above and beyond. I love it."

His lips tingled and the words hit deep. "No, it's not. You deserve the world, Madi. Let me help you get it." Relieved that she liked his present, he removed the silver chain from the box, which Madi handed to her grandmother so she could lift her hair.

"Can't believe you're choosing a honky-tonk tomorrow over me," he teased for her ears only. Doing so kept his brain from racing, his body from liking the way his fingers tingled as he slid the chain around her neck. He fumbled with the fastener but got it secure. "There you go."

She turned toward him and pressed her palm to his chest. He felt his heart leap when their gazes connected. "Maybe I can come over afterward."

Keep things light, he reminded himself. *Don't let her*

know how time stops whenever she looks at me. Or how he wanted to sweep her into his arms. "Uh-huh, we know what will happen if I do."

"Exactly." She grinned and stepped back to retrieve the rose.

"I can't hear you," her grandmother complained.

Madi winked at him. "I was thanking Wyatt for this."

She leaned forward so her grandmother could see the necklace. "Well done," her grandmother said, and Wyatt accepted the compliment with a nod. The hostess returned and, with a "follow me," brought them to a round table that could seat six.

Madi frowned. "Are we expecting others? Grandma, I told you I didn't want a large party and that Alyssa couldn't make it. We're lucky Wyatt could move his schedule around."

Wyatt, ready to pull out Madi's chair, sensed her confusion, and as a couple headed in their direction, he felt Madi stiffen as the pair arrived at the table.

"Madi! Happy birthday, darling." The woman leveled a kiss on Madi's right cheek before wiping away the lipstick with her thumb.

"Madi," the man said, also kissing her cheek, which this time did not leave a mark. "Happy birthday."

These were her parents, Wyatt realized—confirmed when seconds later Madi said grabbed his hand and said, "Mom. Dad. Wow. Hello. I knew you'd arrive at some point but…"

"You didn't think we would miss your thirty-second, did you? Of course, we wouldn't." Despite the light chiding, her mother's smile never wavered. "And it gave us a chance to check on Clarissa and meet your beau."

Madi was clearly surprised to see them, as was Wyatt. He hadn't been expecting to meet her parents. Madi's fingers trembled underneath his and he gave her hand a gentle squeeze. "Nice to meet you," he said. "I'm Wyatt."

Madi's mom arched an eyebrow, a silent reminder for Madi to remember her manners. He gave her hand another reassuring squeeze. "Wyatt, these are my parents, Patrick and Elizabeth Brennan. This is Wyatt Larrabee."

"Of the Larrabee Ranch?" her father asked.

He remembered that Madi's dad had grown up in Legacy Canyon. Wyatt released Madi long enough to return her dad's firm grip with a matching one of his own. "Yes, Dr. Brennan. You might know of my father, Joe. My Uncle Silas. My brother, Caleb. It's a pleasure."

"Same," Madi's dad said, and Wyatt knew using his medical title had scored some points. "My mother says you're a weatherman."

"Meteorologist," Clarissa said, correcting her son. "We don't use that term any longer."

"So you're not on the ranch?"

"I live on the ranch but my brother is the ranch manager. I work for a station in Amarillo. Was in Denver before that."

"I see," her father said.

"Like you, not all of us stay in Legacy Canyon," Wyatt pointed out.

"You went to school with the Larrabees, didn't you?" Madi's grandmother asked her son. Then she faced Madi's mom. "Wyatt's family owns the biggest ranch in this part of the Panhandle," she explained as the group settled at the table, the remaining empty seat and place setting whisked away by the hostess. "You're what, the fifth, sixth generation?"

Wyatt understood this litmus test. "Fifth. My sons are the sixth."

"Wyatt adopted two adorable boys who were a distant cousin's children before she passed," Madi said, reaching over to squeeze his hand. "They're turning nine months old in a few days and positively precious."

Wyatt was never so grateful that the server chose that moment to appear, and Wyatt didn't protest as Dr. Brennan took charge and ordered a bottle of wine for the table. Wyatt was happy to cede control. He reached into Madi's lap, found her hands knitted together and gave them a squeeze. Like him, she didn't like being sideswiped, and the arrival of her parents was akin to a poker player calling someone's bluff. He lifted a strand of her hair and leaned toward her. "How thick do you want me to lay it on?" he whispered.

"Normal. You already won points with the necklace."

"Can do." He bit back disappointment at her points comment. Wyatt hadn't been trying to score when he'd bought the jewelry. He'd wanted her to know how she felt, that she meant something to him beyond friends with benefits.

He straightened and answered another one of her dad's softball questions. They'd get harder, he knew, such as what were his intentions toward Madi and did he know she couldn't stay in Legacy Canyon since she had a job waiting in Boston? Her father might not express things exactly the way Wyatt might envision, but whatever he said, Wyatt predicted the intent would be there. He planned to support Madi in whatever she needed. He leaned back over as her father approved the wine. Gave her hand another squeeze. "I'll follow your lead."

Madi turned toward his direction, her red-stained plump lips within kissing range and sending a rush of blood to his groin. But he refrained and instead laced his fingers back between hers. "Here for you."

Always. The thought flickered and Wyatt brushed it aside. Now was not the time for such declarations or thoughts. And then, as her father asked yet another something, Wyatt left his hand in hers and turned away.

She couldn't believe her parents had arrived in Legacy Canyon without telling her. While she'd expected them at some point, they moved on their own time, her birthday usually an afterthought. How long had it been, anyway, since they'd last visited? No wonder why her grandmother had been so insistent on eating at Henderson's. The town's best restaurant met her parents' expectations—perfect service, delicious food and understated yet elegant decor. When she thought about it, it was difficult reconciling the prestigious doctor seated at the table sipping the restaurant's finest red wine with the boy he'd been in Legacy Canyon, the son of two educators, raised in the same house where she'd been staying. Had his desire for a different life been ingrained? Or had he changed when he'd met Madi's mom?

She was the blue-blood Bostonian with the lineage going back to the country's founding. She'd whipped into shape the country boy from the middle of nowhere who'd gotten into Harvard Medical School. His mother had guided Madi's dad's entry into high society, helped him move through the ranks professionally and ensured that their daughter had had every opportunity to not only succeed, but also excel.

Wyatt sat to Madi's left, and she was grateful that every so often he would squeeze her hand. Few could stand firm in the face of her father's well-ordered barrage of questions, and her admiration for Wyatt increased as he deflected every one of her parents' attempts to knock him off balance. By the end of dinner, he'd even invited her entire family out to the ranch tomorrow afternoon for a tour and dinner, an invitation her parents eagerly accepted.

"No worries," Wyatt told Madi as the evening drew to an end and he drove her to her grandmother's. "My mother can throw together a fancy dinner party in ten minutes. It's one of her skills. When I excused myself to the restroom, I texted her and she responded an enthusiastic *yes*. Don't believe me, check the text messages."

"I believe you. And this will definitely stop me from going to the honky-tonk, an outing of which my parents would not have approved," Madi said. "My mom and dad will love visiting the ranch. I appreciate you doing this for them."

"When I said I was in, I meant it. I'm in, Madi, all in. And you're helping me, too." As if aware that they had an audience, the kiss he bestowed was light, fleeting and left her lips wanting more. "We'll talk when I see you tomorrow, okay? We owe each other that. Happy birthday, Madi."

She watched from the front door as he walked down the sidewalk, climbed into his SUV and drove away. Only then did she go inside, where she found her parents and grandmother waiting for her in the living room.

"He seems nice," her mom said. Since the house had

four large bedrooms with en suite baths, her parents were staying in her father's childhood room.

"He is nice," Madi replied. "He's a great guy."

"He comes premade with two sons?" her dad asked.

"Wyatt comes from an excellent family. You'll see that tomorrow," Madi's grandmother said. She gave an exaggerated yawn. "I'm not used to staying up this late."

It was a little after ten forty. Eleven forty, if on Boston time. "We can regroup in the morning," her grandmother said. "I'll make pancakes. I've got my manager opening and closing, so I'm game for a big breakfast. Might even make some grits."

"Sounds lovely," Madi's mom murmured, though her answer was more about maintaining the peace than an enthusiasm for breakfast. Her mother usually had black coffee and half a bagel, if that. Madi's dad loved a hearty meal, but being a cardiologist, once he'd aged, he'd gotten choosy about what he put into his mouth. He appeared excited about the prospect of pancakes and grits, though. Since it would be rude not to eat them, he was in for a treat. He had eaten some of Madi's birthday cake tonight as well.

Everyone said their good-nights, and ten minutes later Madi's grandmother poked her head around Madi's bedroom door. She found Madi lying there reading a book. "I'm off to sleep. Happy birthday. I hope you enjoyed dinner."

"I did. Surprised, that's all. You could have warned me."

"I learned they were coming right before they boarded the plane. I had to change the reservation. What? I'd made it for three and had to ask for five. Besides, you knew your father would want to come check on me firsthand at some point."

Madi let that partial fib slide. “And my mom came along to make sure I leave.”

Her grandmother tilted her head. “She worries about you. That’s what moms do. You’ll understand when you have your own kids someday. But at some point you have to let your kids live their own lives.”

“I do understand, but because I’m a pediatrician,” Madi said. “I know she means well. And I am going. I told you that I’ve accepted the job pending contract review, which Dad can do in person since he’s here.”

“That can always be undone if you and Wyatt get serious. I’ve known him since he was a boy trying cigarettes for the first time, a story for another time. I’ve never seen him look at anyone the way he looks at you.”

Madi opened her mouth to tell her grandmother the truth. She hated deceiving her. “I can’t stay here.”

“Madi, you can do whatever you want to do. Remember that. You may not have been born in Legacy Canyon, but one entire side of your ancestors comes from here, and we’re as strong as the side that settled Massachusetts. Their blood also runs in your veins. And home is wherever your heart is. That’s more than a cute saying found on the cross-stitch hanging on the wall in the living room. It’s real. Trust yourself. Now, sleep well.”

“Thanks. Good night.” Madi watched as her grandmother closed the bedroom door. Then she heaved a huge sigh. Her parents had paid for her to attend medical school, and she knew how fortunate she was not to have student loans like so many of her peers. That created a deep sense of obligation for a perfectionist who worked for her parents’ approval. Madi fingered the horseshoe charm before taking off the necklace and setting it on the bedside table. The gesture was sweet, but Wyatt was playing a role. Roles required props. That's all this was and best she remember that.

Even if an ever-growing part of her wished it could be more.

Larrabee Ranch needed rain. The entire region did. This once, Wyatt was okay with the last day of January being unseasonably warm and dry. Normal temps were around fifty-four degrees Fahrenheit, but today the temperature was in the low seventies, making it a pleasant, sunny day to sit outside, especially since the constant wind had settled down into a light, rejuvenating breeze. Many people didn't realize that Texas had ten different climatic regions, with the Panhandle seeing four seasons, including snow in the winter and extreme summer heat in the summer. Therefore, while some people in Houston might have their pools open year-round, those in Legacy Canyon, like his parents', were covered and closed.

Despite the fabulous weather and the doors being open to the covered outdoor patio, most partygoers gathered in the two-story great room addition dominated by a floor-to-ceiling fireplace. His parents had added to the back of the house when Wyatt had been eight, and held most of their parties in the cavernous space.

"I thought this would be a small dinner party," Wyatt groaned to his mother. He was used to crowds in their house, but this seemed overboard, especially on such short notice, not even twenty-four hours since Madi's birthday dinner.

His mother's offhand wave sent several caterers moving about. "It is small."

"Fifty to sixty people is small?" Wyatt didn't even bother shaking his head as she walked off to oversee something. He'd asked for a party, and his mother had delivered, and everyone seemed to be enjoying themselves, especially Madi's parents. Wyatt moved next to Madi and wrapped an arm around her waist. Gave her a quick kiss on the cheek. "Sorry I wasn't here when you arrived but I had to check on the boys."

"How are the twins?" Her long lashes made him want to drop kisses on her eyelids. Her blue eyes were pools he could swim in forever. If he whisked her out onto the patio, they could take a fast right turn through the garden and disappear to the cabin, where the boys were getting ready for dinner.

"They should be eating soon. Angelina is with them. They had a big morning crawling everywhere. Suddenly, they have me on the run. I knew this would happen, but man, once they figured out crawling, it was boom. Off to the races."

"They change so fast."

"Too fast," Wyatt agreed. "So what did I miss? Minus that my mom seems to have taken the idea of a small and made it Texas-sized?" A jolt of pleasure went through him as Madi fingered the necklace he'd given her. He liked that she wore it, and how it settled below the collarbones he longed to sample again.

"They're talking about the number of cattle your dad has grazing on your north forty," Madi whispered. "Or something like that. Do you have a north forty?"

"I assume so, somewhere. That's Caleb's department. To my dad's disappointment, I tuned out years ago." His brother had managed to avoid this fray by dropping by, making his excuses and quickly leaving.

Wyatt snagged two glasses of champagne from a roving waiter and handed Madi one. He wrapped his arm through hers. "If we drink enough, we might get through this."

"Cheers, then." When their heads almost bumped as they took a sip, Madi laughed and unwound her arm from his.

He reached for her hand. "No, don't go anywhere. We're a couple, remember?" And he had an overwhelming need to touch her and keep her close.

She nodded. "True. We shouldn't have to pretend much longer. There are things I need to tell you later."

"Sounds ominous." In Wyatt's experience, these types of discussions never went well. Like that one he'd had with his father about how he didn't like or want to do rodeo. Or the one about the state of the ranch and how he didn't want to run it. Or when he'd told his father he was moving to Denver. Or when he was adopting the twins.

We need to talk were words that he hated, since nine times out of ten it wasn't a desired outcome.

"We need to plan our exit strategy," Madi said, her hand a bittersweet yet welcome weight in his. How was he going to permanently let her go?

"I could sneak you out of here right now," Wyatt offered, trying to play things light, even though the idea of her leaving Legacy Canyon didn't sit well. He hadn't liked anyone in a long time, not the way he liked Madi. He'd enjoyed making love to her. He saw how real she was with his boys. She'd be perfect…if she wasn't leaving. He couldn't ask her to stay. Not when they'd met just two weeks ago. Was that really all it was? The idea of falling for anyone this fast was the stuff of those romantic movies his coworkers had loved. He'd turned into the tortured-hero cliché.

Madi's sigh brought his gaze to her throat and a long and creamy neck he wished to kiss. "As much as I'd love to sneak out of here, your mother told me I'm the guest of honor. Well, along with my parents. Speaking of your mother..." Madi trailed off as Wyatt's mom approached.

"Why aren't you two socializing? Go," Jane urged. "People came to see the two of you."

"It's not an engagement party," Wyatt reminded his mother before draining his champagne.

She puckered her lips at him. "Still, you're why we're here."

"Okay. Going." Even though he'd joked about having more champagne, one glass was plenty. He set his empty flute on the end table and offered Madi his arm. "Shall we make the rounds?"

"If we must." She set her glass next to Wyatt's, and within seconds, a server had whisked them away.

"Don't worry if you don't remember any of these people," Wyatt said after they'd met at least three couples before he and Madi were a quarter of the way around the room. "I don't know them well, either. Mostly they're friends of my parents. Some know your dad."

"I'm glad you know their names. I'm overwhelmed and wishing people had name tags on. But everyone seems nice, so it's not so bad. And I'm with you."

"And I'm glad you are. I've missed you."

He felt a moment's panic when she tensed. Her fingers dug into his forearm. "What is she doing here?"

Whew. She didn't mean his confession of missing

her. Wyatt followed her gaze to see Annabeth, who was speaking with both Wyatt and Madi's dads. "I have no idea. Her parents and mine are friends. Let's go say hello, shall we?" He wove them through the crowd, crossing the room in record time. "Annabeth."

Annabeth turned and her face split into a wide smile. "Wyatt." Even with as tall as he was, she landed a kiss on his cheek. He wiped it off. "What a lovely party. Your mother invited me."

Of course, she had. Wyatt drew Madi closer to him. "You know Madi."

"Pleasure to see you again," Madi said, reaching to shake Annabeth's hand.

"Same," Annabeth said. "Wyatt, I can't wait until we film the segments next week." She directed her next words at Madi. "The station is sponsoring a telethon to raise money for fostering and adopting, and Wyatt's playing a huge role. It's quite impressive."

"How lovely." Madi's pleasant poker face hid the coiled tension he could feel. If he didn't know Madi as he did, he never would have realized that Annabeth's presence had unnerved her. She seemed hollowed, as if somehow Wyatt's ex had sucked the joy from her like a candle being snuffed out. Wyatt didn't like that. Madi was fresh. Vivacious. Darn his mother for putting Madi into this spot.

"Wyatt is so generous with his time," Annabeth said. "He's always been that way."

"What's this about a telethon?" Wyatt's father asked, moving to join the conversation.

"Friday, February thirteenth, I'll be one of the hosts of the station's Find a New Sweetheart event. We're featuring homeless pets, fostering and adopting, things to do on Valentine's Day. Stuff like that."

"Wyatt and his boys make the perfect story," Annabeth said. "He has the most generous heart of any man I know. Minus my family, of course."

That was far too thick for even Wyatt to let slide. But before he could speak, Wyatt's dad's brown-eyed gaze landed on him like a sharp dagger. "And you're okay with that? Wasn't that why you came running back here?"

"What's this?" Madi's mom asked as she joined the group.

"I—"

But his dad overrode Wyatt to air the family drama. "My eldest adopted twin boys. Larrabee blood, but not his. Did a segment in Denver on them that had women crawling out of the woodwork to marry into the family. Gold diggers after the ranch. Not that the ranch goes to anyone. It's in a trust."

"I told you how adorable Wyatt's boys are the other night," Madi told her parents. Wyatt appreciated how Madi rode to his rescue, defending him to her mother.

"Fostering and adopting is important," Annabeth said, not to be outdone.

Wyatt kept his temper in check. His dad did not need to continue to stir the proverbial pot. "The only time the segment runs is during the telethon, which is live. We can discuss it at another time."

"Still." His father's frown didn't budge. "None of this would have happened if you had stayed on the ranch, where you belonged." He gazed at Madi's father. "Tradition is important, wouldn't you say?"

Like parents who'd decided their children shouldn't be

together, Madi's dad took Joe's side. "You're one-hundred-percent correct. That's why Madi will be working for one of the top pediatric practices in Boston."

That was news to Wyatt. He knew she was leaving, but she had accepted the job? Was that what she wanted to talk to him about?

"Dad, I said I accepted pending they meet certain conditions. Contract negotiations," Madi said. "I haven't signed the final offer."

"I reviewed the documents. They're ready and awaiting your signature and you're lucky they granted you yet another extension until Monday. No one knows why you're hesitating. It's the perfect opportunity for you."

"I know, but…"

"Really, Madi," her mother chastised gently. "You usually don't drag your feet like this. I know you've met Wyatt, but his life is here and yours is in Boston. Your father worked hard to arrange this."

"What a wonderful career opportunity," Annabeth said. "You're generous parents to help Madi. Madi, I see far too many parents who don't put their children first."

Why was Annabeth chiming in? Wyatt was not planning on dating her again and he'd have to make that clear. "Madi, I see a few people we haven't seen yet," Wyatt said.

"Oh, yes." Madi blinked. Then after a brief hesitation, she turned to her parents. "And the answer to your question is that I'm hesitating because I want to be certain it's the perfect opportunity, what's best for me."

"It is," Madi's mom said with a shake of her perfectly coiffed hair.

"Maybe Madi's found something else she'd like to do better," Wyatt interjected.

Her father's forehead creased. "Is that the case?"

"What could be better than taking over for Dr. Clermont?" Elizabeth Brennan asked, worry bringing perfect eyebrows together. "You've worked your entire life for this. Why haven't you signed on the bottom line? There's nothing in Legacy Canyon."

That had Wyatt bristling. He was here, wasn't he? And Madi, who for a moment had appeared so strong, seemed to wither. She drooped like a flower beheaded by the night's frost. "I…"

"Madi and I are in love," he announced. He'd just blurted out the words, but as soon as he said them, Wyatt committed. What he'd said felt right. Had come more from his heart than a desire to help her. "So since you asked, that's what's in Legacy Canyon. Me."

He gathered her closer as shocked expressions sent ripples through the room. Secondary conversations ceased, as if he'd made his announcement over an intercom. Everyone turned in their direction.

"We haven't known each other long, but when you know, you know. And I know I love Madi. Dr. Brennan, in case you're wondering what my intentions are, let me tell you that I'm planning on marrying your daughter, if she'll have me after I've sprung this on her. But I won't have you or your wife, with respect, sir, pressuring her."

"Wyatt, are you sure about this?" his mother asked.

"I am," Wyatt said, as certain as when he'd signed the papers to adopt the boys. "I guess this is sort of a semi-engagement party after all."

Chapter Eleven

Even as a child, Madi had hated the spotlight. Her father and mother loved being the center of people's attention, but Madi, while not a shy child per se, hadn't enjoyed being the being the focus of curiosity, especially the kind where everyone stared at her as if she'd grown an extra head. She resisted the urge to pat her hair and check.

She could handle this. During college and medical school, no one escaped the gauntlet of professional criticism, that idea of iron shaping iron to create the best medical professionals. That had made things much easier to go through. This was like being a specimen under a microscope, one sliced for closer inspection. As if sensing her turmoil, Wyatt tightened his grip around her waist and drew her closer to him. A strange calm settled. Wyatt might not mean the words of love he'd declared, but Madi appreciated the curious, stunned look on her father's face. That's what gave Madi the strength to push back and play along. "Darling, we didn't intend to tell them this way."

He kissed her forehead, his lips a brand she never wanted to erase. "I lost my temper. I'm sorry. But I won't have them pressure you."

If that was losing his temper, Wyatt was a teddy bear.

He hadn't raised his voice. Hadn't gotten red in the face or huffed and puffed his anger. Madi had seen enough people do those things, and it pleased her that Wyatt could handle adversity without the need to physically erupt. He was like the Texas Panhandle's rattlesnakes, which weren't afraid to strike following enough unheeded warnings, but really simply wanted to be left alone.

"You're forgiven." Madi tilted her head, and Wyatt dropped a kiss on her lips. Another mark of claim, this one short but scintillating, and hinting at far more to come once they were alone.

Annabeth recovered first. "Congrats. I'm happy for you, Wyatt. We'll catch up this week about the segment. Madi." With that she strode off, and Madi couldn't say she was sorry to see her go. While Madi and Wyatt might not be in love, Madi didn't like the idea of him being with Annabeth. Or anyone, really. At least once she was in Boston she wouldn't have to see Wyatt fall in love with another, not that distance would make things easier. She wanted him for herself.

"Madi, I can understand now your confusion," her mother said, finding her voice. "Wyatt, you could always move to Boston, couldn't you? They have weather… meteorologists there. And it's a huge market compared to Denver, right?"

"Ninth largest, where Denver is the seventeenth," Wyatt confirmed.

"Wyatt just took a job here," Wyatt's dad said. Madi didn't like the scowl that was now etched onto Joe's face. "He's also helping on the ranch. We're in a drought. And the ranch is where Larrabees raise their children."

Wyatt tensed, and Madi found it just as ironic that Wyatt's dad could conveniently use the adoption, one he disliked, when it suited him.

"This is problematic," her mother said. "But if they love each other, they'll work it out."

"As long as Madi is in Boston," her father said. "I worked hard to get her this opportunity. Elizabeth, you still have your contacts at the station, right? For Wyatt? We can't let Madi lose out. She deserves the best."

Because, of course, there were other candidates for Dr. Clermont's job. He didn't need to say that aloud, but Madi heard it, anyway, and the rebuke resonated. Those candidates might be even better than she was, especially as she'd missed what should have been an easily diagnosed case of appendicitis, had she done her job correctly and pushed for an ultrasound.

Ever the diplomat, Madi's mom put her hand on her husband's arm. "Look, they've set out the buffet. As Madi's parents, we should start the line so people can eat. In fact, there's Jane. Will you accompany me?" She smiled at her husband and then directed her next words at Wyatt's father. "We can table this until later, once the kids talk things through. Whatever they choose, I know all of us want what's best for them. Excuse us. We can't dishonor your wife by dallying."

As a way to extricate her and her husband from the conversation, it was a brilliant social move, one of those well-executed exits Madi had seen her mother make countless times and wished she could duplicate.

"Are you hungry?" Wyatt asked. "After all, you're the guest of honor."

"I would like something." Madi's knees weakened

slightly as Wyatt led her away. “All I’ve had was the champagne.”

“Same. We definitely need to eat.”

“And talk about what you did and what comes next,” Madi said. She knew he didn’t mean any of his declarations, but they’d landed with the force of a Category 5 hurricane. What would it be like to have a man like Wyatt truly love her? And make that declaration in front of everyone? She wished it had been real, and because it wasn’t, her stomach was in knots.

“Sorry about the earlier drama. You said the other night to be normal and instead I dropped a bomb instead. But our parents don’t get to decide for us. That was the entire point of our arrangement, not to be manipulated.”

“No, and we certainly ran Annabeth off. Sorry about that.”

Wyatt gave her a quizzical look. “What are you talking about? There’s nothing between me and Annabeth, nor do I want there to be. She might be my ex, but that’s done. Has been for like twelve years.”

Hope raced through Madi and she tamped it down. “She might have an idea that there might be something, or the potential for something,” Madi clarified. “And if there is, I don’t want to get in the way of that.”

“The committee probably thought she might be a welcome candidate, especially since you’re leaving. They’re relentless. But, no, I feel nothing. She’s someone I’m working with, that’s all.”

“Maybe they thought I might get jealous,” Madi said. “Up the ante.”

“Are you jealous?”

Was she? One hundred and ten percent. Why did he

want to know? "I'm not sure what the correct answer to that question should be."

"Then there's no need for an answer." Wyatt reached for a porcelain dinner plate and handed it to her. Like her mother, Wyatt's did not use paper, finding it too gauche. The plate was warm to the touch and she loaded it full of elevated ranch fare: slow smoked brisket and pulled pork, grilled lobster tails and portobello mushrooms, a too-pretty-to-eat version of Mexican street corn, roasted red potatoes with garlic and herbs, and a bacon, lettuce and tomato pasta salad.

Wyatt led her outside onto the covered aggregate patio. He set his plate at the head of the large dining table, and Madi placed hers to his left. "No one ever eats out here, and it's too nice to sit inside. What do you want to drink? More champagne? Water?"

"Lemonade would be lovely."

"Coming right up."

As he went back inside, Madi unrolled the black linen napkin surrounding her silverware. She lifted a fork and took a small bite of corn, which was as delicious as it looked. She gazed out at the huge expanse of land. The backyard stretched for about a hundred yards before a white fence separated the yard from the pastures. Several horses grazed, their necks long. One raised its head and stared in her direction before resuming.

She tucked her hair behind her ear. She'd worn it down, and the breeze tickled the ends, taking the wisps and brushing them across her nose and forehead. She heard the door open, and Wyatt set down the lemonade before sitting to her right. "Thank you."

When he smiled, she felt in in her toes. "You're welcome. How is it?" he asked.

"Minus a taste of the street corn, I was waiting for you before I began. And it looks delicious. Your mom went all out."

"My mom called the caterer. Although, the brisket is from our herd, pasture-raised and humanely slaughtered. My brother is big on that. He had to convince my dad and grandfather that fewer cattle could still show a profit, but Caleb discovered that people will pay a premium for organic, free-roam meat. With this drought, the land can't support the large amount of cattle we had before. So the ranch focuses on quality stock now, over quantity. And better marketing to convince buyers to purchase our beef instead of something imported in from South America."

"Probably better for the environment, too."

"Most definitely. The last thing a rancher wants is soil erosion or nutrient runoff. Maintaining the ecosystem is important, and successful ranches as large as ours continually work on their ecological footprint."

"Ranching is out of my wheelhouse. I rode English, not Western saddle. It's hard to picture my father growing up here. My grandfather passed when I was young, so I don't have a lot of memories of him. But my grandmother has always lived in town since she and my grandfather both worked in education."

"She busted me for smoking once."

"She mentioned it, but not the details."

By the time he finished the story, she was laughing so hard she had to wipe the tears from her eyes. She waved her hand in front of her face before grabbing her napkin and wiping her mouth. "Sorry. I know I shouldn't be laughing, but I can picture her doing that. She's a force of nature."

"You could say she scared me straight. Well, that and the fact she called my mother, and then she read me the riot act, too."

"No wonder why my dad wanted to escape. Although, that's more my mom. Her entire family is as synonymous to Boston as the red bricks of the Old State House and Faneuil Hall. Boston is a pretty red city."

"The Red Sox you like."

"The team name is more from the stockings the players used to wear." She gave an amused shake, which made her hair come loose again. "You can tell I'm steeped in my city's history. I've never left. College. Med school. Residency. Minus vacations, it's always been home."

Although her grandmother had said home was wherever her heart was. Trouble was, Madi sometimes wasn't certain she had a firm grip on what her heart might want. Like Wyatt. If she wasn't already in love with him, she was certainly falling. He checked every one of her boxes: handsome, kind. He had a steady job, was caring and tender. He was a committed family man, an excellent lover… She could go on and on. "I can see why you'd want Ethan and Noah to grow up here. There's a sense of wonderment about this place."

The horses had moved deeper into the pasture, appearing more like specks and blobs. "Yeah, it's magical. But I like the city, too. You can't walk anywhere here. In Denver, we could take the stroller, go around the corner and sit in one of our favorite coffee shops. We moved because I want my boys to know their family. My dad was correct when he said that. I don't agree with him often, but another city is not an option. If I'd wanted that, I would have stayed in Denver, or sought out a larger market instead of moving home."

"I understand. I do. There are days I wish I hadn't spent every huge life moment in Boston. My parents' social circle is my social circle. I have to be at a wedding the last Saturday of February. And my onboarding is the twenty-third."

"So at most we have two or three weeks to spend together."

Saying it aloud made it sound so final. "I'll probably leave after Valentine's Day, if that works for you. We can stage some big breakup or something."

"Nah." He pushed his empty plate forward. "No need for that. After my huge declaration in there, your leaving will be enough to break my heart and that'll be enough excuse for the committee. If it's not, I'm a grown man. I can handle them."

"Fingers crossed." She made the motion, and Wyatt reached for her hand and kissed the back of it. Her skin prickled and she fought the shivers as he gazed over their joined hands.

"You and I are victims of circumstances. But until you go, let's not think about things and simply enjoy whatever this is that we've created."

"Sounds like a plan." When he let her hand go, Madi boldly scooted her chair back and angled herself toward him. She placed her hand on his knee.

"Speaking of plans, it might be time for you to kiss me. We've got a bunch of curious onlookers at the windows."

He didn't turn to look, but instead pivoted and leaned

closer. His hands moved to her knees. "We can't disappoint them."

Her breath caught and his lips hadn't even come into kissing range yet. "No. We can't."

"Then we won't." Closing the space, his lips found hers.

The magic began at first contact, and Madi's eyes closed as the ensuing sensations swept her away. The kiss was soft and soulful, the kind that created a slow burn that would simmer long after his lips lifted from hers. Which they did far too soon for her liking.

She opened her eyes to find him watching her, the hint of a smile on his face the only indication of his own pleasure as his gaze searched hers. He thumbed her bottom lip, wiping something away before bending his forehead to hers. "If they weren't here, I'd pick you up and carry you to the cabin and never let you leave."

"And I'd let you," Madi admitted. As he drew back, she reached her hand to his cheek and he leaned into her palm. "You do something to me."

"Same." Wyatt heaved a sigh. "But reality calls."

"That it does." Madi noted that the faces staring out the window turned when she caught them. Pretending they hadn't watched the entire kiss, they headed back into the center of the great room. "It was a good show."

The only problem was she hadn't been pretending.

"So I heard you and Wyatt created quite the stir last weekend."

Madi's fingers froze and she dropped the sticker she'd been stuffing into a red plastic bag covered with pink and white hearts. It was the Wednesday afternoon before Valentine's Day weekend and she and Kay Larrabee were stuffing goodie bags for their pediatric booth in the upcoming Sweetheart Day's fair. A week and a half had passed since the dinner party where Wyatt had declared his love.

Kay Larrabee chuckled. "I can see I've hit a nerve. I wish I could have been there but I had a bridal shower to attend in Lubbock, so I was out of town and this has been the first chance I've really gotten to talk with you since I had to cancel our lunch."

"I'm sorry we've been playing tag. My parents left yesterday. They stayed longer than I thought they would and that kept me busy." And away from Wyatt. She'd tried to see him, but between his schedule and that of her parents, the only time they'd had was chatting on the phone, which they'd done until late at night.

"It seems the introduction of the two families didn't go as well as hoped."

"It wasn't that bad."

Kay paused and shot Madi a dubious eyebrow arch. "Really? You can be honest with me."

"Fine, my grandmother and yours were besides themselves with glee hoping to see an engagement ring, while my father and your brother were in agreement on one thing, that Wyatt and I are better off not dating."

"My brother-in-law fears you're going to steal Wyatt away to Boston. You were the topic of Sunday dinner last weekend. Wyatt got an earful."

"He told me. But his family shouldn't be worried. Wyatt told me he's not moving away from Legacy Canyon."

Kay lifted more empty bags from the box. "Which means you'd have to stay here."

"I can't. I told you about my job offer. My dad stood over me while I signed. It's a great offer. I'd be a fool not to take it." She'd been telling herself that since she'd sent the contract back.

"I'm certain it is. But I'll always be Team Wyatt and Team Legacy Canyon." Kay passed more bags to Madi. Double the size of treat bags, each one contained stickers, a growth chart, a ruler and two samples of healthy snacks. Kay and Madi would distribute the bags to the parents stopping by the booth on Saturday. Madi began putting stickers inside. "You should realize by now how happy you make my nephew."

"I'd like to hope he's happy. It's like we're long-distance already. I haven't had a moment to see him since my parents arrived."

"He told me he filmed the segments with the boys," Kay said. "And completed the other fostering and adoption segments."

"Yes, we chatted about that." And how Annabeth had done hers in the studio, and how she planned to be at the telethon. Madi had no reason to be jealous, but Annabeth had seen him more than she had.

But like Shakespeare had written, jealousy was a green-eyed monster. And while she'd never answered Wyatt's question, Madi was jealous. "I'm Team Wyatt, too," she admitted. "But I don't have the luxuries he does to choose a different path." This past weekend's Sunday brunch with her parents had made that clear.

Kay scoffed.

"Did I say something wrong?" Madi asked.

"No, but don't think that because Wyatt grew up here didn't mean he had it easy. His father practically disowned him when he moved to Denver. There were weeks the two of them didn't speak because of arguments they had. And when Wyatt decided to adopt?"

Kay shook her head in disappointed emphasis. "My brother-in-law was livid. Told him they weren't his own flesh and blood. Whenever Wyatt makes a decision, he learns later that he's disappointed his dad nine out of ten times. He and Caleb aren't exactly close, either, because Joe fostered a rivalry between the two. With Wyatt being more the science-minded older son, the baby of the family—there's seven years between him and Caleb—got the attention. My brother-in-law is not an easy man, and neither is his and Silas's father. We almost lost this ranch a few times during some economic downturns, and there were others when the land was mortgaged to the hilt. Silas was sending home some of his pay to help make the ranch payroll. But by the grace of God, we're still thriving. In the black, with money to spare, and better than ever since Caleb took over. And Larrabees may tend to leave, but they always return home in the end. Silas did."

Madi studied Kay's face. Wyatt's aunt was as serious as a heartbeat. "I had no idea about any of this."

"Families are complicated. The firstborn is supposed to follow in the father's footsteps, like Joe did with his dad, and how his father had done with his, and so on. Joe saw Wyatt's desire to forge his own path as a rejection of his sacrifices, of his hard work to keep everything on the ranch going for the next generation. Like, what was he doing it for if Wyatt didn't want it?"

"My father is the same way but with medicine. Luckily I never have to find out what would have happened had I not loved it the way he did." While part of her had known that truth, Madi hadn't ever spoken it aloud, and it meant she and Wyatt had more in common than she'd originally thought. "You know my dad's parents were teachers."

Kay nodded and continued to fill bags. Madi found she was easy to talk to. "My dad moved to Boston for medical school, where he met my mom. She was this Boston socialite, way out of his league," Madi told her. "Still is. But for some reason, she found him handsome and they fell in love. When she's mad at him, she likes to remind him he's lucky she chose him. He changed for her, and in doing so, he worked his way up to being one of the top heart doctors in the country. Nothing less than the best would do. My dad had to meet her expectations."

"And now, you have to meet theirs. That's a lot of pressure to have on your shoulders."

"They want that same success for me. Can I fault them for that? They've never let me want for anything."

"But that pressure is often at odds with what you want," Kay pointed out.

"True," Madi admitted. "I'm to marry well and, if my mother has her way, preferably into another blue-blood family with a heritage going back as far as our own lineage."

Madi paused, but Kay said nothing. Sighing and hating the silence, Madi continued. "The problem is that I haven't found anyone I liked, much less love. Not that my mom's not on a mission and hasn't set me up on so many dates it's hard to keep track."

"Sounds intense. Especially with medical school. You

do love medicine, though." Kay's tone held an unspoken question.

"I do. But I'm not as great at practicing is as my father is." Madi snorted at the irony. "By my loving being a pediatrician isn't faked. The rest of it? The matchmaking? I pushed back as much as I could, but my mother and her friends could give the organizing committee a solid run for their money. Does the committee keep a database? Because I'm sure my mom does. If not, her friends do."

"I'm positive the committee use a computer spreadsheet now instead of the old Rolodex my grandmother used to have."

"A what?"

Kay's chucked sadly. "Oh, now you're making me feel really old. It's a rotating card file. It was like an address book but it spun and you could write notes on it. Never mind. Have you told Wyatt what you've told me? He did make a pretty passionate declaration, and that's not like him. I've never seen him do that."

"We haven't talked about this. We've spoken every night, as if we're practicing for a long-distance relationship. If we stayed together, would it be fair? He's been busy. I've been busy. He has the telethon Friday night and so I won't see him until the dance." And she couldn't wait, but at the same time worried something would come up and keep them apart.

"The segment with him and the boys debuts on the five-o'clock news tomorrow," Kay said.

"He told me. I've set a reminder so I could watch." Madi wasn't going to miss it.

"I want to let you in on a secret. Wyatt is as hardheaded as his father, so if he's said he loves you, he does."

"He really doesn't." Madi fingered one of the heart bags. She'd spend Valentine's Day with him and then leave soon after. Then she'd try her best to forget him.

Kay gathered the filled bags and set them inside a large cardboard box. "How can you be so sure he doesn't?"

"Can I trust you?" Madi asked. "What I say can't get back to anyone. Doctor to doctor with complete confidentiality?"

Kay's eyebrows knitted together as she tried to contemplate what Madi might want to tell her. "Of course. You don't even need to ask."

"It has to do with the committee," Madi said. "It can't get back to them. Can't get back to anyone."

"This sounds serious. Go ahead. As long you're not in danger and neither is someone else, I'll keep your secret. But if it's something that would make me a mandatory reporter, then you need to keep whatever you're about to say to yourself."

"It has nothing to do with child abuse or neglect," Madi reassured her. If a doctor suspected either of those, the law said it had to be reported to the authorities, and Madi had had to make several of those calls during her residency. "But it does have to do with Wyatt. When we found out our grandmothers were trying to set us up, we decided it was better if we fake dated."

Kay's expression remained confused. "Fake dated? Like you're pretending to date each other? I want to be clear I'm understanding you."

"Yes. Fake dating. We do things together but as friends. But we tell everyone else they are dates."

"I see. Huh. This is a new one. Rather clever. Unless…"

Kay pierced Madi with a sharp gaze. "Unless the two of you have developed actual feelings for each other."

"We can't. I'm leaving."

"That wasn't a 'no' or a 'we haven't.' That was an excuse you're telling yourself."

Madi lifted the box containing the bags. "We don't always get what we want. His future lies in Legacy Canyon. Mine is in Boston."

"I see. It probably felt good to unburden that."

"Thank you. It did. I haven't put you in an awkward spot, have I?"

"No. Your secret is safe with me."

Madi nodded, and she and Kay let the conversation drop. Madi carried the boxes out to Kay's SUV. She'd store them until Saturday. They loaded everything, the lights from the liftgate and the parking lot illuminating their efforts to pack everything in.

An SUV came to a stop a short distance behind Kay's and Wyatt climbed out. "Saw both your cars. Do you need any help?"

Madi glanced at her watch. It was half past seven.

"We're done now." Kay pressed the fob and the liftgate lowered. "But thank you. Tell your mom and dad I said hi."

She gave them a wave and drove away. Madi shivered. The weekend's warm weather had dipped back to being a few degrees above freezing. "Where are you off to now?" Wyatt asked.

"I was headed home." As his face fell, she added, "But I'm not doing anything. Would you like me to come over? We've never had that talk."

"We don't have to talk about that for me to want to be

with you. I've missed you and I would love to see you. Why don't you follow me?"

Ten minutes later, Madi parked behind Wyatt's SUV. They went inside and discovered the nanny had heated a casserole. The boys were both already asleep.

"Can you believe she was my nanny, too?" Wyatt asked as he and Madi left the nursery. "She's been a godsend. So great with the boys."

When they entered the great room, Wyatt found Madi's hand and drew her closer to him. "And you. You are a sight for sore eyes."

Oh, the excuses she could give, such as there was no one watching, so no reason to playact. Instead, Madi went into his arms. Let her lips find his. Then, he broke the kiss. "Are you hungry?"

"I had dinner at Kay's clinic. We were stuffing the bags so she ordered in. So, no, I'm not hungry. At least not for food." He was the only thing she wanted. Thankfully, Wyatt agreed.

"Then I can think of far more interesting things to do than eat," Wyatt said. "The only thing I want right now is you."

Knowing their time was limited, Madi tamped down her brain's logical side and let the deliciousness of his kisses swallow any warnings of regrets. She let herself enjoy how her skin tingled as his mouth trailed over it. His fingers made short work of her clothing, and Madi returned the favor. She returned his explorations with her own, memorizing the nooks and crannies of his body. She embedded into her subconscious the texture of his skin, his scent and the heft of him inside her mouth.

The best word for their lovemaking would be *tran-*

scendent, and even that didn't come close to the connection she experienced when joined with Wyatt. In bed, they were more than in sync, they were as close as two people could get, sharing a moment that only they could create, a mystical synthesis of two people who'd discovered they'd been made for each other, as some elemental life force had destined them for each other.

They remained wrapped together long after they'd floated down from a post-orgasmic high. Wyatt propped himself on his elbow and used his free hand to move her hair from her face. "Have I told you how lovely you look today?"

"You mean my slightly sweaty afterglow?"

"Matches mine." Wyatt dropped a kiss on her lips and then lifted her hair off her face and kissed her forehead. "Let me run you a shower if you want and I'll check on dinner. It was in the oven keeping warm, so I'm sure it's fine."

Ten minutes later, the ends of her hair slightly damp, a barefooted Madi padded into the kitchen. "That pasta smells delicious."

"One positive thing about the members of the committee, they can cook." He pulled out a chair. "Wine?"

"Just water. It's too late for a glass. I'm already as limp as those stuffed noodles. If I drink anything I'll fall asleep."

"Would that be so bad?" He was serious. "You can stay with me."

"And do a walk of shame into my grandmother's wearing what I wore the day before? No, I'll go home tonight."

He placed her plate on the table. "Then stay over on Saturday night. Come home with me after the dance. I'll let my mom take the boys for their first overnight with Grandma. She'd be ecstatic and so would I."

"Wyatt." She put her fork down instead of digging into the meat-filled cannelloni. "What are we doing? I know I started this, but I'm leaving. I signed the contract and..."

"Madi." He used his foot to spin the counter stool on which she was seated. He drew her up so he could wrap her in his arms. "We are doing whatever feels right. I want to wake up with you at least once. And if one more night is all I have, then that's all I have and I want it to include everything. Do I want more? Yes, I admit it. I do. If you were staying, I would make my move. Ensure that you would be mine, that this dating we're doing becomes as real as this casserole we're about to eat. We'd take things one day at a time to see where they would go. Because those words I said at the party? I think I meant them."

He'd told everyone he loved her. She ran her fingers along his jaw. "I think I'd like that."

"But we don't have that kind of time or that kind of future."

She hadn't yet bought her plane ticket. For a perfectionist who'd always met a deadline and usually completed things early, when it came to the job and returning to Boston, Madi had been definitely dragging her feet. First time for everything, she guessed. "I wish things could be different."

"Me, too." He let her go and rounded the kitchen island to serve himself. Madi dropped into her seat and began to eat. Wyatt sat beside her, and by unspoken agreement they didn't speak about their relationship again. Instead, they discussed Wyatt's news segments, sitting long after they'd both eaten their fill.

"I'm hoping we get traction and that people step up. We'd love to see more people volunteer to be foster parents, but for those who can't, those in foster care wrote out wish lists, and donations can be made to make those wishes come true. We're also focusing on Big Brothers Big Sisters as well. People can become 'Bigs' and change a child's life."

"It's wonderful what you're doing. Adopting the boys was wonderful. You're a good man."

"And a sexy one, too, I hope?" The mood had gotten heavy, so he lightened it with a joke.

"Well, my clothes keep coming off around you," Madi teased back.

"I like that idea." As he dropped a kiss on her lips, a sharp cry sounded through the baby monitor. When a second one came, Wyatt groaned. "But it'll have to wait. That sounds like Ethan."

"I'll go with you."

They found Ethan wide-awake. Wyatt checked his diaper and turned his face away. "This one's going to be bad."

Madi caught a whiff and calmed her gag reflex. "I can help."

"I'm going to owe you."

"I'll figure out way to make you pay."

He caught her sexual teasing. "That'll be the bright spot in all this."

Together they cleaned Ethan. Wyatt checked his temperature, and then Madi put her hand on Ethan's forehead as well. "Doesn't feel warm."

"Here," Wyatt said. "How about you take him and rock him? That way I can straighten the kitchen."

"Of course." Madi settled onto the glider and Wyatt placed Ethan in her arms. Ethan gazed at her and then snuggled closer, his lips sucking his pacifier. Wyatt dimmed the lights and turned on some classical music. By the time Wyatt returned, Madi's arm was numb and Ethan was sound asleep. But Madi wouldn't have had it any other way. Was this what it would be like if Ethan was hers? Or when she had her own children? This overpowering and wonderful sense of protectiveness and love?

Wyatt placed his son in the crib and assisted Madi from the glider. She moved her arm to get the blood flowing. "Happens to me all the time. Come on." He took her hand and led her into the living room. "I know you have to leave, but sit with me for a minute."

It was almost eleven. "If I do, I'll never leave. I'll plan on staying Saturday."

"Thank you." He kissed her gently and, wanting more, Madi deepened the kiss. Finally, before she lost control, she wrenched her mouth from his.

"I'm going now."

Ever the gentleman, he helped her into her coat. "I'll call you."

It wasn't a line—he meant it. And her heart overflowed and didn't stop until long after she'd driven back to her grandmother's house and climbed into bed. The next night, Wyatt did call, wanting to know what she thought about his segment on the news. She told him she'd loved it. He'd hit a home run.

"The station is really pleased. Tomorrow's the telethon, and I'll be working a twelve-hour day. But I'm off Saturday, and I can't wait for our date."

“Me, either,” Madi told before she ended the call. She lifted the book she’d been too giddy to read the night before. Still too distracted, she returned the paperback to the bedside table. One more day until she’d attend another dance with Wyatt.

She wiped away the sad tears that prickled. Tried for the cool Boston reserve that had gotten her through crisis after crisis, but this time failed to find. She was in love with Wyatt. In love with his boys. In love with Legacy Canyon. And he might love her back. Everything she wanted was within reach, except for one fact.

On Sunday, she’d say goodbye forever.

Chapter Twelve

"Thank you for joining us." Jill Sears handed Madi another roll of red crepe-paper streamer. Using her thumb and forefinger, Madi held both the white and red streamers and taped them together. Then she began twisting them. When done, the alternating colors of twisted streamers draped from the front of the check-in table. "We know dance decorating is not that exciting, and it has to do double duty because we're hosting the wellness fair first."

"It's okay. Wyatt's doing the telethon tonight so we won't see each other until tomorrow."

"That's right, the telethon. I donated online," Jill said.

Someone had the live stream going on a computer in the main hall, but every time Madi had walked by, some musical act or comedian was performing.

Michelle unfolded two easels and propped foam boards onto them. One board contained a map of the wellness booths and another was a list of sponsors. "Last night's news segment was so moving! His boys are so cute."

"They are," Madi agreed. While she'd held dozens of babies as part of her job, holding Ethan had been different, as if he'd fit too perfectly, like her arms were designed for cradling him and Noah.

"Would you and Wyatt have your own kids, too?" Jill asked.

Startled, Madi dropped the crepe paper and had to go catch it before it unrolled. "I think that's getting ahead of ourselves," Madi replied. She wasn't opposed to being a mother. But despite how delightful it was to rock Ethan, motherhood wasn't on her radar. Not yet. Not for a long time. Although the idea of having Wyatt's children created a longing for something she couldn't have. A baby boy might have his dimples and wide eyes. If her daughter got his thick and luxurious hair, she'd be blessed.

Before Jill and Michelle could say more about the merits of having children with Wyatt, Madi went into the main hall and began to set up her and Kay's booth, which was little more than an eight-foot banquet table covered with a red-and-white-checkered cloth. An easel and foam board to the side of the table announced the booth's purpose. Madi soon had the brochures and goody bags set out. For the most part, everything was ready. Kay had apologized for not being able to help with the setup, but she had a conflict with an event she couldn't wiggle out of in Amarillo. She promised she'd be on time tomorrow when the wellness fair opened.

Around the hall, other booths came to life. There was even an indoor play area. Her phone buzzed, and she reached for it. Normally she didn't answer unknown numbers, but this was an 806 area code, meaning the call at almost 9:00 p.m. on a Friday night was coming from the somewhere in the Texas Panhandle. Thinking it might be Wyatt calling from work, she answered. "Hello?"

"Madi? It's Jane. Wyatt's mom."

"Hi, Jane." A sense of foreboding made Madi's fingers tighten around her device.

"I think something might be wrong with Ethan, and Kay's in Amarillo and Wyatt's at the telethon. We can't bother him, especially if it's nothing. Will you come?"

"Of course." Ethan hadn't felt well the other night—he'd had a diaper blowout—and Noah had had a virus not too long ago. With the booth ready, Madi grabbed her purse and headed toward her car. "What are his symptoms?"

"He's not wanting to eat. I've tried everything. And his diapers are dry. He's had a few sniffles this week, but it's been nothing much, so I told Wyatt not to worry."

"I'm on my way." Madi ended the call. Her fingers trembled as she opened her car door. It took her an extra second to buckle in as she missed getting the latch plate into the slot on the first try. She started the engine and gripped the steering wheel. Took two deep breaths. She'd be no help to anyone if she crashed along the way.

When she arrived, Jane opened the door to the cabin the moment Madi stepped out of the SUV. "Madi, thank goodness."

"How long has Ethan been like this?"

"Maybe it started last night? Wyatt came home late so the boys were already in bed. And then he left early. I figured Ethan had had a big meal, which is why he didn't want to eat. Or that he had a little cold, which is why he slept most of the day. I tried one of those electrolyte drinks, but he didn't want it. Spit it out."

"It's going to be okay," Madi told her as they passed the play yard, where Noah sat chewing on a teething ring even though it was past his bedtime. When he saw her, he grinned. Madi glanced at the television, where the telethon was on. Wyatt was on camera looking as handsome as ever, with Annabeth standing by his side. Madi ignored the figurative knife stabbing her heart. "Let me take a look at Ethan."

She entered the nursery and found an awake Ethan lying on his back. "Hey, buddy. Why aren't you eating?"

She put her hand to his forehead. He didn't feel warm, but that didn't mean anything. She took his temperature. One degree above normal. If he wasn't eating or drinking, and hadn't the entire day, he was at risk for dehydration, and dehydration was a catch-22. The more he didn't drink, the worse he felt. The worse he felt, the more he wouldn't eat or drink. A quick exam showed that Ethan's lips and mouth felt as dry as his diaper. His skin was paler than she'd seen it, and his eyes slightly sunken.

"We need to take him to the emergency room for IV fluids," she told Jane. "He's got mild to moderate dehydration, and the sooner he gets fluids, the sooner he will feel better and we can figure out the underlying cause. It could be as simple as he didn't feel well so he stopped eating. By doing so, he made himself even worse. Not eating is a common reaction for babies when they don't feel well, but it's the wrong thing to do."

"This is horrible. I feel terrible. Has it been going on long?"

"He didn't feel well the other night but Wyatt thought he'd improved." Should she have noticed? She'd obviously missed something. What kind of a doctor was she, anyway? "I know Wyatt's in the middle of the telethon, but you need to call him and tell him to meet us at Legacy Canyon General."

Jane bustled from the room. "It's going to be okay," Madi told Ethan as she lifted him from the crib. She dressed him for the journey and carried him into the living room. Jane had strapped Noah into his car seat.

"I'm not leaving him here and the nanny is off tonight." Jane drew on her coat. "I didn't think I'd need the car seats I bought for my car so soon. I'll call Wyatt on the way."

"Let me drive," Madi said. Now that she knew what was going on, her doctor persona had kicked in and taken over. Even though her mind raced, her nerves had steadied, same as they did when she saw any other patient. She was in problem-solving mode. She took the keys from Jane and they went outside. The wind was brisk as they rounded to the garage. "Does Joe want to come?"

"He's in Amarillo, too. Bunch of business meetings or something. I'll text him."

Fifteen minutes later, Madi parked at the hospital. The nurse triaged Ethan quickly. Legacy Canyon General had a separate, small area for pediatric ER patients, and Madi unstrapped Ethan and put him in the crib. Noah slept in his car seat, which Jane had set on the counter.

The doctor entered. He was maybe in his sixties with a full head of gray hair. "Mrs. Larrabee. Kay's sister-in-law, right? I'm Dr. Irwin. What's going on?"

"It's my grandson." When Jane looked helplessly at Madi, Madi took over.

"Hi. Dr. Madi Brennan, pediatrics. Family friend. My initial exam showed dehydration."

"Let's take a look." As the doctor began his exam, he asked more questions, which Madi answered.

"I'm going to start an IV," he said, confirming what

Madi had told Jane. "Let me go out and get that ordered."

A nurse came in and whispered something to the doctor. He turned to Jane and Madi. "Your son is on the phone. I'm going to go speak with him."

With that, he left.

Jane was beside herself. "Oh, Madi, I can't believe I waited. I should have called you immediately."

"It's okay," Madi soothed. A few nights ago, she hadn't seen that Ethan was beginning to come down with something. She should have, but she'd missed it, same as she'd missed the appendicitis.

"I've texted my husband," Jane said. "He's on his way. We at least need to get Noah home, so when he gets here, I'll leave."

"How about I take him?" Madi asked. "You and your husband should stay with Ethan until Wyatt arrives. He'll need you. They both will." And she wasn't family. She was a friend with benefits. A doctor that hadn't even diagnosed his son's illness, a sickness that had the power to hurt Ethan had it not been caught.

As the nurse returned to start Ethan's IV, Madi took Jane's spare keys and lifted Noah. At least she could babysit. Hopefully she wouldn't fail at that.

Wyatt had finished introducing a segment on teenage fosters looking for a home when his producer came to get him the moment the camera light stopped blinking, meaning they weren't live. "You need to call your mother," Caroline said, handing Wyatt the silenced cell phone he'd left out of visual and audio range. "She called the station and said it's an emergency."

"What is it?" Annabeth asked. The entire night she'd

been his partner for the telethon segments touting the benefits of fostering or adopting.

"I don't know." Wyatt began a fast swipe through his texts and hadn't made it far when his phone rang. The moment he saw that the caller ID read Legacy Canyon General, his stomach dropped. Had something happened to his grandfather? Then it hit him. He'd been so prepared for bad news about his grandfather because of the cancer, he hadn't thought of his twins. But they were with his mother. Panic consumed him and his hand shook slightly. "I have to take this," he told Caroline and Annabeth before moving off set. He swiped the phone open. "This is Wyatt."

"Wyatt, this is Dr. Irwin. I'm one of the pediatricians at Legacy Canyon General. Your mother brought Ethan in and..."

Wyatt tried to concentrate as the doctor began to outline what had occurred. Ethan was dehydrated? When? How? "Yes, of course, administer the IV," Wyatt said. "Do whatever's necessary. I'm on my way."

He strode back to his producer. "Ethan's in the hospital. I've got to go."

"Oh, no! That's terrible. What about the segments?" Annabeth asked.

"We'll get them covered," Caroline reassured her. Whatever either of the women said next, Wyatt didn't hear, as he was already on the move.

Within minutes he was in his car, driving enough over the speed limit to cut the time but not enough to be pulled over or get into an accident. He called his mother using the car's hands-free mobile device and learned Madi had diagnosed Ethan and that she'd taken Noah home. He tried calling her, but she didn't answer.

He pulled into the hospital parking lot and sprinted toward the door. Several minutes later, he entered the exam room. Despite the lower lights, saw Ethan sleeping in a crib, an IV taped to his son's hand. His mom stood. "Wyatt!"

"Mom." He gave her a huge hug and they turned to look at Ethan. "How's he been?"

She'd finished telling him when a nurse entered. "Mr. Larrabee." She checked on Ethan. "I'll let the doctor know you've arrived." Then she was gone. Soon the doctor arrived. Besides the dehydration, Ethan had an ear infection, one severe enough to warrant antibiotics.

Those and a painkiller were soon administered through the IV port. The doctor also said that until Ethan was fully hydrated, they wanted to admit him to a room in the pediatric ward. "We'll have a recliner in there and you can stay with him," Dr. Irwin said. "Someone will come get you when it's time to move out of the ER into the patient room."

"I'm so sorry," his mother said once they were alone again.

Wyatt raked a hand through his hair. "It's not your fault. If anything, it's mine for not noticing." Which made him a horrible father.

"I'll go home and relieve Madi so she can go home. She's probably wondering what's going on."

"I tried to call her but she didn't answer." Which also made him worried. After learning his son was in the hospital, Wyatt's anxiety meter had gone off the charts. He'd already contemplated multiple scenarios, all bad, like Madi being in an accident on the way home. Then he'd lose both her and Noah, which turned his blood cold. "When you get there, tell her to call me. I need to know she and Ethan are okay."

Before his mom could answer, Wyatt's dad burst in. "They almost didn't let me come back."

The room seemed to shrink. His mother went into her husband's arms. "I'm glad you're here."

"What's wrong with him?" his dad asked.

"Virus. Ear infection. Dehydration." Wyatt's words came out clipped.

"You should have paid better attention. If you weren't at the telethon, you might have noticed. You need to decide, Wyatt. Are you a dad or a broadcaster?"

His mother gasped, and Wyatt bit back the retort as a young woman in scrubs entered. If she sensed the tension, she didn't lose her friendly yet professional attitude. "Hi, I'm Sawyer, your CNA. Let's get you and Ethan to your new home in the pediatric wing. Would you like to hold him or me?"

"I'll carry him." Wyatt lifted Ethan, who whimpered but didn't wake.

Sawyer grabbed the IV pole and rolled it to come alongside Wyatt. "Shall we?"

Ignoring his father, Wyatt leaned to give his mother a kiss on the cheek. "I'll call you as soon as I can."

"Do you need anything?" she asked. "What can I do?"

"Nothing. Go home and check on Madi and Noah. I have a change of clothes in the car. Once I get Ethan settled, I can grab them." Wyatt followed Sawyer from the room, down the hall and into the elevator.

"He's such a cute little guy," Sawyer said. "Probably be right as rain tomorrow afternoon after he's had enough fluids and the antibiotics. Don't worry, Dad. We see this all the time."

"Hopefully he'll recover that fast." Once on the floor, Wyatt settled Ethan into a crib and Sawyer adjusted the IV line so he wouldn't dislodge it.

"Your nurse will be by in a few minutes to introduce himself and touch base. Feel free to sleep in the recliner tonight. You'll need your rest, too, Dad."

Dad. She'd called him that twice. Wyatt was a dad, and a terrible one at that, according to his own father. He remained standing after Sawyer left. He bent over the railing and ran his hand over Ethan's forehead. His son slept on, his little mouth moving slightly. Around him, machines hummed and beeped. "I'm sorry about this, buddy. So sorry I wasn't there."

Grown men weren't supposed to cry, but the tears fell, anyway, and he angrily brushed them aside. Was Wyatt's father right? Would it have changed anything if Wyatt hadn't had a thirteen-plus-hour workday? If he hadn't been at the station? His long work hours were why he'd left Denver in the first place. He'd come to Legacy Canyon so he could be around for his sons, be a better father than his own dad had been for him. He'd already failed by failing Ethan tonight. He'd failed his son when it mattered most.

He would never forgive himself for that.

When she heard the front door, Madi rose and turned off the television. "How is he?" she asked as Jane walked in. The front door closed with an ominous click.

"Ethan's spending the night at the hospital so Wyatt's going to stay there. I'll stay with Noah."

"Did the doctor say what it was?"

"A virus?" Jane shrugged out of her coat. "Ethan has a double ear infection, so they're giving him antibiotics. Wyatt says he's tried to call you."

"My phone died. Normally I don't let the battery run down." Another mistake on her part. She handed Jane the baby monitor. "I'll text him when I get home."

"Please. He's already worried, and he'll worry until he hears from you. He cares for you, Madi."

His affections were so misplaced. She didn't deserve him. Madi grabbed her coat. "I promise to call him the moment I have battery."

"I'll message him as well so he knows."

"Thank you." Madi escaped to the privacy of her car. Tried to calm her hands, which were shaking. She started the car and made it home to find her grandmother still awake.

Her grandmother's "How are you?" turned immediately into a "Come here" and she drew Madi into a tight embrace. Madi realized the committee was good for something. At least she didn't have to explain what had happened. "Everything is going to be alright. You'll see," her grandmother soothed.

"It's my fault. My gut told me something was wrong and I ignored it." Instead, she'd rocked a sick baby to sleep.

Her grandmother straightened her arms and drew back. "Honey, did I ever tell you about your dad?"

"What? My dad misdiagnosed something?"

"No. During a checkup, your dad's pediatrician missed the fact that a couple of red spots on your dad were the start of a very nasty case of chicken pox. No one is perfect. Not even the best doctors. Missing chicken pox isn't malpractice. Neither is you not being able to diagnose Ethan without having the proper tools."

"But what you mentioned was back then. We have better testing. Vaccines. Antivirals."

"And aren't the germs and viruses and whatnot still evolving and mutating and whatever they do? Humans aren't perfect. Diagnoses are sometimes wrong. Sometimes it takes a long time for doctors to figure out what's wrong with a patient. No one is infallible. Once I had pneumonia and it took a CT scan to find. You need to stop blaming yourself."

Madi knew that, but she couldn't wrap her head around the idea of letting go. She was driven to succeed. Had crashed and burned because of it. Telling her grandmother that this was personal—that Madi had failed Wyatt and his son—would fall on deaf ears. Her grandmother wouldn't, perhaps even couldn't, understand. Madi hadn't known the girl whose appendicitis she'd failed to diagnose. But she knew Wyatt. Had loved him with her body. Loved him with her heart.

Which made her failure a million times worse.

"I need to plug my phone in and text Wyatt," she said. "His mom said he's worried since he hadn't heard from me."

"Go," her grandmother urged.

When Madi texted Wyatt—How's Ethan doing? How are you?—she received no answer. She glanced at the clock. It was far later than she'd thought. He'd been up all day and was probably trying to sleep while Ethan was.

She had to make things easier for him so she sent

him another message: Don't worry about taking me to the dance tomorrow. Family comes first. Hope Ethan is feeling better soon.

The text left with an audible whoosh, a noise she wished took heartbreak and indecision with it. If she couldn't handle a virus, how would she handle the bigger issues of her patients? Her parents would be so disappointed.

Her phone pinged a short time later: He's better. Thanks for calming my mom and bringing him in. I owe you. Will you come over tomorrow instead of the dance? After the health fair? If he continues to improve, we should be home. I'll understand if you don't want to, but I want to see you. Please.

She should tell him no. But his saying "please" tugged her heartstrings, and she wanted to see him and the boys. Check on Ethan herself. Goodbyes also needed to be said in person. She sent him one word back: Yes.

The next day, Madi's heart was heavy. Despite tossing and turning, she at least managed to fake smile her way through the health fair, enduring the you're-too-kind well-wishers who kept telling her how awesome she was for "saving" Ethan. She hadn't done anything. If she'd paid better attention when she'd examined him, he never would have deteriorated enough to go to the hospital.

It was Kay's praise, though, where Madi pushed back. "I didn't do anything," she told her. "If I'd noticed Ethan's symptoms earlier, I could have warned Wyatt. Told him what to watch for."

Kay brushed aside Madi's concerns. "Viruses are tricky. Sometimes they aren't there, and twenty minutes later without any warning, you've got a child vomiting in their bed. It happens, Madi. Don't be so hard on yourself."

"You sound like my grandmother."

"She's right. Did I ever tell you I had a fusion?" Kay lowered the crew-neck sweater she wore and Madi could see a faint line on her neck. "I was in a car accident when I was in my twenties and had to have a herniated disk removed. When I went into my surgeon as a follow-up two weeks later, he was like 'everything looks great.' I showed him my right leg and said it seemed swollen. He wasn't worried. Thought it was most likely water retention. The next day my leg looked like a two-by-four. My primary care doctor got me in immediately. He checked my blood pressure and found it was low. An ultrasound done that afternoon showed blood clots in my inner-thigh region. Let me tell you, the protocol for dissolving those is not fun."

"I didn't know that had happened to you."

"I'm telling you this because the day I saw my surgeon, my blood pressure was fine so he didn't think it could be blood clots, probably because he's a specialist and he'd taken all precautions during surgery—a successful surgery, I might add. My internist, however, recognized the problem immediately because it had fully manifested the next day. You can't blame my surgeon for not catching it, just as you can't blame yourself for not expecting whatever sniffles Ethan had would develop into an ear infection two days after you saw him. He might have been well on Thursday and come down with something else on Friday."

Not wanting to accept Kay's explanation, Madi changed the subject. "Wyatt texted he was doing better. That they're on their way home. The fluids and intravenous doses of antibiotics worked."

"Good to hear. I dropped by the hospital this morning. You came through when needed. Madi. You can't blame yourself for the days before, so stop."

"I'll try."

"Do. I'm sorry you'll miss the dance, but glad you're going to see Wyatt. He cares for you. I know you've decided to go back to Boston, but if you ask me, you'd be a fool to throw what you and Wyatt share away. A man like Wyatt is hard to find."

"So everyone tells me," Madi murmured.

"If you had a job offer here, would you stay?" Kay asked. "Because I can make that happen. My practice is bursting at the seams. We're ready to expand. You'd be a perfect fit and I'd welcome the chance to mentor you. To tell you things are alright when you worry they aren't."

The offer tempted, but Madi rejected the idea. "And then if Wyatt and I broke up? How awkward would that be for everyone? No. It's best I go as planned."

"Sometimes going places where you least expect you should be going is actually the better way to go, the right path. The reward is far greater. Think about it."

If Kay planned to say more, she didn't have the opportunity as a crowd of moms pushing strollers approached the booth. The committee had declared the fair a success, and once it ended, a large group of volunteers began to move the tables and transform the hall for the dance, one she'd miss.

Melancholy consumed her as she drove to Wyatt's. Monday, her grandmother's doctor would declare her fully healed, and Monday afternoon Madi would fly back to Boston. To combat her procrastination, her mother had purchased the first-class ticket and the airline had emailed the confirmation. Tomorrow, technically, was her last full day in Legacy Canyon.

Always anticipating and watching, Wyatt opened the door the moment she stepped onto the porch. "Hey there." He gave her a kiss on the lips before holding the door wide. "Come on in. The boys are asleep and Ethan is doing much better."

He'd decorated the cabin for Valentine's Day. While nowhere near as fancy as the committee's transformation of the festival hall, his effort astounded. He'd placed Valentine's decorations around the room. The dining room table was set with fancy china, linen place mats, fan-folded napkins and flickering candles. Soft, classical music, complete with harps, played from hidden speakers. "I won't admit to cooking," Wyatt said. "Still have those casseroles in the freezer, and the bunkhouse cook made the fresh bread this morning. She sent some over."

"I'm certain whatever it is will be delicious."

He held up two bottles of wine. "Red or white? It's a chicken dish."

"White, then," she said, watching as he uncorked a chilled Riesling. He handed her a filled glass and she took a sip. "This is perfect. Thank you."

"I'm glad you like it." He poured himself a glass and set it by his plate. She trailed him into the kitchen, which contained the savory aroma of garlic and basil. "It's garlic-basil chicken over rice," he said, confirming her suspicions. "Every other casserole has been delicious, so this one should be, too. What will I do when I run out of food?"

She arched an eyebrow. “Cook?”

He laughed. “I’m the king of reheating and carryout, not much more minus baby-food prep. I’m have a feeling I’m going to end up like my mother, who always had Angelina make extra. I see the wisdom in that now. As Angelina’s also the kids’ nanny, when she fears I’m about to starve she’ll probably start putting food in the fridge.”

“How’s your mom doing? She was really upset the other night.”

“Better. She didn’t want to let me down, let Ethan down.” He reached for Madi and drew her into his arms. “Thank you for being there. It helped. I can’t tell you how much it means to me.”

“I should have seen he didn’t feel well, that something was coming.”

“Same, but I didn’t, either. None of us are perfect.”

“That’s easy for you to say.” She began to draw back. Stopped. “Let’s not rehash. It’s our last night together. I don’t want to be any sadder than I already am.”

“Feels weird,” he admitted. “I’m just getting to know you and have to let you go.”

“We always knew it would come to this. I have to return for the wedding I have to attend. I have the onboarding for the new job, and my parents…”

When she trailed off, he searched her face. “Madi, what do you want?”

“I don’t know.” She stepped out of his hug, immediately missing the comfort of his arms. “I keep asking myself that question.”

“I understand what it’s like to have the weight of expectations on your shoulders.” He swept his arm. “This ranch, my parents. My sons. Last night, my father accused me of not putting them first. Of putting my own ambition before everything else. Today, all I've done is soul-search. Am I as awful of a dad as my father said I am? He was no winner, either. And I'm asking myself, what do I want? The answer is I don't know. That scares me, Madi, and I didn't think I would be scared of anything. But I'm afraid of failing those boys like my dad failed me."

She had no advice for that, which added to the depth of her own failure. But a timer dinged, and Wyatt removed the casserole from the oven. Soon they were sitting at the table where by unspoken agreement they talked about other things, such as the telethon's success, the pony Wyatt's brother was buying for his daughter, the effects of the drought and the Valentine's Day dance they were skipping, but really wouldn't miss at all. After a dessert of strawberries, pound cake and whipped cream, Wyatt gathered Madi into his arms and said, "The dishes can wait."

They danced together to a rhythm all their own, not caring if their steps didn't match the music. When he kissed her, a sense of making this moment last fought with the bittersweetness trying to creep in. "Take me to bed," she whispered and, leaving everything as it was, he scooped her into his arms and carried her to the place where they created endless magic.

Except that even that type of magic did end, and later they cleaned the kitchen and checked on the boys. "Stay," he suggested as they moved into the living room. "You said you would."

But that had been before Ethan had been sick, before she'd failed, before she realized how much she loved them. "I can't. I'm up early." Even to her ears, the excuse sounded lame. "Be my date to the wedding. Come to Boston that weekend."

He dropped a kiss on her forehead. "I can't leave the boys."

"I know." His excuse was far more understandable than hers. She pressed a palm to his chest. "Thank you."

His brow creased. "For what?"

She bit back tears. "For this. For everything. For being all a girl could want. For understanding. For just being you." To her embarrassment, her voice cracked.

He stroked her hair. "Ah, Madi. I wish things could be different."

"So do I." Madi accepted the long, lingering kiss he gave her. "So do I."

As was his habit, he walked her to her car to check that she was secure and safe to drive. "Don't be a stranger."

"I won't." But as she drove away, leaving him behind to be enveloped in darkness, Madi wished she hadn't made a promise she couldn't keep. Seeing Wyatt again, seeing him dating someone and being happy, seeing the boys all grown, seeing what she was leaving behind—any of those things might break her. She'd always thought herself made of stronger stuff, able to put aside personal feelings and get the job done. Yet, as she turned left onto the main road and left the ranch for the last time, a piece of her heart stayed behind. And Madi said a prayer that she hadn't just made the biggest mistake of her life.

Chapter Thirteen

By the end of the first week back in Boston, Madi knew three things. One, she'd pleased her parents by coming home. Two, the pediatric practice where she was going to work was top-notch. She'd shadowed two of the pediatricians, noting they saw at least three patients an hour, sometimes up to five. That translated to about twenty-to-thirty patients a day, give or take, depending on the schedule. The third thing Madi learned was that the practice had also decided to hire the second-place candidate. "We've discovered we can add two doctors," the office manager had said. "With two of you, we can take more patients."

The practice had the patient rooms and more than enough space as it took up an entire floor in a medical building near the hospital. The doctors mostly kept to themselves and the office staff to themselves. Each doctor had an office, and there was a doctors' lounge. The office staff had their spaces and their own break room. "It'll take some time to get to know everyone," her father had told her over dinner. "But I've heard great things about your first week."

Even in Boston, word traveled. But Legacy Canyon had spoiled her. Boston felt impersonal. More structured and rigid. Things that used to feel comfortable, like the city's ways and customs, now felt confining. She loved Boston, so she didn't understand the disconnect. Maybe it was because Legacy Canyon was the type of place where she'd made friends quickly, not that Boston wasn't friendly. But she missed Alyssa. And Kay. Most of all she missed Wyatt.

They'd texted a few times, but Madi hadn't known what to say. A few times she'd reached for her phone to call him to hear his voice, but then remembered that with the hour time difference, he'd most likely be on the air. She'd heard from her grandmother a few times, and it was different not seeing her every day and sharing the gossip in person.

"Madi?" Her mother came into the living room. Madi planned on moving out once she'd passed her probationary period, but for now, it was easier to stay at home. At least she had her own floor. "We're headed out. Are you sure you don't want to come?"

"No. Too tired. It's been a long week."

"You'll adjust. What did you decide to do about the wedding?"

"I'm going. When I RSVP'd, I told her I'm a single, so she's going to put me at that table for the reception."

"Madi, I told you we could have you attend with the son of one of our friends. Ian Ellison already has a date, but I can arrange for someone else. That's easy enough."

"Mom, I'm really tired. Could we discuss this tomorrow?"

"Of course." Her mother placed a hand on Madi's forehead, as if checking for a fever. Then she kissed Madi's cheek. “It’s been an adjustment to be back, I’m sure. Tomorrow we’ll do brunch at the club.”

“It’s on my calendar.” One thing about this new job, if Madi didn’t have a patient in the emergency room, she worked a standard business week of Monday to Friday. She retrieved the remote control and pressed a button. Turned on Netflix and scrolled. Finally chose to rewatch a British historical that she’d seen at least three times, and a story that had been remade at least five or six times. As she watched Captain Wentworth and Anne Elliot finally declare their love, Madi wondered what it was about society that kept people from saying what they meant. But would it have helped if she’d told Wyatt she loved him? Actually said the words? Not everyone got what they wanted. If they did, children would never be sick. Grandmothers wouldn’t break their arms. And Wyatt and Madi would have figured out how to make it work. Enough was enough. She clicked off the TV. Time to focus on the future, even if it wasn’t what she’d envisioned.

“And that’s a wrap.”

As the light indicating which camera was broadcasting was extinguished, Wyatt removed the microphone and stepped off the news set. Once he checked his email and filmed a few forecasts for the web, he was free to go home. After Ethan’s illness, he’d switched his shifts, and the Monday midday broadcast was finished. The producer seemed happy with the new schedule, as was Wyatt. For the first time ever, with the exception of when he’d need to stay to report on severe weather, he worked an eight-to-four shift.

As for the forecast, he'd told viewers a thunderstorm was in the forecast starting as early as 5:00 p.m. The entire Texas Panhandle needed rain, and the storm had the potential to give the entire region a long soaking and much-needed drought relief. While the rain wouldn't cure all the area's ills, the amount they'd get per hour shouldn't cause any destructive flash flooding, which was a plus when the land was so dry.

Wyatt retrieved his cell phone and checked his texts. Madi hadn't sent anything today, but his mother had sent a picture of the twins. Hard to believe a full week had passed since she'd left. He missed her.

Be home soon, he texted to his mom. She'd really stepped into the breach. As for the committee, when word got around town that Madi had returned to Boston, leaving Wyatt single, his mother had been the one to shut down their efforts.

"He needs time," she'd said. "He needs space." Amazingly, the committee had done what she'd wanted and backed off, meaning his and Madi's plan had worked.

The only reason Wyatt knew this was his grandmother had told him what his mother had done. His grandmother had also called him a bloody fool for letting Madi go. But what choice did he have? She had to be free to make her own choices. He couldn't hold her back from her dreams, dreams that didn't involve Legacy Canyon or him.

When Wyatt arrived home around 5:00 p.m., he parked and walked over to the main house. Since it was Emma's third birthday and even though the entire family had gathered for Sunday dinner last night, his mother was hosting a dinner complete with presents and a cake. Hard to believe that his sons would be one soon. In the past week, they'd both been pulling themselves up in their cribs. Wyatt had walked at ten and a half months, and his mother said she expected both of his boys to do the same.

He found Caleb in the family room, and his brother handed Wyatt a beer. "How are things?"

Wyatt shrugged. "Same old." He went to the play yard and scooped up Noah. He tried to alternate which son he grabbed first. "Hey, buddy."

"Da da!" Noah grinned. Then he began to string together more random sounds in an attempt to talk.

"He's got your name down," Caleb said before taking a swig.

"Yep. Not that he knows what it means yet," Wyatt confirmed. "Can't wait for him to really start saying things."

"Be careful what you wish for." Caleb gestured an elbow toward Emma, who was showing her grandfather her new doll. "Once they start, they never stop."

"Hush," their mother said. She took Noah from Wyatt and settled him onto her hip. "Don't listen to your uncle."

"Grammy! Grandpa likes my doll!" Emma called.

"Of course, he does," she said. Wyatt retrieved Ethan, who'd held up his arms. Soon, they had everyone seated around the dining room table. Their grandmother was there, but not their grandfather.

"He wanted to rest," Wyatt's grandmother said. "Today's chemo wiped him out."

Wyatt hoped the doctors would have positive news next time his grandfather went in for testing. "So how's Madi?" his grandmother asked once they were done singing "Happy Birthday" and eating sprinkled birthday cake. Ethan and Noah remained in their high chairs, but Emma had left the table to play with some of her new toys.

"Madi's fine. I haven't really heard from her lately."

His grandmother's eyes narrowed. "Why is that? You're friends, aren't you?"

"She's busy. It was her first work week." Wyatt lifted his fork. Set it back down. Pushed it even with the bottom of the square plate.

"Well, her grandmother said she's miserable."

Wyatt's mind raced. Was she? "That's an exaggeration. This was her dream job."

"No more an exaggeration than you moping around here for a week." His grandmother doubled down, showing the ferocity she was known for. Very few had ever won an argument with Clarissa Larrabee, and Wyatt doubted he'd be one of the few tonight.

"I miss her," he admitted, suddenly not caring his whole immediate family minus Kristen sat at the table.

"Then do something about it," his grandmother snapped. She sipped her water. "She was perfect for you. Perfect."

"She was." The truth slipped out. "But I'm not leaving Legacy Canyon."

"Then convince her to come back here," Caleb suggested, deciding to help.

Frustrated by his missing Madi, Wyatt narrowed his gaze on his brother. "You have no room to talk."

"Look, I don't know what happened between me and Liv, but I tried to call her. I went by her house and they told me she'd gone to California. I tried, Wyatt. Madi didn't ghost you. She didn't disappear without a trace."

That was true. “We started dating to get the committee off our backs. But it became real.”

To his surprise, no one seemed shocked by that announcement. Then again, were there really secrets in Legacy Canyon?

“Madi told Kay and she told me once Madi left and she saw how heartsick you were,” his grandmother said. “And your mom used your love for Madi against the committee, told them Madi’s the one for you.”

“That’s how I know she loves you,” his mom said.

Why didn’t everyone see how hopeless this was and leave him alone. “Who, Kay?” Wyatt asked.

“Madi, you fool,” his grandmother retorted. “She told Kay the truth because she couldn’t keep the secret anymore, and because she loves you. Are you sure you’re my grandson?”

“Of course, I am.”

“Then you should do something about it.”

Wyatt shifted in his chair. Those words had come from his father. “What do you mean?”

His dad stared at him. “You’re a Larrabee. I may not like the fact that you don’t work on the ranch like Caleb, but I respect it.”

Wyatt folded his arms across his chest.

“Okay,” his father conceded, “I don’t respect it. But I do respect you. You have pursued your goals and your dreams. You want something, you go after it. You wanted to be a meteorologist and you went for it. You wanted a larger market and you got it. You wanted those boys and they’re yours. I don’t understand why, if you want the girl, you haven’t pulled out the stops to win her.”

“Like you did?” Wyatt replied.

"Exactly like I did."

As if sensing what was coming, Wyatt's grandmother and mother began to clear some plates and headed into the kitchen.

"This is a lesson for both of you. You're Larrabees. We don't settle. We fight for what's right and for what we love. I yelled at you in the hospital because the thought of you losing one of those boys scares me and I lashed out. I shouldn't have and I'm sorry. If you can look past that, then maybe you'd see that I'm trying to tell you to go after what you want. See, I'm not so bad."

Wyatt wondered if his mouth was as agape as Caleb's was. Had their father ever been so forthright or straight? Or so revealing of his feelings? If he had, Wyatt couldn't remember it.

"It took me a bit to win over your mother," his dad continued. "What did she want with a cowboy? Hollywood makes us appear sexy and romantic, when that's the furthest thing. It's hard work taming this land. We have to wrestle Mother Nature daily, dealing with whatever she throws our way, and we'll continue the fight until our dying days because the land is our lifeblood. It's who we are. But it's not an easy life for an outsider. But when you're soul mates, and, yes, I'm man enough to use that term, like I am with your mother, you don't let her go. I told your mother once that if she ever wanted to move to the city, I'd leave this place behind because I love her more. I'm lucky she's never cashed in that particular poker chip. But I'd do it in a heartbeat. Would you go to Boston for Madi?"

"I would," Wyatt said. "But it's different. I have my

sons to think about. I want to raise them in Legacy Canyon."

"Then convince her to come here. If you love her, that can overcome a lot. Your mother and I haven't always had it easy. I'm not the most affectionate man, as you know. But your mom, she knows my heart. I'd like to think it's in the right place."

Maybe his father's heart was in the right place, Wyatt realized. His father was gruff and exacting because he cared. Maybe they could forge a new way forward after this, a new bond, if both of them were willing to try and change.

"Son, figure out what you want," his dad urged. "Do the distance thing. Move to Boston. Just stop moping around here like a melancholy loser. We're Larrabees. That's beneath us and I can't respect that behavior. You're better than this."

Ah, there was the father he knew and loved. The one who was often demanding and frustrating, the one who demanded greatness from his sons. "I'll see what I can do."

"You can start by going to the baby store," his grandmother said as she returned to clear more plates, and because she'd been listening at the door. "Tell Madi's grandmother how you feel and ask for her help. She'll have advice for you."

"Madi did ask me to attend a wedding with her next weekend."

"There you go," his grandmother said. "Your mother and I will take care of the boys. It's good for them to stay with us every so often, and you should get away once in a while. You need your life, too."

He could argue about that point, that he didn't have a life, but family support was the entire reason he'd moved to Legacy Canyon. And he'd have a life if he could patch things up with Madi. "Okay. I'm going."

His father nodded in a rare show of approval. "It's settled. Go win back your girl."

"So you're a doctor?"

"Uh-huh," Madi answered the guy to her left as she pushed around the piece of steak, letting the portion soak in some of the juice. The wedding reception was at one of Boston's toniest hotels, one with a top chef and where the meals cost a pretty penny a plate, and yet the steak fell far short of what she'd had in Legacy Canyon.

"What's your specialty?" the man asked. He'd told her his name but Madi had forgotten.

"Pediatrician."

"I'm in banking." He seemed nice, but Madi couldn't muster the energy to maintain a conversation.

"Interesting." Madi put the bite in her mouth and chewed, grateful that her single-word answers had him turning to the woman on his other side. She didn't want to be rude and tell him "this isn't happening," not when he was the son of a friend of one of her parents. At least they weren't on a date. They'd been seated by virtue of a seating chart, nothing more.

Not that there was anything wrong with the man. He seemed nice and sweet. Wore his tux well. Had a pleasant face. But he wasn't Wyatt. She sipped her champagne and finished the last bite of wedding cake as the newlyweds and their parents finished the first dances of the night.

Her parents were making the rounds and they came

up behind Madi. "Chad. We see you've met Madi," her mother said.

"Dr. and Mrs. Brennan." Chad rose. Madi couldn't fault him for bad manners—his were impeccable. As he began to speak with her parents, Madi wiggled out the other side of her chair and excused herself to the restroom. She dabbed some water on her face and used the soft towels the hotel provided to pat her face dry. She reapplied her lipstick. She'd worn a midi formal gown in a blue-and-silver floral pattern. Knowing she couldn't hide in the luxury women's lounge forever, she reentered a banquet hall that had been draped in enough fresh greenery and twinkling fairy lights to make it feel like an enchanted forest, which was somehow related to a wedding theme Madi couldn't remember.

She headed back to her table to set down her purse. Most of the table was empty, but Chad waited. "I thought you might like to dance."

Madi caught her parents in her peripheral vision. She'd never hear the end of it if she turned him down. One dance wouldn't hurt. Thankfully, it wasn't a slow song. "Sure."

They headed out to the dance floor and joined a group of people around their age, making her and Chad's dance seem like they were more part of a blob than dancing with each other. The band played one of Madi's favorite songs, so she threw her arms into the air. Might as well enjoy this part. When the dance ended, she could call a taxi and no one would fault her for leaving.

"Okay, we're going to slow this down now," the singer said, and Madi readied to exit the dance floor.

Not ready for her to desert him, Chad reached for her hand. "Shall we?"

"I'm sorry. But her dance card is full."

She knew that voice intimately. As another hand reached for her, Madi's gaze ran up the tuxedo sleeve to a shoulder, to a chin she'd caressed, and lips she'd kissed until she'd lost herself. When he smiled, she flung herself into his arms.

"Wyatt! What are you doing here?"

"I believe you asked me to be your date. I'm sorry I'm late." He wrapped his arms around her waist. "Forgive me."

She ran her hands over his face. "I can't believe you're here or that you're crashing this wedding."

"Shh. Don't tell anyone."

She laughed. "As if. The scandal! But seriously. You're here." She fingered his lapels. "Really here."

"I am." He loosened one arm and used a curved finger to lift her chin. "I've missed you."

"Me, too. I can't believe you're here. Why? How?"

"Well, they have these things called planes," he teased. "I bought a ticket and..."

"Are the boys here?"

"No, they're in Texas. It's just me. I came for you. Because I love you and I don't want to spend another moment apart from you."

"You love me."

The song ended, and Madi glanced around. Thankfully, few in the crowd had heard him. But they couldn't talk here. "Come on." She led him from the dance floor. As they passed her table, she grabbed her purse and walked out into the hallway. "We need to find a quiet place before my parents notice we're gone."

"Oh, they saw us," Wyatt said. "They know I'm here. I already talked to them."

She stopped short. "What?"

His hand still laced in hers, Wyatt used the other to remove a keycard. "Come with me."

She'd follow him anywhere. As they stepped into elevator, a shyness overtook her. It was true. She wanted to be with him. And not just for tonight.

The lift opened on an upper floor and Wyatt opened the door to a junior suite. The king-sized bed was covered in rose petals. Two crystal flutes stood next to a silver bucket containing a bottle of champagne. She set down her purse and turned to look at him. "What's all this?"

Wyatt threw the crash bar across the door. He loosened his bow tie and wrapped his arms around her. "A seduction of sorts."

"You don't have to seduce me. I've always fallen into your arms willingly. Each and every time."

"I don't want a night, Madi. When I said I love you, I meant it. I want it all. You. Me. The boys. A family."

"But how? My job…your job…"

He slid her hand under his suit jacket, resting it on top the shirt covering his heart. "I love you. The rest is mere details if you love me the way I love you. I'm a Larrabee. My dad told me Larrabees go after what they want. And I want to marry you."

Under her fingers, she could feel the *thump thump* of a heart beating faster than normal. Despite his outward calm, he was nervous. Laying it all on the line for her. "You'd leave Legacy Canyon for me?"

"Yes. You are what I want, Madi. You. I'm not happy unless I'm with you. Why should the place matter? That's exactly what I told your dad downstairs."

"You told my dad that."

"Well, it's the twenty-first century. Women don't need their parents' permission to marry. The only one I want to ask is you. If you love me like I'm hoping you do, will you marry me, Madi? I don't need an answer right away. But I need you to know my intentions. It's everything. The better or worse, the sickness and health, the death-do-us-part stuff. Not that I'm planning on dying anytime soon. I have two boys to raise, and I hope you'll raise them with me. And any other children we may or may not decide to have. Do you want me on my knees?"

"No. What I want is for you to kiss me. Do you know how much I love you? My heart has been breaking since I returned to Boston. I like my job, but I love you more, Wyatt. And, yes, I'll marry you. Ask me again, though. Wait, did you bring a ring?"

"Would any self-respecting man fly to Boston from Amarillo without one?"

She laughed and planted kisses on his cheeks and lips before stepping back. "Then I change my mind. Down on your knees, sir."

"Yes, ma'am." Wyatt didn't hesitate. He took a knee and held both her hands. "Madi Brennan."

She trembled with excitement, her heart so full and impatient it was bursting. "Yes, Wyatt Larrabee?"

"Will you marry me?"

For the briefest second Madi thought about biting her lips and teasing him, but then she saw the ring in his hand. He'd chosen a single solitaire set into a gold band.

Two sapphires the color of Texas bluebonnets sat on each side. “Yes. Yes. Yes, I will marry you.”

And with that, everything clicked into place. The moment was perfect, but before he could stand, she sunk to her knees.

“My heart and my boys,” he told her as he slid the ring onto her finger. “That’s what the stones represent. I love you, Madi.”

“I love you.” She studied her ring before throwing her arms around him. He was her hopes, dreams and future, and she’d love him forever. “Now, kiss me and show me how much.”

Epilogue

September in Legacy Canyon was known for the Lasso for Legacy charity rodeo. Six months and two weeks after Wyatt had put an engagement ring on Madi's finger, the start of September would become known for something else—the best wedding the town had ever seen.

The bride's family would settle for nothing less if they were bringing a hundred of their fancy Boston friends to the Panhandle of Texas. They'd also insisted on paying; after all, it was their only child getting married and she deserved the perfect day. Madi's parents weren't thrilled that she'd moved to Legacy Canyon and taken a job working with Wyatt's Aunt Kay, but in the end they'd wanted their daughter's happiness more than her to live in Boston, and so they'd accepted her decisions.

Not to be outdone, the Larrabees had also risen to the occasion, turning the ranch into a showcase. Wyatt and Madi were being married in a barn-turned-banquet hall, but the venue rivaled anything found in a five-star hotel by the time the decorators and caterers were done. After a honeymoon, Wyatt and Madi and the boys would move into their own house on ten acres, their homestead a part of the Larrabee Ranch acreage set aside for them.

"You ready, son?" Wyatt's dad asked. He clapped Wyatt's shoulder to help calm his son's nerves.

"I am." Wyatt loved Madi more and more each day, and couldn't wait to make it official.

"Then it's time to get out there." His dad made a tiny adjustment to Wyatt's bow tie. "Proud of you, son. Your grandfather is, too."

Wyatt didn't know how much longer his grandfather had, but he was outside in the front row ready to see his eldest grandson wed.

"I know I don't say it enough, but I love you, son. And I really am proud of the man you've become."

Hearing words he'd never thought he'd hear from his dad, and words that he knew his father truly meant, a speechless Wyatt nodded his thanks. As if on cue, his mother came and retrieved her husband. A short five minutes later, Wyatt stood at the front of the aisle, his brother to his left. Madi's friend Alyssa stood at the ready. In the front, his almost seventeen-month-old sons struggled to keep still despite both of their grandmothers' best efforts. Emma came down the aisle as flower girl, tossing out red rose petals.

Then the music changed, and Wyatt swore his heart stopped as Madi appeared. She floated down the aisle like an angel until she stood before him. "Hey," he said. He kissed her cheek. "You are beautiful."

"You're not so shabby yourself."

"Mama!" The noise came from Ethan, who slipped loose.

Not to be outdone, Noah wiggled free. "Dada!"

Wyatt scooped up Noah at the same time Madi lifted Ethan. "Seems fitting," she said, shaking her head at the grandmas who came to retrieve their grandsons so the wedding could start. "We are a family. We should do this together."

Balancing Noah, Wyatt reached for Madi's hand. Ethan was snuggled to her. "It does seem perfect," he told her. "Just the way it should be. Now and forever."

"Now and forever," she repeated.

And holding their sons, throughout their vows, their married lives began.

* * * * *